I'LL GET BY

I'LL GET BY

Janet Woods

This first world edition published 2013
in Great Britain and in the USA by
SEVERN HOUSE PUBLISHERS LTD of
19 Cedar Road, Sutton, Surrey, England, SM2 5DA.

British Library Cataloguing in Publication Data

Woods, Janet, 1939-
  I'll get by.
  1. Great Britain. Royal Navy. Women's Royal Naval Service–
  Fiction. 2. World War, 1939-1945–Women–Fiction.
  3. Aristocracy (Social class)–Fiction. 4. World War,
  1939-1945–Cryptography–Fiction. 5. Love stories.
  I. Title
  823.9'14-dc23

  ISBN-13: 978-0-7278-8272-1 (cased)

All Severn House titles are printed on acid-free paper.

Severn House Publishers support The Forest Stewardship Council [FSC],the
leading international forest certification organisation. All our titles that are printed
on Greenpeace-approved FSC-certified paper carry the FSC logo.

MIX
Paper from
responsible sources
FSC
www.fsc.org FSC® C018575

Typeset by Palimpsest Book Production Ltd.,
Falkirk, Stirlingshire, Scotland.
Printed and bound in Great Britain by
MPG Books Ltd., Bodmin, Cornwall.

Welcome to
Taylor Charlene O'Connor
Born on 22nd October 2012.
Nice Timing, Taylor!

One

March, 1939

The damp breath of London pressed against Meggie Elliot's skin. Scarf held over her mouth to prevent the vapours from invading her lungs, she shone the thin beam of her torch on the house numbers as she walked past them.

Every house looked the same, like soldiers on parade. The one the Thornton family rented stood shoulder to shoulder with its neighbours on either side, as did all the buildings in the street. Three steps bridged the basement and led into the porch.

'Aunt Es lives along here somewhere,' she muttered. At least, she had the last time Meggie had visited. And she was definitely in the right street.

The street lamps were far from comforting. They sprouted like gallows from the pavement into the fog, a mustard-coloured miasma. Though their arms lacked a hanging noose it didn't take Meggie's mind long to conjure up a couple of sinister corpses swinging back and forth. A glass helmet topped by a decorative spike protected a flickering flame of gaslight.

Jack the Ripper came to mind. Meggie shivered, crossing her fingers in front of her in the time-honoured gesture to ward off vampires. 'Begone, else I'll breathe garlic fumes all over you.' She hoped that would dispose of ghosts as well.

Then she told herself, finding comfort in her own voice, 'Jack the Ripper hasn't committed a crime for forty years or so and is probably dead. Besides, I don't believe in ghosts.' She placed her suitcase down, trying not to believe her own lie. Nevertheless, with her imagination travelling at full flood she felt exposed in the circle of lamplight while she checked the small map she'd made.

She yelped when a man appeared from the fog like a genie from a bottle.

'Are you all right, miss?'

'I was all right until you appeared, now I'm having a heart attack.' She noticed his helmet and made a face. 'Lord, you're a bobby! Now I'm in trouble.'

'Why is that . . . are you committing a crime?'

She relaxed. At least he sounded human. 'Certainly not, but my mind jumped back to when I scrumped an apple as a child, and I felt guilty.'

'I won't tell anyone if you don't.'

'Did you hear me talking to myself?'

'About Jack the Ripper? No, I didn't.'

She grinned. 'Thank goodness for that.' It was reassuring to note that the policeman was big enough to see off a dozen Rippers. More reassuring was the swift flash of a smile across his face. She waited until the panicky clang of her heart settled to its reassuring, regular tick, and, resisting the urge to turn and run like a rabbit, said, 'I was looking for number forty-three.'

'It's an odd number, so it's on the other side of the road, and forty-three is in the opposite direction to where you were facing. Do you know somebody who lives there?'

'My aunt and uncle do. I should have got a taxicab from Waterloo station, really, but the rank was empty and there was a long queue, so I decided to go on the underground to save money. I've never travelled on it by myself before, and it was like being a ferret down a burrow. Not that I've ever been a ferret . . . or even been down a burrow, come to that.'

'Quite,' he said.

But Meggie hadn't finished relating her actions. 'Then somebody told me that the train didn't go to this area, and I'd have to get off at Highgate and catch a bus. When I got off it was misty, and it just got thicker, and I walked and walked for what seemed like miles, until I eventually found the street. I got a bit disorientated and then you came out of the fog just when I was thinking about Jack the Ripper. You gave me quite a start.'

'And no wonder.' He sounded slightly bemused when he picked up her case. 'All the same, ferret or not, I can't leave you wandering around in the fog by yourself. Come on, I'll see you safely to your destination. What's the name of your aunt?'

'Esmé Thornton. Her husband is Doctor Leo Thornton. They're very respectable.' She hesitated, reluctant to mention her relatives, no matter how law-abiding and honest they were. 'You're not Jack the Ripper disguised as a policeman, are you?'

His laughter was spontaneous but relaxed, and it had a pleasant low rumble to it like far off thunder. She couldn't see all of his face. Shaded by the helmet, which was a little on the large side, only his mouth and chin were visible. He looked fit, and appeared to be fairly young. His voice was deep and yummy . . . rather posh.

'You've got a vivid imagination, miss, but I can't say I blame you in this fog. Don't worry. Jack the Ripper doesn't operate in this part of town; he prefers Whitechapel. How old are you?'

'Seventeen. You must think I'm stupid. Don't you ever lose your way in the fog?'

'I grew up around here, so not often. The police station is just around the corner, and no, I don't think you're stupid. It was only by chance that you chose a foggy evening in which to get lost.' After a few minutes of walking in silence he turned into a porch, placed her suitcase down and rang the bell before moving back on to the pavement. 'Here you are then. The light is on. I'll wait until you're safely inside.'

'Thank you, Constable . . .?'

'Blessing . . . Sergeant Benjamin Blessing.'

He seemed to be rather young to be a sergeant, or even Jack the Ripper come to that. 'What a wonderful, saintly name . . . are you one?'

'Only on Sundays. Do you have a name?'

She laughed. 'I'm Meggie Elliot. Actually, I'm Margaret Eloise Sinclair Sangster Elliot. I was adopted, you see. My real father was a war hero called Richard Sangster.'

She didn't realize that the door had opened behind her until she heard her aunt laugh and say, 'Meggie, I believe you've confused the poor man enough.' She glanced at the policeman's chevrons. 'I do hope she hasn't been chattering, Sergeant. You could have let yourself in, Meggie.'

He gazed past Meggie's shoulder to where her aunt stood, and smiled, a brief, appreciative flash of white teeth.

Men always smiled at Aunt Esmé, she was *too* beautiful for words. At the moment her long legs were captured in a pair of beige slacks, and she wore a baby pink jumper and a long matching cardigan with pearl buttons. Although her aunt was not very tall – Meggie was half-a-head taller – she was slender in a way that suggested elegance rather than fragility and had long shapely legs. Her hair was a bob of glossy brown waves and Meggie wished she looked just like her.

Her observation of her aunt was disturbed by the rumble of the policeman's voice, 'Just a little, ma'am, and I'm not in the least bit confused.'

Meggie's interest was piqued. 'I expect you get heaps of information from encouraging people to talk, that way you learn who all the crooks are.'

A small sigh escaped from him. 'Some people don't need any encouragement to talk, but you're right . . . you do learn a lot from them.'

'You mean me, I suppose.' She shrugged and turned to her aunt. 'This is Sergeant Benjamin Blessing who kindly rescued me, but now wishes he hadn't, because he now can't wait to get rid of me.'

His chuckle had a touch of spice to it. 'I didn't say that, miss.'

'You gave a long-suffering sigh, which meant almost the same thing.'

'It's because I *am* long-suffering. I've just finished a ten-hour shift, with only a corned beef sandwich for lunch, and my mother will be waiting with my dinner.'

A sweet little old lady sitting in a parlour, her hair in a straggly grey bun, and with a ginger cat on her lap came inconveniently to Meggie's mind. 'Poor you, I expect you're as ravenous as a werewolf. This is my aunt I told you about, Mrs Esmé Thornton.'

Esmé cut in smoothly, 'Thank you for bringing my niece home. I was getting a little worried, and was just about to ring her parents in Dorset to see if she was on her way.'

'I'm pleased to be of help, ma'am. Good evening Mrs Thornton,

and to you too, Miss Margaret Eloise Sinclair Sangster Elliot
. . . Meggie for short.'

She laughed. 'You do have a wonderful memory. You must
drop in for morning tea sometime, then you can tell me all
about being a policeman. I'm sure my aunt wouldn't mind.
You won't mind, will you, Aunt Es? Wednesday would be a
good day?'

'Wednesday is my day off and we're going shopping, so
nobody will be in. Friday would be better, my husband will
be home then.'

'Thank you, ma'am. Friday also happens to be my day off.'

He turned, and three steps saw him swallowed by the fog.
It struck Meggie as odd that he was wearing brown shoes with
his uniform. 'Abracadabra! What a wonderful disappearing act,'
she called after him.

Esmé took her by the arm. 'Let's get this door shut before
the house fills with fog. It stinks.' When they were inside they
exchanged a hug, and then Esmé held her at arm's length and
gazed at her, head to one side, and smiling. 'You look wonderful
Meggie Moo . . . so grown up. How is everyone?'

'They are all well, as usual. My stepfather is working his
fingers to the bone. Luke is taking an interest in girls, and
invited that horsey looking creature for Sunday high tea. Angela,
I think she's called. Luke pushed Adam to the floor when he
teased him about her, and accused him of being jealous. Adam
went all red. They began to wrestle a bit and rolled down the
stairs to the first landing. Daddy had just come home and had
to separate them. They were breathing out cinders and flames,
just like dragons.'

When Meggie dragged in a breath to replace the expended
one, Esmé slid in a chuckle. 'Nothing's changed then.'

'Anyway, the boys didn't speak to each other for days. Then
Angela started making eyes at Philip Slattery. Luke walked
around with a face as long as a donkey's tail for a while.

'Then on his day off Daddy took the boys into his study
and gave them a serious man-to-man talk that started off, "Now
listen to me, gentlemen. I will not have this behaviour."

'*Gentlemen!*' she snorted. 'I was listening at the keyhole. I
gathered that the process of becoming a man is just as fraught

as one becoming a woman. Now they keep looking in the mirror to see who gets the first whisker growing on their chins. How absolutely pathetic of them. Luke's bound to win, since he's two years older.'

'Don't be so hard on your brothers, whiskers are very important to young males. It's a yardstick towards adulthood.' But Aunt Esmé was laughing. 'They will grow up into fine young men like their father. Are you sure you don't want to follow the family tradition of entering the medical world? We haven't got a dentist in the family yet.'

'Just the thought of blood makes me feel squashy, let alone ripping out rotting teeth with a pair of pliers. Ugh! That's utterly ghoulish. I don't know what I want to do yet. Well . . . yes I do, I suppose. I think I might like to take after my father.'

'But you said you don't want to enter any branch of medicine.'

'I meant my real father . . . Richard Sinclair Sangster.'

'I don't understand, Meggie. Richard was in the army, he was a soldier.'

'Well, I could join the land army, couldn't I? Someone has to grow vegetables and milk the cows. That horrid khaki uniform is unflattering though. It makes the women's thighs appear gigantic.'

'You're thinking of becoming a farmer?' Her aunt looked so mystified that Meggie giggled. 'Lord no! Haven't you forgotten my father was a lawyer before he took up soldiering.'

Esmé made a face at her as the penny dropped. 'Of course he was. What does Livia think of that proposition?'

'Not much . . . my mother said that hardly anyone would consult with a woman lawyer, even if any man would be willing to take me into their law practice, and that was the end of that conversation. But anyway, I sat the entrance exam for Girton College, and I'm waiting to see if I'll be called up for an interview. So that's a start.'

'You're aiming for Cambridge? Good lord, how very clever of you. I'm impressed.'

'So am I. Some of the women sitting the exam were terribly earnest, and didn't look as though they could conjure up a

laugh between them. I haven't told mother about it yet. She'll
probably kick up a fuss. But if there's a war I shall probably
leave and do my bit, anyway.'

'But how will you afford university?'

Meggie shrugged. 'There's the Sinclair legacy. It's not much
use having a legacy if I can't make use of it. I'm going to see
Mr Stone while I'm in London and sort it out. Once I have
all the finance arranged nobody will be able to object. I only
met him once, when I was ten. He was past middle-age then,
so he'll probably resemble Methuselah's grandfather by now.'

'Seven years isn't long. But as I understood it, you can't
have control of your legacy until you're twenty-one.'

'Oh, I don't want control of it. I just want a good education
from it. After all, Uncle Chad did, and he wasn't even a Sinclair.'

'That was because Chad managed to get a scholarship, and
your father and stepfather opened a trust fund for him when he
was young to see him through his training. He looked on that
as a loan, and has paid most of it back now he's practising.'

'Yes . . . Daddy told me. The point is, Aunt Es, although
they sponsored Uncle Chad, they didn't think to sponsor you,
and you were his twin. It was probably because you were a
female. And nobody has given my education a thought either,
though Luke and Adam seem to have their futures all mapped
out. The parents are dreadfully old-fashioned. I'm a girl, so
I'm expected to have a temporary job, and then get married
and have children. Daddy said if I do a secretarial course I
could probably get a job at the hospital. I can already type and
take shorthand, since I did the course at school. I want more
than that, though. You do see, don't you?'

'Yes . . . I do see. You've always had a lively mind and
learned things easily.' A wistful note came into her voice. 'I'm
quite happy being a nurse and midwife but I'd be just as happy
to give it up and have babies of my own.'

'Then why don't you?'

'Leo and I decided to both work and save our money, and
then wait until we got back to Australia. Leo's contract runs
out at the end of the year, and it's ages since he saw his family,
so I think we'll be going then. I'm looking forward to seeing
Minnie again, especially now she's my sister-in-law, and settling

down in my own place. We'd planned to deliver each other's babies, but Minnie is expecting her second child.'

Meggie voiced what Esmé thought. 'If Leo keeps extending his contracts you might never go back. When they meet, my mother uses emotional blackmail on him, and tells him how much they'll all miss you.'

'Leo knows that. He might appear easy-going, but he doesn't bow to that sort of pressure, and we have no intention of staying here permanently. Livia will get used to us not being here. After all, she has plenty to keep her occupied with the boys . . . and she has you, and Chad will be nearby.'

'Oh . . . I don't want to live at home, though I love them all to pieces. I want to do something exciting. Perhaps I'll join one of the women's services. The Women's Royal Naval Service has a smart uniform, and I heard someone on the train saying they were reorganizing the service, just in case. Do you remember a time when you were going to be a dancer, and the fuss everyone made.'

'Yes, there was a bit of a to-do over that, wasn't there? My sister tends to be overprotective, but she means well. I did give it a try, but I made a better nurse than I'd ever have made as a dancer.'

'And you might have made a better doctor than a nurse if you'd been given the chance.'

'Oh, don't let's get into this women's rights thing when you're hardly through the door. I wanted to be a nurse ever since I can remember. Take your case up then come to the kitchen. I'll make us a cup of tea. Unless you'd rather make your own, now you're independent and filled with idealistic notions about improving the world.'

'It's called progress, Aunt Es.'

'There's not much progress going on as far as I can see. Still, they say that while men are talking they're not fighting. It's about time we women were consulted, but don't tell anyone I said that.'

Meggie smiled. 'I do love you, Aunt Es. You never talk down to me or think I'm still a child.'

'You're not a child, Meggie. You're a little immature at times, but that's to be expected since you haven't been out of the family circle much, and we all have our moments of rebellion. I know you were joking, but being part of the women's naval service wouldn't do you any harm. Don't close your eyes to what's going on around you, but yes, do look to the future. The world is in a mess. Most people are convinced there will be another war.'

'Do you think so?'

'It seems to be heading in that direction. Your generation will have their work cut out putting the world back together again afterwards, and you will need some useful skills. I went into nurses training at your age, and although it was good to get out from under the family scrutiny and experience some independence, I soon learned that I knew very little. Having a family to turn to was comforting.'

Her aunt gave her a hug. 'But here I am, lecturing you already. No doubt university will broaden your social life and open your mind to new ways of thinking. I just hope you haven't based your career choice on your need to prove your independence, though. There's much to be said for being a wife and mother. You only have to look at your own mother to see that.'

Meggie hadn't based her choice on anything, but now the idea of joining the navy had appeared in her head it was proving to be quite an attractive proposition. The trouble was, she kept changing her mind. She shelved the idea for the moment. 'I've thought it over seriously. I was going to ask you to talk to Mummy on my behalf once I've sorted everything out. She always listens to you. Would you mind?'

'Who's a little scaredy-cat then? Yes, I actually do mind being used as a go-between now you're an adult. You owe your mother the respect of discussing it with her, Meggie. You know she doesn't like me to interfere.'

Meggie sighed. 'I thought you'd say that.'

'Then why ask? How are my sister and brother?'

'Mother is well. She's helping Uncle Chad redecorate Nutting Cottage, so when he and Sylvia are married, they'll be able to live in it until they can afford to buy a place of their own. Wasn't Sylvia your friend at school?'

'She was one of them. We were part of a small crowd, and

we had a lot of fun together. Her parents moved to Bournemouth in our final year at school, and we lost touch when I started my nurses training. Sylvia and Chad should suit each other. She was quiet, but capable, and good at organizing people.'

'You'll be coming down for the wedding in September, won't you?'

'Would I miss my twin brother's wedding? I've already booked a weekend off and so has Leo.'

'I'll miss you when you go to Australia.'

'And I'll miss you. Now off you go and unpack. Leo will be home soon.'

'If he can find his way.'

'He will. He uses the underground and has got built-in radar. A bit like your policeman.'

'Do you suppose the sergeant will come for tea on Friday?'

'I hope not.'

'Why . . . didn't you like him?'

'He has charmer written all over him, and he's too old for you, Meggie. You shouldn't have encouraged him.'

'Goodness, how could you tell his age . . . I couldn't even see him under that monstrous helmet. Besides, I'm not about to have an affair with him. Just give him a cup of tea and a scone to thank him for helping me.'

'Well, if you do decide to have an affair with him talk to me first so I can educate you about methods of birth control, which will help to avoid unwanted pregnancy and disease.'

Meggie blushed a fiery red and pressed her palms against her cheeks. 'As if I'd even consider having a love affair! Goodness, my mother would have had a fit if she'd heard you say that.'

'It looks as though you're already having one. Believe me, mother nature has her own way of dealing with such matters, and I doubt if your mother would be consulted over it.' Her aunt caressed her cheek and smiled. 'Come to one of the clinic lectures run by the alternate nurse tutor. Other women are bound to ask the questions you might be too shy to ask for yourself.'

'I'll think about it.' Picking up her suitcase Meggie headed upstairs, knowing she wouldn't think about it for long.

Esmé watched Meggie go, a smile on her face. She loved having her niece to stay. The girl looked a little old-fashioned for a seventeen-year-old. Her hair was too long, and a little make-up wouldn't go astray. She'd also buy a new outfit for her, a classic suit with padded shoulders and a sweet little hat to top it off – smart but not too fussy.

Meggie seemed to have no idea how to enhance her appearance. She vaguely resembled her mother, only was more animated when measured against Livia's air of calmness. Her curiosity about everyone and everything, along with her smile, came from the Sangster side of the family.

Esmé turned when she heard the key in the latch, smiling when she saw the outline of her husband through the glass. Despite his boast of his navigational ability, she always worried when it was foggy. They worked in separate hospitals and quite often, one, or both of them, would sleep over.

Whipping off his brown trilby Leo went through his ritual of throwing it towards the hallstand. It hit the hook, spun round it and fell on to the floor. 'Almost,' he said. Taking off his coat he hung it on the hook, scooped up the hat and set it on top. His mouth crinkled into a smile when he saw her. 'Ah . . . my favourite woman. Come here and give me a kiss.'

Leo had lost some of his Australian accent in the time he'd lived in England, but he still flattened his vowels a little. He hadn't forgotten how to kiss her, his mouth travelling in a tease from her mouth to her nose on to her forehead, and then landing on her mouth again, for something longer and more lingering. 'You taste delicious, like spotted dog.'

'We're having it with custard for pudding. I tested it first. How was your day?'

'The Jenkins' boy is minus an appendix and out of danger. I do wish parents would bring their children in earlier. Another hour or so and we could have lost him. You?'

'I had one delivery this morning, a beautiful little girl who arrived just before the clinic began, which was rather convenient of her, since I managed to get back for it. They're calling her Rosemary.'

They both liked positive days, and rarely discussed the negatives of their professions. It was wiser not to get involved emotionally with patients. The fact that Esmé loved all the babies she delivered didn't count, she told him.

'That's different,' Leo had said. 'It's the herd instinct. Females protect other females' babies. It's a mindless sort of thing, an instinct. Men are physically stronger and more predatory. They protect both, especially if they can get something out of it for the effort. Slaves to till his fields, extra female to see to his comfort . . . a favourite wife to massage his feet . . .'

That statement had earned him a cushion in the face.

Now she returned his kiss and said, 'I'm still your favourite woman, then.'

'Always. What's been happening, anything I should know about?'

'Meggie arrived. She had a police sergeant in tow carrying her suitcase.'

He raised an eyebrow.

'She took it into her head to use public transport and then lost her way in the fog. She invited him for morning tea as a thank you, and I suggested he come on Friday, which is your day off. You don't mind do you, darling?'

'You want me to babysit Meggie on my day off?' He groaned. 'Am I wrong in believing she's an adult at nearly eighteen?'

'And still has the smell of the schoolroom on her. Sergeant Blessing is an attractive man . . . and twenty-five at least.'

He grinned. 'Ah yes . . . twenty-five. I remember it well.'

She poked a finger in his stomach. 'Not too well if you value your life.'

'Does she fancy the bobby then? The last thing I want to deal with is a lovesick teenager.'

'Not yet . . . but she will if he works at it, because she's of an age to fall in love for the first time.'

'Do you want me to see him off?'

'Men understand the nuances of men much better then women do. When a woman sees an attractive man her brain immediately sizes him up as a possible mate and her hormones begin to rumba.'

'And I thought it was my Australian accent that made you rumba. Just tell the policeman to bugger off . . . he should understand the nuance in that, whoever delivers it.'

Laughter filled her. 'Stop grumbling like an old bear. I more or less told you to do the same thing on several occasions. You took no notice.'

He laughed. 'Your dancing hormones must have deafened me . . . besides I knew you adored me right from the moment we met. You just needed a little encouragement.'

'You're encouraging me to beat you up at the moment. Stop being so provocative. Will you keep an eye on Meggie, or not?'

He nodded. 'I'll hang around like a bad smell and glower.'

When he demonstrated she kissed his ear and whispered, 'I adore it when you glower, you remind me of an amiable bloodhound.'

Footsteps clattered down the stairs before he had time to howl, and Meggie burst through the door. Smiles radiated from her like sunshine as she flung her arms around him. 'Hello, Uncle Leo.'

'You're strangling me,' he grumbled, but he hugged her back and kissed her cheek before they let each other go.

'Are you pleased to see me?'

He gave her a stern look. 'Since I value my peace and quiet, certainly not. I understand you've been dragging stray coppers in off the streets.'

'Only one; I'm not going to make a habit of it.'

'Good answer, Meggie.' Esmé could have kissed him when he said, 'I hope he doesn't stay long because if the day is clear I intend to hire a Tiger Moth and take you flying. It will take us half an hour to get to the airfield.'

'Oh . . . that's absolutely wonderful. You're the caterpillar's clogs, Uncle Leo.'

'Good Lord, am I? That takes some thinking about. Thank you, sweetheart . . . I think.'

'It's my turn to cook the dinner so I'd better get on with it,' Esmé said. 'It's grilled lamb chops, boiled vegetables and gravy. The vegetables are prepared, so it won't take me long.'

'Can I help?'

'Yes . . . you can set the table if you like, then take Leo a glass of white wine. He likes to relax and listen to the radio before dinner.'

'Why don't you relax with him while I cook dinner? I often cook it at home, and that's for six of us. I'm quite good at it, I promise. Besides, Leo looks as though he needs some company.'

'Especially the company of a good looking popsie like you, Es,' he invited.

Esmé bestowed a smile on him. 'That would be lovely, Meggie. Thank you so much. I'll fetch the wine.'

Leo gazed from one to the other and grinned, as though he'd realized that having two women in the house looking after him might be good for his comfort.

An hour later, when Meggie went into the sitting room, it was to discover Leo sprawled untidily on the dark red couch, asleep. In the same state, her aunt was hugged against his body, her head resting comfortably in the crook of his shoulder. Two empty wine glasses stood on the coffee table and Victor Sylvester's orchestra was a melodious low hum coming from the radio.

They looked so sweet and relaxed; Meggie thought it would be a shame to wake them. For a moment or two she wallowed in the love she felt for them.

She closed the door gently, then knocked and called out, 'Dinner's ready, you two.'

Two

It was Wednesday.

From the outside steps leading to the basement of the boarded-up house opposite, Nicholas Cowan had watched the man kiss his wife and leave in the green Morris car that had been parked outside the house. An hour later the two women emerged, laughing together. They hooked arms and headed for the underground station around the corner, walking in step.

It had been nice of them to tell him when they'd be out for the day.

Giving them a few seconds to turn the corner Nicholas

crossed the road, and stood in the shadows of the porch at number forty-three, Queen's Road.

'You could have let yourself in,' the Thornton woman had said to the girl. That meant the key was concealed somewhere. It wouldn't be on the ledge over the door because it was too high for the women to reach.

A cement pot supported limp vegetation that bore an unsavoury sprinkle of grey berries. It smelled vaguely of cat's spray, and was the most obvious place. Wrinkling his nose he forced his fingers into the dirt and raked gingerly through it. When he was rewarded with a small slice of metal, Nicholas smiled.

The door opened quietly. Nicholas doffed his hat and for a couple of moments he stood there, his mouth opening and closing as if he was talking to someone who'd opened the door to him. It was a precaution in case a neighbour passed by. He pushed the door wider with his foot, so it looked as if he was being allowed entrance by someone on the other side, and slid through the gap. He closed the door quietly behind him.

He stood in the hall for a couple of minutes and listened. Apart from the tick of the clock, all was quiet. Unlocking the door to the basement he went down the steps to the abandoned kitchen, now turned into a junk room. Some of these roomy houses had been converted into small flats, but this one had escaped so far.

The house wasn't in bad repair but there was no mistaking the signs of neglect. Bubbles of faded paper disguised the occasional damp patch and the paint and plaster were flaking. Some of the floorboards groaned under his weight. The fire grates had wide chimneys of the type that sucked out the heat rather than allowed it to radiate with cosy warmth into the room.

He turned the key in the lock and pulled back the bolts to the outside door, in case he needed to escape quickly through the basement.

It had been lucky that he'd run into the girl. He'd learned a lot from her. She was a good-looking young woman with fine skin, and dark, astute eyes . . . a little on the awkward side yet, but outgoing.

Her aunt was a corker. He grinned, shaking his head. She

was just the type he liked, but he had a rule never to mess
with married ladies. He wasn't about to break it.

Taking the stairs two at a time he went back up to the hall
then on up to where the bedrooms were situated. Only two
were furnished. The bigger bedroom had a sage green eider-
down. He went to the man's dresser first, found fifty pounds
in a wallet and a pair of gold cufflinks to pocket.

The woman's jewellery box was on the dressing table and
yielded some gold trinkets. He didn't have time to sort out
the dross, so he tipped the contents into his handkerchief, tying
it securely. There was also a purse. It had a fiver, and five
separate one pound notes in it. He pocketed three of the pound
notes and left the rest, mostly because he'd liked the owner.
Besides, he'd made a good haul earlier.

A creamy pink satin nightdress hung over the footboard,
and a flimsy flower-patterned scarf lay on the floor. He picked
up the scarf and held it to his face, closing his eyes as he
inhaled the scent. He hadn't enjoyed a woman for some time!
She was the feminine type who wore silk and lace under
her clothes. Rifling through the top drawer confirmed it. Her
husband was a lucky dog.

There was the swift tock tock of heels on the pavement
outside. Fingering the curtain aside a chink, he gazed through
it. Damn . . . the women were coming back! While the girl
stayed on the pavement, her aunt called out. 'I won't be a jiffy,
Meggie. I'm sure I left it on my dressing table.'

Nicholas dropped the scarf and purse on to the bed. The
nightdress slithered to the floor. Swiftly he moved across the
landing to the empty room opposite. The floorboards creaked
a couple of times. He held his breath as he gazed through the
crack in the door.

She slowed down when she neared the top of the stairs as
if she'd heard the floorboards give under his weight, caution
in her expression. She was so close he could have reached out
and touched her. He experienced a vicarious thrill when she
moved through the open bedroom door. His heart began to
work overtime when he caught a whiff of her perfume in the
current of air she left in her wake.

Through her open bedroom door he watched the woman's

pert little backside as she went to the dressing table. She looked round, gazed at the purse for a moment, then snatched it from the bed and placed it in the brown leather handbag she carried over her arm. She frowned as she bent to pick up the night-dress from the floor, and gazed at it for a few minutes before hanging it back over the foot of the bed. Pulling the bedroom door shut she rattled it to make sure the latch had closed, and then padded off down the stairs, her footsteps as light and agile as those of a cat.

Back at the window, he gazed at her through the net curtains. As if she could sense his presence, she gazed up at the house, her glance suspicious, and moving from window to window. He kept very still when her eyes seemed to gaze into his, but she couldn't see him in the shadows.

Then she shrugged and the pair linked arms and hurried off again.

He went back to her bedroom and dropped her nightgown to the floor again, leaving the door open when he left. He wanted her to know he'd been there – watching her. It would teach her to be more cautious of strangers.

The man couldn't find much else worth taking. There were no collections of knick-knacks, silver or household goods. The couple lived with the basics, as though they were temporary tenants rather than permanent homemakers.

There was a ring in a trinket bowl on the bedside table in the second bedroom, which obviously belonged to the girl. It had garnets in it. They weren't worth much, but the setting was gold.

A folded newspaper was on the bed, cryptic crossword face up. She was young to have mastered the cryptic. One clue was left unsolved. 'Lively movement noted in the pit,' he murmured. The s and h were filled in. He smiled, and unable to resist he picked up the pencil and supplied the rest, coming up with the answer. Scherzo.

When he went downstairs the street was empty, except for a man and woman walking away from him. Pulling his hat down to shade his eyes he left via the front door. The key was dropped into the pot plant and he smoothed the earth over it when he pretended to do up his shoelace. The visit would have hardly been worth the risk in monetary terms, but it was the thrill of possible discovery and the touch of danger by being so close to his victim that he'd enjoyed. He certainly didn't need the money.

But now it was time to go and lunch with his uncle at their club. No doubt the old boy would be tedious and would want to discuss politics, and his future. He'd have a heart attack if he knew.

Esmé wore a thoughtful air on the way to the bus stop.

'Is something bothering you, Aunt Es?'

'Yes, actually . . . you might put it down to my imagination, but I think we have a ghost in the house.'

Meggie grinned widely, 'How exciting; what did it look like?'

'I didn't see it, but I had this weird feeling that I was being watched when I went in. And I heard a creaking sound, as though someone was treading on a loose floorboard.'

'Does a ghost weigh enough to make creaking sounds?'

'Trust you to come up with a question like that. I've never weighed one. All I know is the hairs on my neck and arms prickled. And I was sure I'd left my purse on the dressing table, but I found it on the bed.'

'Have you checked the contents?'

'That's a thought.' Esmé opened it and gave a quick look. 'There's still some money in it, though I thought I had two or three pounds more.'

'Perhaps Leo borrowed it.'

'Yes, that must be it, though usually he tells me. I'll have to go to the bank before we shop.' Esmé shrugged. 'I could have sworn my nightgown had been moved, too.'

'Now you're spooking me . . . if I see your nightgown floating around the house by itself I'm going to run a mile.'

Esmé grinned, looking slightly shamefaced. 'So will I.'

Meggie spent a wonderful day with her aunt. She had her hair trimmed and fashioned into a style with easy, shoulder length curls. They had lunch in Lyons Café, and then went shopping at Selfridges.

At the cosmetic counter Esmé advised. 'Buy the Ponds cold cream and vanishing cream. It's inexpensive, but a good product, and it smells nice.' She added a powder compact, a pink lipstick and a bottle of flowery smelling cologne.'

In the clothes department, Meggie fell in love with a blue checked dress with a velvet collar and cuffs, but couldn't afford it. With a sigh, she hung the dress back on the rack.

Her aunt bought her a serviceable grey suit with a slightly flared skirt, and two blouses, one white with a lace yoke and one in pale pink dotted with ruby coloured rosebuds, murmuring, 'You can wear anything with this suit. Go and change back into your other clothes while I pay for this, then we'll go and find some shoes.'

There were dark grey shoes with heels and a matching handbag. A small brimmed hat trimmed with a pink silk rose and net completed the purchases.

They forgot Esmé's ghost until they arrived home, just as it was getting dark.

'Whoooooo . . . watch out for the ghost,' she said as her aunt inserted the key in the lock.

'Dry up, Meggie Moo else I'll make you go in first in case something's waiting there to eat us,' she warned.

The house was cold. They stood in the eerie dimness of the hall hugging their bags and looking at one another in the gloom, ears strained to collect every alien sound. Meggie gave a nervous giggle. 'We're being stupid. Come on let's summon up some courage. We'll take everything upstairs and then we'll light the fire in the sitting room and have a cup of tea.'

Meggie unpacked her new clothes, smiling over the blue-checked dress that her aunt had slipped into their purchases. She was arranging her beauty products on the dressing table when she noticed that her garnet ring was missing.

She looked everywhere, and then went downstairs. 'Remember that garnet ring you gave me? I can't seem to find it. I'm sure I left it in the trinket bowl, and I've looked every-where else.'

'Perhaps you put it in my jewellery case. Remember, how you used to keep it in that secret compartment before I left home. Go and have a look there.'

She did as she was told, and then went back downstairs, feeling scared. Her aunt was in the kitchen making the tea. 'You know you said you thought you felt a ghost in here?'

Esmé nodded, then laughed. 'Don't tell me you've seen one.'

'Your jewellery box is empty.'

Her aunt gazed at her, eyes wide. 'Are you sure?'

'There's nothing wrong with my eyesight, and I know what empty looks like.' She lowered her voice. 'And someone finished my crossword.'

'Finished your crossword? Oh, come on, Meggie, if you're trying to scare me, you're succeeding.'

'No . . . really. There was one clue left that I hadn't got. It's been written in, but the slope of the handwriting is opposite to mine, as though the person was left-handed.'

'So now we have a left-handed ghost that does crosswords. That's a bit too far-fetched.'

'Not a ghost but a burglar. I'm suggesting that someone has been in the house while we were absent. Doing cryptic crosswords is addictive. An unsolved clue would have been almost irresistible to anyone who enjoys doing them.'

Her aunt took a rolling pin from the drawer. 'We'd better have a look around the house before it gets totally dark. We'll switch all the lights on.'

When Meggie picked up the carving knife her sister said, 'Put that back in the drawer. It could kill somebody.'

'So could the rolling pin.'

'Not if I hit him on the knee or calf. Besides, you don't like blood, and that thing will have us wallowing in it. Bring the wooden spoon instead, you can use that in self-defence if you have to, but avoid hitting anyone on the head.' She didn't mince words. 'Crack him one in the groin instead, men are vulnerable there.'

'The giggle Meggie gave was from nerves rather than anything else. I imagine he'll be gone by now, but can't we wait for Leo to come home?'

'That's not for two hours. Come on, Meggie, be brave. I'm pretty sure you're right and he's gone. But we have to make sure.'

Fully armed they headed out. The first thing they noticed

was that the bolt on the door leading to the stairs down to the basement was unlocked. Her aunt shot the bolt across. 'That's always kept locked, but I'm not going down there to check on the door to the street in the dark. It's full of creepy-crawlies.'

They crept cautiously from room to room, switching on lights. The house proved to be empty of strangers.

'Should we call the police?'

'Not until Leo arrives home and we've listed everything that's been stolen; I think his gold cufflinks are gone.'

'What about that policeman . . . Blessing? Perhaps I could telephone him.'

'Later. We'll let Leo handle it. Men take more notice of men. Let's drink our tea then we'll start on the vegetables.'

They were sipping their tea when her aunt placed her cup into the saucer, buried her face in her hands and began to cry.

Meggie went to where she sat and slid an arm round her shoulder. 'Don't let this upset you, Aunt Es.' She placed a hand over her aunt's. 'At least you were wearing your wedding and engagement rings, so he didn't get those. And I was wearing my silver locket.'

'We had such a lovely day together, and now this. It's horrid to think that a complete stranger has violated my home and rifled through my things. Everything in the drawers was in disarray. I feel so . . . *grubby.*'

'He's the grubby one, not you,' Meggie said fiercely. 'I wonder how he got in.'

'The basement, I expect.'

'He couldn't have done. It was bolted from the inside. And you keep the door to the street bolted, too.'

They gazed at each other and Esmé said almost inaudibly, 'He must have found the key in the pot plant.'

The sound of a key scraping in the lock made them both jump. Exchanging a look they picked up their weapons and headed for the hall at a run.

'Leo, thank God it's you.'

'Yes . . . I managed to get off early.' His vivid blue eyes sharpened when they took in Esmé's face. His smile faded and he gazed at the rolling pin. 'You look as though you're about to flatten a cockroach. What's happened, my lovely girl?'

'We've been burgled. My jewellery box . . . money . . . your gold cuff links.'

'I wondered why the house was lit up like a Christmas tree. I thought you'd turned them on to guide me home.'

When her aunt gave a bit of a sniffle Leo drew her close. 'All right, Es, tell me about it.'

'I think he was in the house before we caught the bus . . . I'd forgotten my purse you see, and we came back. I'm sure I left it on the dressing table but it was on the bed when we came back. I thought some money was missing, but I wasn't certain. I could sense his presence too, and one of those shivery feelings . . . as though someone was watching me. I picked my nightgown up and put it back on the bed, and I closed the bedroom door when I left that second time. I rattled the handle to make sure it had latched. When we came back from shopping the nightgown was on the floor again, and the door had been opened and left open. It was as if he'd wanted to make sure I knew he'd been there. He could have been hidden under the bed or in the wardrobe that first time.'

Leo's other arm came protectively round her when she shuddered. He pressed a kiss against her forehead, as if she was the most precious thing in the world to him. Meggie hoped that one day a man would love her as much as Leo loved Esmé.

Leo's gaze wandered her way, and he held out his arm and drew her into the circle. 'How are you holding up, love . . . scared?'

'Not any more, but I'm angry. The rotter stole the garnet ring Aunt Es gave me. I feel a bit safer now you're home. Aunt Es thought it was a ghost at first,' Meggie said with a shudder. 'We were laughing about it all day . . . until we arrived home. We were just about to check and see if the spare key was still in the pot plant, in case he comes back.'

'That was an invitation to come inside if ever I saw one. I'll telephone a locksmith and have some new locks fitted to the front and back doors. They might have time to do it now.'

They promised to come the next morning.

★   ★   ★

By six o'clock the basement had been checked, the house secured and the spare key plucked from the pot. A list was made of the missing goods and the police informed.

A thin man verging on middle age and answering to the title of Constable Duffy arrived. He accepted a cup of tea and a couple of ginger biscuits to go with it.

'There have been a few burglaries recently. Another house further up the road was robbed a couple of days ago, not long after the fog rolled in. Luckily there was a police sergeant at hand. He said somebody had reported seeing a man loitering. He checked the house for the owner while she waited on the pavement. The robber got away with a large amount of money. The police officer wasn't one of our chaps.'

'His name wasn't Sergeant Benjamin Blessing, by any chance, was it?' Esmé asked.

The constable offered her a sharp look. 'That sounds familiar. Do you know him then?'

'I've met him . . . on the same day you mentioned.'

Meggie chimed in. 'He helped me find my way here that same afternoon in the fog. He told me he worked at the station round the corner.'

'There's nobody by that name working in our patch.' The man took out his notebook and licked the end of his pencil. 'Do you have a description of this man? Miss Elliot . . . Mrs Thornton?'

Meggie went first. 'He was about six feet tall. His helmet was too big, it shaded his face.'

'He was polite and his voice was quite . . . cultured, I suppose,' Esmé offered.

'And he did cryptic crosswords.'

Meggie was the recipient of a surprised look. She shrugged. 'He completed the one in my bedroom.'

The man wrote it down. 'Anything else?'

Meggie stole a glance at his sensible black boots and remembered. 'Sergeant Blessing wore brown shoes with his uniform . . . brogues, I think. I thought it odd.'

'Why did you think it odd?'

'Perhaps I should have said a coincidence more than odd. My stepfather has a pair just like it.' She hesitated, and then said. 'No . . . I did mean odd. Daddy paid nearly eleven pounds for his, and grumbled about the price all the way home. I thought a policeman might not earn enough to be able to afford a pair of expensive shoes. I know that sounds snobbish, and he might be a well-off policeman for all I know about him. I suppose there are some.'

'That might be true, but I've never come across one. Besides, he should have been wearing regulation uniform.'

'Perhaps he won the money to buy the shoes with a bet on a horse.'

The constable licked his pencil again and gazed at her, his expression bland. 'Do you have a description of the winning horse, miss?'

Uncertain, she gazed at her aunt who was in the process of exchanging a smile with Leo. She giggled. 'I think you're all perfectly horrid, including you, Constable Duffy.'

'I'm sorry but I couldn't resist it, young lady.'

'Oh, I forgot. I think the burglar was left-handed. His writing sloped as if he was.'

Constable Duffy wrote it down and closed his notebook. 'Actually, you've been most helpful, and observant. You'd make a good detective, were you a man.'

The lightning bolt Meggie sent his way bounced off him.

'At least we have a definite suspect now. It's possible your Sergeant Blessing is impersonating a police officer.'

'You mean he might be the crook?' Though he'd denied he was Jack the Ripper. 'He's coming to morning tea on Friday. You can come and meet him if you like.'

The constable smiled. 'If he keeps the appointment telephone me.' Finishing his tea, he stood, and picked up his helmet. Unless your goods happen to turn up, which is highly unlikely, you won't hear from me again. Thank you for your hospitality, Doctor and Mrs Thornton. Miss Elliot. I never say no to a cup of tea.'

After he'd gone Leo gazed at his watch. 'Get your coats and lipstick on ladies. As I'm not on call tonight I'm taking you both out to dine at a restaurant.'

'What if the burglar comes back?'

'He's already taken anything that's worth having, so he might as well have the rest of it?'

'Don't think this will let you off when it's your turn to cook the dinner,' Esmé told him as they scrambled off up the stairs.

Leo gave a martyred sigh. 'As if I'd be so devious.'

'As you once told me, there's a first time for everything.'

'So I did, Mrs Thornton, so I did. I remember the occasion clearly.' He winked at her and consulted his watch, grinning when colour touched her cheeks. 'You have exactly ten minutes.'

Three

Sergeant Blessing failed to turn up for morning tea.

Meggie felt guilty for encouraging him into the house, and said so to Leo.

'You couldn't help getting lost in the fog, my angel. He certainly had his eye on the main chance. Two houses within sight of each other . . . I could almost admire him for his nerve.'

'Do you think Aunt Es will be all right? She was really shaken up.'

'She'll be fine now the locks have been changed. My Es is made of strong stuff.'

Meggie slid him a look. 'You really love her, don't you?'

'I'd walk a mile over hot coals if it made her happy. Luckily it wouldn't.' His smile lit his eyes. 'Go and put your slacks on while I fetch Esmé's leather flying gear for you to wear.'

Excitement filled her. 'We're definitely going flying then?'

'With a vengeance, since I've got the plane booked. It's a good day for it. I hope you're ready for some excitement this time because I won't be doddering about up there.'

'I thought you just mentioned it because Aunt Es wasn't keen on having that fake policeman in the house.'

He slid her a gaze. 'You don't miss much, do you? As it turned out, Es was right to distrust him.'

'I feel such a fool. I practically invited him to rob us.'

'Don't beat yourself up over it. He was a con man, and

they're usually experts at what they do.' He changed the subject. 'How are your driving lessons coming along?'

'Famously.'

'Good . . . you can drive us to the airfield then, as long as you're careful.'

Meggie smiled at the thought. She'd had six lessons, so was fairly confident. 'I'll be careful, I promise. You'll have to tell me which streets to turn into.'

And she *was* careful. She'd never driven in a city before, and guided the car through the traffic, honking the horn to warn anyone when they got too close, or when they turned a corner.

When they were out of the traffic she sent a glance Leo's way, looking for a word of praise. He'd put his flying helmet on and was hunched in his seat, holding the flying jackets bundled firmly against his chest with white-knuckled fists.

Her smile faded. 'Was my driving that bad?'

'Well, not bad for a female, I suppose. Luckily, every driver on the road was more experienced today. They must have been warned about you in advance. You can't just honk at everyone and expect them to get out of your way.'

'Why not? It worked.'

He began to laugh. 'So it did. I'm of a mind to get a bit of my own back for that little ride. This is supposed to be my way of unwinding after a stressful week, and I'm as tight as a spring. I'm going to throw us about a bit when we get up there, but if you're scared use the speaking tube and tell me.'

He was as good as his word. The plane was fuelled up and waiting for them. They spent the next hour or two zooming about in the clouds, and doing turns, so the sky and land rolled around them and at first Meggie's stomach flattened against her spine, then they were upside down and she seemed to be hanging by her straps and heels like a trapeze artist. The air was cold against her cheeks, but the leather jacket she wore was lined with sheepskin, and quite cosy.

She had been up with Leo before, but this was different from the last sedate outing. It was exciting, and she squealed when he took her up as far as the plane could go. They fell in a slow banana roll before straightening up and coming down to earth, landing as gently as a gadfly. The front wheels touched down lightly, and when they'd slowed sufficiently they were followed a few moments later by the tail wheel. They coasted towards the hanger, the propeller ticking over until they came to a halt.

Four young men stood in a group, watching. They were cadets judging by their appearance. They clapped as Leo stepped out on to the wing walk and turned to help her out.

'That was quite a show you put on. Well done, sir,' one of them called out.

Pulling off his goggles and helmet, Leo dragged his fingers through his hair, setting his dark unruly curls free. He smiled at them. 'Thank you.'

A tall young man stepped forward and offered Leo a hand. 'I'm Edwin Richards.'

'I'm Doctor Leo Thornton. Air force trainees, are you?'

'No, sir, we're sixth formers at Armadale College. This will be our first hands-on session in the air today. It's a school initiative and we're very keen to get up there. It doesn't hurt to be prepared in case war breaks out, does it?'

'It certainly doesn't. Is all your class undertaking the course?'

'We had a choice of three options. Some joined the naval cadets. They learn to tie knots and sail on the river. The army cadets march around a lot, and shoot air rifles at targets.' This was stated with a slight air of disdain.

'Good luck with your lessons then. Learning to fly isn't all that hard.'

Aware that a couple of boys were eyeing her Meggie followed Leo's lead and released her own hair from its leather confines. She automatically shook it back into its new style with a toss or two of her head.

Leo chuckled and turned away, and when Meggie followed his lanky form towards the hanger one of the boys gave a soft wolf whistle.

'Schoolboys . . . *honestly!*' she scoffed.

Leo grinned at her. 'They're going to find it hard to keep their minds on their lesson after that small display of feminine come hither. You ought to practise getting a bit of a sway to your hips as well, then the boys will be after you in droves.

Like this.' Holding out his arm, his hand hanging limply, he waggled his rear end as he walked.

A giggle tore from her. 'You're perfectly horrid Leo Thornton. You look as if you've dislocated your hips.'

'And you're being precious.'

She'd always been able to argue with Leo without getting upset. 'I'm evolving. Preening and artifice is part of the female nature. It happens naturally, and helps women to attract a mate and reproduce.'

'Evolving, is it? Good Lord, what have you been reading, and what are you evolving into?'

'A woman of course. It was an article in a magazine about being feminine.'

'You're feminine by gender. The trouble with those types of articles is, if you take them as gospel and make a habit of ogling men they get the wrong idea of what you're all about. Just be your natural self and let men do the chasing; resistance brings out the hunter in them.'

'I wasn't ogling men, and I don't want to be hunted, especially by a bunch of spotty schoolboys. They did all the ogling.' She picked up speed and headed for the car, face hot with the beginnings of temper.

Catching her up he brought her to a halt. 'I was teasing.'

'I know, I'm not angry with you. I'm angry because I hate being whistled at, like a dog being brought to heel.'

'Get used to it, Meggie. You're a lovely-looking girl, and men are going to whistle whether you like it or not. It's a compliment. And if you're going to act like a child and flounce off in the middle of a conversation I'll send you back home to be taught some manners.'

'You wouldn't.'

'Try me.'

Noting the amusement in his eyes she grinned; she couldn't help it. 'Aunt Es would flatten you if you did.'

'So . . . you're calling my bluff with your secret weapon, are you?'

When she nodded he placed a kiss against her forehead. 'Well done for that, but the next time you feel like flaring up do me a favour and count to ten and think about it first. At your age you should be able to handle such situations, and your moods, without resorting to being rude.'

'Sorry Leo.' And she was.

'Good . . . end of lecture.'

They'd been on the road for ten minutes when he said, 'Those young men, they're not just spotty schoolboys . . . or even spotty come to that. They have families who love them. And although they've hardly enjoyed what life has to offer yet they're learning to fly so they can help defend this country should it be needed. You should have some respect for that, Meggie.'

'Like my stepfather and my father did in the last war.'

'Exactly . . .'

'Did you meet my father?'

'No . . . he'd already died when I met your aunt.'

'I should have liked to have known him.'

'Apparently he was a good sort, if that's any help.'

'Yes . . . it is. I'm glad people liked him. It means people will be more inclined to respect me because of it . . . as if my father acts as a reference.'

'Only to the people who knew him and that can work two ways. They might measure you against him. The way you dress, speak and mostly, how you conduct yourself, will make a lasting impression.'

She drew in a deep breath and whispered, '*One . . . two . . . three . . .*'

'What are you doing?'

'Counting to ten. I thought the lecture was over, Leo.'

When he laughed, so did she.

'See . . . counting to ten obviously worked, and you only made it to three,' he said.

Her brothers came into her mind, and the thought of war no longer seemed like an adventure concerning heroes and villains. It was real and dangerous. Her own father was an example of that. It was a defining moment for her, a moment when her childhood seemed to fall from her shoulders.

Her brother, Luke, wasn't much younger than the youths at the airport, and fear trickled through her. Her mother would be devastated if she lost any of her children, and what of Leo?'

'If there's a war will you have to go and fight?'

'I guess that's going to be the way of things, Meggie.'

'Oh, God . . . I can hardly bear to think about it. But you're a doctor, Leo, surely you wouldn't have to physically fight. You'd work in a hospital and heal the wounded, wouldn't you . . . like my stepfather did.'

'That's a possibility.'

'And Luke, my brother . . . what about him? He's young yet, but in a year or two he'll be . . . an adult.'

She stitched the two together in her mind, Luke all tattered and torn from the battlefield and Leo in his starched white coat, a dedicated doctor, his eyes as blue as love-in-the-mist. Leo took Luke's temperature and miraculously declared when her brother emerged from his imaginary coma, 'He'll live.'

Before she came completely down to earth she whispered, 'Thank you Leo, you're a hero.'

Meggie hadn't meant to say it out loud but it had been in so quiet a whisper she was sure Leo couldn't have heard it. It had been ages since her mind had created such a dramatic scene, something she'd grown up with. It reminded her that she'd once wanted to be a writer, and perhaps she would be one day. Following the example of her late father, she kept a daily journal to write her experiences in . . . just in case.

'Thanks,' Leo threw at her.

'For what?'

'Calling me your hero. A chap needs all the encouragement he can get when he's showing off in a plane. I didn't hear you scream once.'

Leo had absorbed the hero bit, dissected it, and sensing something personal might be in it had turned it into something harmless. He must have lots of nurses making sheep eyes at him, and had probably developed a way of turning anything remotely personal aside. 'I thought it was fun.'

'As for Luke, he'll find the courage inside him to do what's required if the need arises.'

'There's been talk of war for over a year now. You can't help but feel the inevitability of it.'

They fell silent for a while, and then Leo gently squeezed the back of her hand. 'It might never happen, but don't be in too much of a hurry. Neville Chamberlain is negotiating with the powers that be, so war might yet be avoided. If it isn't . . . then I guess we'll have to get by. In the meantime we'll carry on with our lives as normal, try to find some collective sense of human decency within ourselves, and be of service to the less fortunate people we meet in our everyday lives.'

Two days later Meggie, feeling confident in her grey suit worn with the chic little hat and rosebud blouse, presented herself at the legal offices of Anderson and Stone in Temple Bar.

A fading woman of about fifty was behind the reception desk, and she smiled warmly at her. 'May I help you?'

'I'm Miss Elliot. I have an appointment to see Mr Stone.'

'*Miss* Elliot is it?' She drew an invisible line down the page with her finger and taking up a pencil altered a mark on it, tut-tutting. 'Ah yes . . . I see. A mistake was made in writing it down. I'll just check if Mr Stone is ready to see you, yet.'

He was – well almost. He was removing a file from a cabinet, with his back to the room, and he called over his shoulder, 'Please be seated. I'll be with you in a moment or two.'

She arranged herself on a chair in front of the desk, crossing one leg elegantly over the other, like her Aunt Esmé did – though her aunt had long legs to die for. Placing her gloves and bag on the green leather-topped desk in front of her she gazed round her. Apart from the desk there were three chairs and a wall of filing cabinets. A window offered a view of a garden square surrounded by buildings.

He turned to gaze at her, and her expression must have shown the same surprise as his, when he said, 'Unless you've changed your gender you're not Doctor Elliot!'

'I'm his stepdaughter, Margaret Elliot . . . and you're not Simon Stone.'

'I'm his grandson . . . Rainard Stone.'

'As in Reynard the fox?'

'Exactly as . . . but spelled differently because I was born in a deluge.' This was accompanied by a smile.

'Really . . . how odd.'

He shrugged, looking slightly embarrassed. 'It was supposed

to be a joke to relax the client with. I was actually named after a long dead ancestor.'

'Curiouser and curiouser,' she said, with a smile, quoting from *Alice in Wonderland*. 'That's a joke to relax the solicitor with.'

'We must have been brought up on the same nursery stories. Most people call me Rennie.'

'Has your grandfather retired?'

'Simon Stone died last year, I'm afraid, and my Anderson grandfather has a couple of years left in him before retirement. My father is away at present and the receptionist is at home with a streaming cold so I'm a bit pushed. That was my mother at the front desk helping out.'

'Oh, I'm sorry . . . about Mr Simon Stone. I met him when I was a child and he struck me as being a lovely man.'

His smile was spontaneous, and disappeared as quickly as it came. 'He was. Now then, Miss Elliot, is there something I can help you with?'

'I hope so. It's about the Sinclair legacy.'

'I really don't think that's something I should discuss with you.'

She fixed him with a gaze, mentally doing the ten count. 'Why not, when I'm the beneficiary?'

He opened the file and gazed down at it then offered her a smile. 'I see you must be the young lady who was born Margaret Eloise Sinclair Sangster.'

She nodded. 'Elliot is my adopted name.'

'I still can't discuss it with you. Doctor Elliot is the trustee acting on your behalf until you're of legal age.'

He was infuriating. Skipping numbers five to seven she jumped straight to number eight. 'I see. Then we won't discuss it. All you have to do is listen, so you'll know what my side of the argument is when Doctor Elliot brings it up with you.'

He didn't mince words either. 'Let's get one thing clear to start with, Miss Elliot. I don't care much for that hostile tone you're using. I'm not the enemy.'

She must have sounded like a spoiled brat. 'I'm sorry, Mr Stone. I didn't mean to make you feel uncomfortable. The thing is, I've grown up with this legacy yet nobody ever consults me about it, or will even listen to me when I want to talk about it. I've also never been one to use six words when one will suffice. It often gets me into trouble.'

His eyes were a glow of amber flecked with brown, and as alert as those of the fox he'd been named after. He picked up his fountain pen. 'Forewarned is forearmed; let's get on. Just expect me to bite back. You won't mind if I take notes, will you?'

'You won't need to since I can say it all in two or three short sentences, which won't waste your time. I want to study at Cambridge if they'll have me. Assuming I'm accepted, I'll need money to pay the fees and support myself. Will I be able to use money from the Sinclair legacy to pay for that purpose?'

'It depends. We must be careful not to incur a debt that you'll be liable for in the future.'

'I thought you couldn't discuss it with me, and after all, it's my money to spend.'

He sighed. 'That may be, but I can't . . . not until I've been through the file and then informed the trustee of the enquiry with my recommendations. To be honest, my grandfather thought that the Sinclair trust had just about exhausted its capital during the depression. He said the estate had been neglected and no effort had been made for it to be productive. I will need to study the file in some depth to give you a definitive answer. I believe there's a house involved.'

'Yes . . . Foxglove House. It's been boarded up for years. My stepfather tried to find a tenant for it, but it's terribly expensive to run because it's not a house that can be managed without servants. I can't imagine ever living there myself, though I visit from time to time. It's a bit of a hidey-hole for me. The place is rather sad. It's filled with the past lives of my relatives, yet I never met any of them, including my father. Sometimes I feel like an alien, as though I'm on the outside of the family trying to get in. And sometimes the estate feels like a millstone hanging round my neck. If I could sell it I would. I imagine I'll give it to charity when I'm old enough to have some say in the matter.'

He didn't quite hide his smile at her meandering explanation. 'Do you think you might have felt warmer towards the place if you'd grown up there?'

'Yes . . . I suppose I might have. But I didn't and I don't. Actually, I'm glad I don't because that will make it easier to dispose of.' She offered him a rueful smile. 'Thank you, Mr Stone. I really didn't mean to be churlish. You certainly know how to bite, so you were well named I think. I shall behave myself when I'm around you from now on.'

His shrug was almost apologetic, his eyes agleam with amusement. 'I'll be in touch.'

'I'll be in London until halfway through April.' Plucking the fountain pen from his fingers she wrote her aunt's number on his notepad. 'There.'

When she reached for her bag and gloves, he stood, saying, 'Perhaps we could go out one night while you're in the capital. Do you like dancing?'

She liked his direct approach. 'Yes, but I don't dance as well as my Aunt Es does. That would be nice though . . . perhaps we could make up a foursome with them. They would want to meet you, I imagine.'

Rennie looked as though the inclusion of Es and Leo was the last thing he'd expected. 'Is having your aunt and uncle along a condition?'

She chuckled at the thought. She was seventeen, after all . . . and *inexperienced*. She'd already misjudged one man who'd indicated that he'd represented the law. 'I don't really know the protocol. I've never been out with a man before.'

The corner of one eyebrow twitched. 'Never?'

'Never . . . at least . . . not a strange one.'

'I'm hardly strange.' He sighed 'All right, seeing as how your aunt and uncle are acting *in loco parentis* on this occasion I'll ring them.'

'Will you wait until I've informed them of that fact then.'

He laughed and hurried across the office to open the door for her. He stood in the opening, partially blocking it, the quizzical look back on his face. He was of a comfortable height. Her eyes were on a level with the firm jaw, and the curve of his mouth. 'I'll have to think of something more memorable than a quick shuffle around the dance floor of the Hammersmith Palais for your first date. Why do you want to go to Cambridge? You never said.'

She admitted, 'I'm trying not to offer information because I was conned by a man disguised as a policeman last week.

He went in the house while my aunt and I were out and he helped himself to some money and our jewellery.'

The expected scoff of laughter at her stupidity didn't come. Instead, he said, 'You have to be careful in London. There are a lot of disadvantaged people who will steal out of sheer necessity.'

'This man wasn't so poor that he couldn't afford expensive shoes. He probably stole those from somewhere, too.'

'I hope he didn't get much?'

'He only took a garnet ring from my room, but he stole all of my aunt's jewellery and some cash. Just the thought that a stranger has been through the house and handled everything is disconcerting. It made my aunt feel . . . *grubby*.'

'Yes . . . I suppose it must have. I'm so sorry you and your aunt had to go through that. Cambridge?' he reminded.

'Ah yes . . . Cambridge. The plan is that I might decide to study law as a career eventually and I thought that having a degree of sorts would be an asset.'

'*The law?* You're an enigma, do you know that, Margaret. However, I do love it when the occasional lady lawyer emerges from the ranks and splutters of outrage go around the old boys' clubs. Good luck to you.'

Meggie could only remember one person who'd called her Margaret. That had been her grandfather. She'd always thought it to be an old-fashioned name because it had been her Sangster grandmother's name. But if the name was good enough for an English princess then it was good enough for her, and she was grown-up, after all.

She decided that she liked Rennie Stone, and wished she hadn't been so bumptious.

Four

Meggie discussed the outcome of her meeting with her Aunt Esmé. 'Rennie Stone was quite nice, but he didn't tell me anything, except to say that he thinks the estate isn't worth much now. He wants to go through the files to familiarize himself with it. I expect he'll consult my stepfather because he acts on my behalf. Then I'll be in trouble.'

'You could always ring Denton yourself. He's not unreasonable.'

'I know . . . but he's always so busy, and Mummy likes him to relax when he's not working.'

'As we're all inclined to do with our men. But Denton is trustee of your legacy, and that is your business and his. You have no choice, Meggie. Denton will be much more inclined to see reason if you explain things to him personally. Ring him now.'

'He won't be home yet.'

'Then ask your mother to pass on a message for him to ring you.'

As luck had it, Denton was having a rare day off. He sounded pleased to hear from her. 'Meggie . . . this is a surprise. Your mother isn't in. She's at Nutting Cottage with Chad, measuring up for some new curtains.'

'It's you I wanted to talk to,' and she drew in a breath and plunged in. 'I went to see the solicitor handling the Sinclair estate. He'll probably ring you before long.'

There wasn't even the slightest censure in his voice when he asked, 'Is there anything important I should know about?'

'Well . . . I don't suppose you'll think it that important. Did Mummy tell you I wanted to go to university . . . to become a lawyer?'

There wasn't even a blink of silence. 'No . . . no, she didn't, but what's that to do with the Sinclair estate, poppet?'

'If I'm accepted I'll need money to support myself with.'

'Good lord, yes, I suppose you will. Nothing comes cheaply these days. So you're going to follow in your father's footsteps, are you? Richard would be delighted.'

She felt a little teary. 'You don't mind, do you? What if the Sinclair estate can't afford the fees? I'm given to understand that Girton College is dreadfully expensive. I don't want to sound selfish or anything because I know you have the boys to educate—'

'You're not responsible for their education, Meggie. Besides,

Grandfather Elliot left them a legacy, enough for their education. We can only wait and see what Mr Stone comes up with. I'll discuss it with Livia, too. She might have some thoughts on the matter. Poor Meggie, we haven't given your future much thought, have we? What have you been up to in London?'

'Leo took me flying . . . it was such fun. We did all these twists, turns, and somersaults in the air. He said it helps him to unwind after the stress of his job.'

'Working with sick children can be extremely stressful, as well as rewarding. Children have such fear along with the trust in their eyes when they look at you. Knowing you're going to have to cause them pain to effect a cure doesn't lessen the guilt you feel. I have a great deal of respect for Leo. How is your aunt?'

'She's well, though a bit rattled at the moment. I adore them both.' Not only did she adore them both, Meggie now had a great deal more respect for what both Leo and her stepfather achieved in their respective professions.

'What's Esmé rattled about?'

'Oh yes . . . I nearly forgot to tell you. A man disguised as a policeman robbed us . . .' She related the incident and finished with, 'Aunt Es keeps a rolling pin handy when she's here alone, in case he comes back.'

He laughed. 'Good for Esmé. By the way, I never grumble. I'm perfect. Your mother has been telling me so for years.'

'You're not a bad old Daddy Bear, at that.'

'Thanks . . . was much taken in the robbery?'

'Cash and all of Aunt Esmé's jewels, and that ring she gave me with the garnets in . . . the one that famous dancer gave to her, only I can't remember his name. By the way . . . Mr uh . . . Stone wanted to take me out dancing. I said yes. I suppose that's all right, isn't it? He seems quite a decent sort.'

'Isn't Simon Stone a little *grandfatherly* for someone of your tender years? He's old enough even to be *my* father.'

She grinned at the note of censure in his voice. '*That* Mr Stone died a year ago. I'm talking about Rainard Stone . . . his grandson. He said he was born in a deluge of rain, and that's how he got his name. What an odd thing for a parent to do, though his mother looked quite normal.'

'Oh yes, I remember . . . I did receive a letter from him. Your mother did something with it; probably put it in a file somewhere. It's amazing how many pieces of paper one collects in a lifetime. You reminded me just as I was about to put my fatherly foot down.'

'It would have ended up in your mouth.'

'It often does, which is why I leave most things to your mother. She finds it easier to say no than I do. What were we talking about?'

'Me going dancing with Rainard Stone.'

'You don't need my permission to go out dancing, you're old enough to decide for yourself.'

'I've never been asked out by a man before.'

He chuckled. 'Then it's time you got some practice in. How do you feel about it?'

'I feel unsure.' She grinned at the mouthpiece. 'I was flattered to be invited though. It was probably because I looked smart. I wore the new suit and court shoes Aunt Es bought me . . . also some lipstick. I suggested we make up a foursome with Aunt Es and Leo. Rennie didn't seem all that keen on the idea, but said he'd ring them.'

'Good idea, there's always safety in numbers . . . and once you get to know this young man better I expect you'll have more confidence in yourself.'

'Exactly what I thought. I do seem to have a tendency to say the wrong thing at the wrong time and he ticked me off. So did Leo. So that was twice in one week. I'll have to try and train myself to be pleasant. Men are awfully touchy, aren't they? Leo told me I should count to ten before I speak. So far I haven't got past five.'

Now he guffawed with laughter. 'Good luck then. Don't be too hard on yourself, my love. I've always thought you to be perfectly all right as you are. Give my love to Esmé. When you come home bring me a packet of those special mint humbugs she buys from Fortnum and Mason, will you?'

'Will do. Bye, Daddy, you're a brick and a half.'

'That was worth knowing,' he said and blew a kiss down the line before he hung up.

Meggie turned to find her aunt grinning at her. 'From your response, it sounds as though everything went well.'

'My stepfather is a gem.'

'I've always thought so. What was that about us going dancing with your solicitor? That's the first I've heard of it.'

'He hasn't telephoned you, yet. I hope he hasn't forgotten, or changed his mind.'

'It sounds as though you like this lawyer of yours.'

She shrugged, but couldn't hide the faint grin she gave. 'He's all right, I suppose, but I don't want to form any attachments with men. As soon as women get married they're expected to stop work and stay home, unless they have a job like yours. It's not fair.'

'I agree.'

'Will you teach me how to do the foxtrot?'

'Now . . . when it's my turn to get the dinner ready?'

'After dinner will do fine. In return I'll cook it for you. What's more, tomorrow, when it's my proper turn, I'll make a lamb hotpot with suet dumplings.'

Es grinned. 'Mmmmm . . . you're on.'

Nicholas Cowan's eyelids barely quivered when his father looked over *The Times* newspaper at him and announced, 'Sir James Bethuen will have an opening in his department in a month or two. I've put your name forward. It will be an opportunity for you especially if war breaks out, since it's a desk job. At least you'll be out of the fighting, unless Hitler manages to set foot on English soil, then every man, woman and child will take up arms.'

Nick had known his idle life was coming to an end. He'd spent two years settling into his manhood, mostly on the Continent, supposedly studying but doing very little apart from living the life of a well-heeled young viscount with very little responsibility. Nick never did anything by half. He sailed the Mediterranean coast, picking up awards for his skills in the racing circles, entertained a smart crowd of several nationalities at his villa, and collected a smattering of languages along the way, something that came surprisingly easy to him. His father, who had an eye on the diplomatic service for him, had called him home six months previously.

'If war breaks out I want you this side of the English Channel. In the meantime I'll keep an ear open for an opportunity for you.'

Carefully, Nick cut a generous strip of crisply fried bacon from his rasher, dipped it into his egg yolk and ate it. The egg was just as he liked it, the yolk not runny, but not quite firm either, and the outside edge of the egg browned, but not burned.

Dabbing his mouth with a linen napkin he gazed at his father – at his handsome face and the grey moustache he'd recently grown. He reminded Nick somewhat of Anthony Eden, who'd resigned the year before as secretary of state after a disagreement with Chamberlain. The Italian dictator Mussolini had referred to Eden as, 'The best dressed fool in Europe.' Something Nicholas was inclined to agree with. 'What does Sir James have in mind?'

'Who knows? Some sort of information gathering, I think. Nothing that would stretch your intellect to any great degree I should imagine, since James was a duffer at school. He hints at cloak and dagger stuff to attach importance to himself. Anyway, he can fit you in the day after tomorrow. Lunch at his club one p.m. He owes me a favour so don't be late. It doesn't pay to rub civil servants up the wrong way.'

When Nicholas nodded in reply his father folded the page back and ducked down behind the paper again. The crossword was in full view and Nicholas slanted his head to one side. He'd solved several of the clues in his mind and had eaten most of his breakfast before his father turned to the next page and informed him, 'That burglar has been at it again . . . the one who disguises himself as a policeman. This time somebody saw him and gave a good description. He's an ugly looking customer. Apparently he has dark staring eyes, crooked teeth and a flattened nose, as though it had been broken. They've put a drawing of him in the paper.'

Nick didn't think he'd have anything to worry about, since his eyes were grey, his teeth straight and his nose as handsome as that of a Roman senator . . . or so his mother had told him.

He had a short, poignant memory of her hugging him tight, his handsome nose pressed against the tickling fur flung over one shoulder, and breathing in her perfume as he fought against the urge to sneeze. He'd been about thirteen. '*Never forget that I love you. Promise you'll be all right without me, my lovely boy . . . and be good for your father. You can come and visit me in the holidays.*'

'*I promise, mother.*'

It had been a rainy April day, the park opposite scattered with daffodils. A man had stepped from the cab and kissed her red mouth. Nick had cleared a space in the misted window and watched as her cabin trunks were loaded into the cab. Then she'd turned to look up at the window and her mouth had wrinkled and puckered, as though she'd grown old before his eyes. She'd blown him a kiss.

He'd realized then that she was leaving for good, and turned his back on her. At that moment he'd never wanted to see her again.

He closed his eyes as the memory began to fade. She'd been wearing a diamond ring, and for a moment the sun had emerged from behind a cloud and it had gleamed with cold fire.

Three months later his father had taken time out from his busy schedule to travel to the school. He'd cleared his throat and said, 'There was an accident dear boy . . . the car your mother was in. It went off the road into a ravine. They had been drinking. Perhaps it's just as well . . . the scandal, you know.'

He'd been in the middle of exams, and was angry with her for dying before she'd proved she loved him by coming back. 'You could have telephoned,' was all he found to say.

His father had a woman with him, small, with bright hair, pert breasts, and the same red mouth as his mother. She was about eight years older than Nick.

'This is Jane. We're going to be married when you come home for the hols.'

Jane took it on herself to teach Nick the facts of life during the first week of his holiday. She learned that blood was thicker than water when word just happened to reach his father's ear via an anonymous letter.

Opening his eyes, Nick gently smiled. Ah yes the scandal . . . something not to be tolerated at all. It was all done quite gentlemanly . . . a birching from his father followed by a quick trip to a professional lady with many tricks, and honour was satisfied. The woman and her belongings disappeared overnight, never to be mentioned again. He wondered what had happened to her.

'I'll have a quick look at the burglar after breakfast so I can keep an eye out for the cad. People are silly leaving their valuables where they can easily be found.'

'Quite . . . I hope you're free the day after tomorrow, Nick?'

'I've joined the martial arts class at my club.'

His father's head popped up again. 'I've heard of it but never known exactly what type of art it is.'

Nick tried not to grin. 'It's actually the art of self-defence. It's a method of defending yourself by disabling your opponent with a series of kicks, holds and throws if you're attacked.'

His father gave a huff of laughter. 'Yes, of course it is. I was making a joke. Martial arts . . .?' He laughed and slowly shook his head to cover his embarrassment. 'A good one, what? It certainly had you fooled. Personally I've always thought a good jab to the stomach with my stick does the trick just as well. It disables the buggers by robbing them of breath, you know. Not that I've ever had to use it.'

Nick did know.

Folding the newspaper his father threw it on the table and pushed back his chair. 'Right, I'm off then, I've got an appointment with my tailor before my meeting with the bank's board of directors. In case we don't see each other for a day or two don't forget your luncheon engagement, Nicholas. I'm very keen that you should get this position . . . especially when I went to so much trouble to set it up. Apparently, Colin Foggerty's son is after it. Wasn't he at school with you?'

Michael Foggerty was short and plump. He was friendly, but had a rather ingratiating manner. 'Foggerty comes from Irish stock. Doesn't his family still have property there?'

His father chuckled. 'So he does, Nicholas. How sharp of you to remember. Be sure to work that into the conversation with Bethuen. He has definite opinions where the Irish are concerned.'

And unfortunately, none of them were good. Nicholas sighed and reached for the newspaper before the door was completely shut. With some distaste he delicately lifted a blob of rough-cut marmalade from it with the blade of his knife and flicked it at the portrait of his mother, which hung over the fireplace. It landed somewhere on the former countess's scarlet gown, where it blended perfectly.

Turning to the page where the felon was featured, he chuckled. On consideration, far from being exposed by this poor likeness, Nicholas should feel insulted, since it was nothing like him.

Amused, he began to compose a letter to *The Times*, drawing himself up to his full height and spitting out in a pompous manner:

> *Sirs,*
>
> *Since when has* The Times *indulged in such sensationalist journalism as to present a totally fictitious account of the supposed burglar? The sketch of said villain, which was presented as an eyewitness description, is so poor a likeness it is laughable to the extreme. It can only be compared to a caricature devised by the devious brain of the current editor of* Punch, *the excellent Edmund Knox.*
>
> *Sirs, you are liars! Far from being the low, ape-like type of lout depicted on page two, observation in the bathroom mirror allows the felon to give you a more accurate and objective descrip-tion. Handsome? Most definitely. His eyes are blue, his teeth straight and he stands at just over six feet – a prime specimen of British manhood in fact. As for the nose, it has never collided with the fist of a would-be pugilist, and its roman ancestors would abhor the very notion of insult being afforded to such a noble work of genetic nostrology.*
>
> *Your faithful servant,*
> *The right honourable. Anonymous.*

Of course, he wouldn't write a letter, or even send it, he thought, sinking into his chair and folding the paper into precise crossword-and-clues working mode. But the publicity *did* make it difficult to get rid of the accumulated loot.

The thought came again. He could hand it back to the owners. That would present a greater challenge than stealing it in the first place, since they would all have changed their locks. His almost photographic memory gave him an instant recall of what had been gathered from whom.

He could always use the post office for delivery. In fact he could be his own post office. He smiled to himself as the idea took hold . . . after all it was almost April Fools' Day.

A maid came into the room and began to busy herself with the dishes on the buffet. She was square and solid, a middle-aged spinster with nobody to care for except her employer's family.

Where did she go for her annual fortnight's holiday? he wondered. Did she take the train down to Bournemouth to spend her time in a genteel, but dull hotel? There, she'd sit at a table for one in a conservatory that impersonated a dining room. It would have potted palms instead of curtains to give it a tropical look, and beach sand gritting the threadbare carpet. Would she hire a striped deckchair for tuppence, and breathe in enough sea air to last her another fifty weeks while she dreamed of retirement and read an Agatha Christie novel from behind a pair of sinister-looking smoked glasses?

The scrape of his knife against his plate brought the maid whirling round and she nearly dropped the dish she was holding. 'Oh . . . I beg your pardon, sir. I didn't see you when I came in. I'll return later.'

He felt a sudden surge of pity for her. He had no intention of putting the routine of the household out so he could indulge in a few more flights of fantasy. 'There's no need, Anna. I'll have another cup of coffee to drink while I'm doing the crossword. If I move to the fireside you can get on with whatever you want to do. Pass my compliments to the cook, if you would. My bacon and eggs were exactly as I like them.'

Her face turned pink with pleasure. 'It's the cook's day off, so I did the breakfast today, sir.'

He'd learned that a servant travelled a long way on a word of praise for fuel. 'Well, good for you, Anna.'

'Thank you, sir. I'll try not to disturb you. Will you be in for lunch?'

'Not today. I'm going to mess around on my boat; the brass needs polishing. I dare say you'll be glad when I'm out from underfoot.'

Anna tittered. 'Oh no, sir. You're such a pleasant gentleman, and no trouble at all.'

'Glad to hear it.' Taking a pencil from his waistcoat pocket he slid into a leather wing-backed chair, there to be fully absorbed for the fifteen minutes he'd allowed himself to ponder on the harder of the clues. The time limit proved quite a challenge, but he beat his own record with seconds to spare.

When the long clock in the hall chimed nine he swallowed his lukewarm coffee and rose. Time to get on, he supposed, and wondered what James Bethuen had in mind for him.

One thing he was sure of, although the man wasn't the fool his father had made him out to be, he wasn't far off.

Five

They had forgotten to set the alarm clock.

Not that it mattered to Meggie, but her aunt and uncle were scrambling around in panic, snatching gulps of tea and tearing bites from the bread she'd toasted under the grill and spread with butter and marmalade. An apple was placed in each hand as they headed for the door. It was more nutritious than what they'd eaten so far.

'Eat them in the car,' she said.

'I'll drop you off at the station,' Leo told Es, because from there they'd be travelling in different directions. He kissed Meggie on the cheek as he went past and grinned. 'Thanks, Mum.'

Her aunt grabbed up the handbag Meggie held out for her and did likewise.

'Don't forget to comb your hair, Aunt Es,' Meggie called after her, and make sure you both eat a good lunch.

'No . . . we won't forget. What are you going to do today?'

'I'll do the immediate chores first then go to the markets to do some food shopping. This afternoon I'll do the ironing.'

'I feel guilty leaving all this work.'

'Don't feel guilty, since I'm responsible for some of it. Off you go now else you'll be late.'

The pair gazed at each other and laughed.

The Morris engine was a bit reluctant to wake up, too. After it offered him a couple of sluggish dry coughs Leo stuck his head out of the window and called out, 'Wake up you cantankerous old cow else I'll heave your rusting arse into the scrap yard.' The engine spluttered with indignation then fired.

'Leo's got a wonderful way with engines,' Es told her from the passenger seat, and they both giggled when he snorted.

Giving a last wave when the car reached the corner she went back indoors.

Silence descended when she closed the door. She could smell smoke. *'Holy Moses . . . my toast!'*

She made a dash for the kitchen, pulled it out from under the grill and threw the charred, smoking mess out of the back door, flapping as much smoke as she could out after it with the tea towel. Mostly though, it had risen to the high ceiling, where it hovered like a drifting grey cloud of bad breath. From experience she knew the smell would linger for several days.

It had been the last of the bread, and the carter hadn't been yet. Neither had the milkman. She sighed and ate a cracker spread with marmite, washing it down with the lukewarm remainder of her aunt's leftover tea, to which some hot water was added to weaken the strong brown brew.

After dressing, she went into a flurry of housework. There came the hum of the milk float and the chink of milk bottles on the doorstep. She got there before the blue-tits pecked through the top to help themselves to the cream, placing the two bottles on the larder shelf.

Not long afterwards a horse plodded down the road, and she bought a couple of loaves from the cart to place in the bread bin, and a bun with a sprinkling of shredded cheese melted on top to supplement her meagre breakfast.

'Nice weather for March innit, missus?' the carter called out. 'Not much wind and rain abat lately.'

She nodded, though she thought the sky to be dull and overcast, and the temperature fairly cold.

She smiled at him before she closed the door, not bothering to correct him about her single status, because in her apron and with a scarf tied turban style around her hair to keep it tidy, she felt like a mother who'd just got her children off to school and was rushing through her chores so she could go out for morning coffee with her girlfriends.

An important-looking envelope came through the letterbox, hit the floor with a thud and skidded across the hall. It was in reply to her request for information after reading an article about the Women's Royal Naval Service. Quickly she read through it. They were taking the names of women who were offering their services should they be needed.

She filled in the form, listing name, age, educational qualifications and skills, including all the hobbies she could think of . . . driving, typing, flying, cryptic crosswords, dancing, writing fiction. Before she could change her mind she signed the form, placed it in an envelope, and dashing to the post box at the end of the street she watched it disappear into the square red mouth, just before the collection van came around the corner.

Back home, she turned the radio up loud and waltzed around the room in practice for the weekend dance date, until a sudden thought brought her to a halt. She didn't have any girlfriends. She just didn't seem to attract females. Susan, once her best friend at school, had started work as a junior shop assistant in the children's book department at a Bournemouth bookshop. There, she earned a wage of twelve shillings a week, and had started going out with a 'crowd'.

Being by herself didn't bother Meggie, since she was content with her own company most of the time, and her own thoughts. All the same, it would be nice to have a friend she could talk to – one who understood the odd flights of fancy she indulged in. Susan hadn't been able to do that. She had turned into a prim little miss who thought it was weird that Meggie even thought silly things. Her aim was to meet a nice boy, then get engaged to be married.

The telephone rang.

She pinched her nose and assumed a nasal whine. 'Good morning. Margaret Elliot speaking.'

'Ah, you're home, Margaret . . . good. It's Rennie Stone. I wondered if you'd be free for lunch today. By the way, what's wrong with your voice; do you have a cold?'

'No. I just talk like this on Mondays. It was nice of you to enquire, though.' She grinned when he made an impatient hissing noise through his teeth. 'We're seeing you at the weekend for the dance, aren't we? Are you ringing to cancel it?'

'Certainly not! That's got nothing to do with it. Don't you eat lunch?'

'Of course I eat lunch.'

'Good, then let me ask you again. Are you free for lunch today?'

'Well yes . . . but I've got to go to the market first, else we won't have anything for dinner, and it's already eleven thirty.'

'Is there any reason why you can't go to the market after lunch?'

'Well no, but—'

'I'll pick you up at noon then . . . that is, unless you need an adult's permission.'

'You're being rude and sarcastic.'

'So I am.'

'Well . . . you can apologize if you want to take me out to lunch.'

'Ah . . . an ultimatum. I hadn't expected one.' There was a moment of silence that indeed felt like a stand off, then he said, and quite gently, 'I'll see you at noon then, Mags.'

'Don't bother,' she flung at him, and hung up half-a-second after he did.

Just in case he hadn't heard what she'd said, she began to get ready. It took all of twenty-five minutes to wash, roll on her stockings, don her checked dress and arrange her hair. She followed up a light dusting of face powder with lipstick, then dabbed cologne behind her ears.

Meggie felt self-conscious and on edge waiting for a man she hardly knew to take her out. She thought she heard a car, but her bedroom didn't look out over the road and she wasn't going to appear eager, even to her own eyes, by rushing to have a look.

Not that she expected Rennie to turn up, she thought, gazing at the clock's large hand, which quivered on two minutes to the hour. When it took a sudden leap forward her heart jumped with it.

She would give herself a couple minutes to make sure, in case the clock was fast, she told herself. But anyway, she couldn't go shopping looking scruffy.

'When the doorbell rang exactly one minute later she had her coat on and her shopping basket on her arm. The hall clock gave its usual whirring sound and began to chime the twelve strokes of noon. Resisting the urge to run, she sauntered down the stairs and feigned surprise when she opened the door on the last stroke. 'Oh . . . it's you. I told you not to come. I didn't expect . . . actually, I was getting ready to go to the market.'

His eyes impaled her, the reddish brown autumn of them guarded by sooty spikes of lashes. 'Liar, you were doing no such thing. You were waiting for me to turn up on the doorstep. Stop playing games.'

She choked out a laugh. 'I hope you're not going to be grumpy all day.'

He smiled and brought a posy of sweet smelling violets out from behind his back. 'I apologize.'

She was captivated. It was the best apology she'd ever had. 'They're beautiful . . . thank you so much.'

'You're beautiful.' Much to her annoyance she blushed, and it was his turn to laugh. 'You're also very sweet, you know. It's not often I get to take out somebody as young as you.' He took the basket from her. 'We can leave this in the car.'

'Will you wait a moment until I put these in water? I don't want them to wilt.'

Meggie had expected to be taken somewhere local, but they motored to Southend, which was about forty miles away. They sat in a café overlooking the long stretch of beach and eating fish and chips washed down with mugs of hot tea.

'This was a long way to come for lunch,' she said.

'After working in a dusty office I needed some clean, fresh

air in my lungs, and I hadn't seen the sea for a while. That's
one of the penalties of being part of the legal profession.'

There was a blustery breeze coming off the water and grey
clouds scudded across the sky. The air smelled of salt and the
seagulls wheeled above, giving raucous squawks.

'I've never seen such a long pier.'

'It's the longest in England. Would you like a walk to help
blow the cobwebs away? In half an hour we must set off back
home again.'

It was obvious he needed to walk. Outside, he took her
hand, entwining his fingers with hers. She could have pulled
her hand away, but instead she enjoyed the moment for what
it was. He was ahead of her. 'We can go to the market up the
road, the one we passed on the way in here. The one you
usually shop at will be closed by the time we get back to
London.'

The shopping was done quickly, but they got the late
bargains. As they drove home the clouds built up and the sky
darkened. Now and again handfuls of rain splattered the wind-
screen. By the time they arrived at the house the sky was
thunderous and the air charged. The house looked gloomy,
and she didn't want to go inside by herself.

'Thank you for a wonderful day, Rennie,' she said, not
wanting to leave the safety of the car.

He smiled. 'I enjoyed it.'

There was a flash of lightning and she jumped. 'Will you
come in for a cup of tea?'

He glanced at his watch.

'Please,' she said when there was a rumble of thunder.

His glance measured her. 'You didn't strike me as a person
who'd be scared of thunder and lightning.'

'I'm not usually. I just don't want to go into a dark empty
house by myself. Not after the burglar. Silly, isn't it? I'll be
quite all right once I've turned the lights on, and Aunt Es and
Leo will be home in a couple of hours. If you can't stay will
you just wait until I've turned the lights on before you drive
away?'

'Actually, I'd love a cup of tea.'

She felt an enormous sense of relief when he followed her

inside, and placed her basket on the kitchen table. The kitchen smelled deliciously of violets from the posy he'd given her. She held them to her nose for a moment. Afterwards she put both the kettle and the radio on.

They were just in time to hear the newsreader say, 'News has just come in that German troops have occupied Czechoslovakia.'

She gazed at him. 'Do you think there will be a war?'

He nodded. 'I think it's inevitable, don't you?'

'I keep hoping it will all go away. Will you have to . . . well, you know . . . *fight?*'

'I imagine I'll be called up eventually.'

'And would you go?'

'It would be compulsory. But anyway, I'd probably enlist if war happens to be declared. Even if given a choice it wouldn't be fair to leave the fighting to all the other chaps. In fact it would be rather cowardly.'

'You know Rennie, if there's a war I think I'll forget about going to university and join one of the women's services instead. I can type and do shorthand, so I could make myself useful. My studies could probably be deferred until a later date.'

'Yes, you could. You know, Mags, becoming a lawyer isn't all fun, especially for a woman. Promise me you'll think carefully about it, because once you've committed to it you'll discover it hard work for the most part, and without much time left over to enjoy what life has to offer.'

'Like war, you mean?' She touched his cheek, feeling a bit weepy at the thought of him being placed in danger. 'If you're called up you'll take care, won't you? Don't do anything dangerous or heroic.'

'I'm not naturally brave, so I'll try not to.'

'My father was a war hero. He died before I was born. Everyone who knew him said he was a wonderful man. I wish I'd known him too.'

They gazed at each other for a moment, and then he drew her into his arms. When she gazed up at him in surprise he kissed her. It was unexpectedly tender and undemanding. 'Thank you for caring about me.'

'That's the first time I've been kissed . . . properly, I mean. It was nice.'

He avoided her eyes. 'Don't read anything into it. I shouldn't have encouraged you. You're much too young for me.'

She wouldn't have objected to an encore, but he'd probably kissed hundreds of girls, and she didn't want him to think she was one of those fast types.

'I'll grow older.'

A laugh choked from him. 'I'm sure I'll keep up with the age gap.'

They drank their tea in the kitchen while the storm threw bolts of lightning about the sky. Thunder rumbled up through the soles of their feet as though they were part of it. Eventually the noise lost its intensity, but it left in its wake a howling gale and a heavy downpour of rain.

'You'd better wait until this is over,' she said.

There was the sound of the key in the lock and Leo and her aunt were blown into the house on a gust of wind, laughing together. Leo called out, 'We're home, Meggie, and soaked through.'

'I'm in the kitchen.'

Leo's voice got louder as he moved towards them. 'Es started to walk home because I wasn't there on time to pick her up, and the bus had gone. The storm got to her and beat her up before I did.' He deposited a kiss on her cheek and gazed over her shoulder. 'Hello . . . who's this?'

Rennie had already risen to his feet. He held out a hand, 'Rainard Stone. I'm the solicitor handling Margaret's legacy.'

Aunt Es came in after Leo, her stocking clad feet leaving a trail of wet footprints behind her. Her hair was a draggle of rats tails. She smiled ruefully as she shed water all over the kitchen floor. 'It's nice to meet you before we go dancing together at the weekend.'

Rennie smiled at Esmé. 'You look rather wet, Mrs Thornton.'

'I am rather. I must go upstairs and change.'

'And I must go too. I hadn't realized how late it was.'

'Must you, when we've only just met? Unless you have a prior engagement, stay for dinner. We've bought enough sausages haven't we, Meggie?'

Rennie protested. 'It's tempting . . . but you haven't had time to cater for a guest.'

Aunt Es won the argument with her killer smile. 'Nonsense, I won't hear of it. It's bangers and mash day, with lashings of onion gravy on top, and there's always plenty.'

'That will be followed by one of Meggie's delicious apple crumbles and custard, I hope,' Leo said, shamelessly ingratiating as he got his order in for a pudding.

Rennie grinned at that, 'It sounds more tempting by the second. May I use your telephone?'

'Of course you may. I'll leave you with Leo to sort it out,' Esmé said, drifting off in the direction of the stairs. 'I'll change into something dry, and then come down and give you a hand, Meggie.'

'Are you quite sure?'

Meggie laughed. 'Not another word, Rennie. I bought some lovely fresh runner beans at the Southend market, and some carrots.'

Leo raised an eyebrow. 'Southend?'

'Rennie took me there for lunch today. He needed some fresh air.'

'It's a long way to go for it, but there's plenty of that at Southend,' Leo said.

'He didn't really give me the option of saying no.'

Leo laughed. 'Well done, Rennie. Let's leave the kitchen to the women and go and catch up on the news. We'll crack open a bottle of wine while I give you the third degree. Since I hold the position of guardian while Meggie is in London, I don't want to disappoint her.'

The thought mortified Meggie. 'I'll never speak to you again if you do. Besides which, apple crumble will be off the menu . . . and for ever.'

'Now that's what I call a punishment.'

Rennie chuckled when she said. 'Honestly, Leo, you must be the most convincing liar on earth. And to think I actually believed you.'

'You take everyone at face value. In fact, your lack of guile is quite refreshing. Don't worry, love, I won't embarrass you.'

The two men disappeared towards the hall, where Rainard had a short conversation on the telephone with someone. She couldn't help but overhear some of it in the space created when the door opened to allow Aunt Es through, and it closing behind her.

'I'm sorry, Pam, my sweet, but I'm dining with a client.'

Meggie wondered who Pam was.

Her aunt had changed into navy slacks and a lacy pink twinset with pearl buttons. Her hair was drying into its natural curls as she reached for an apron from the hook behind the door, and tied it around her. As she began to scrape the carrots she said, 'Rennie Stone seems rather nice. Did you have a good time today?'

'Oh . . . rather. At first I thought we were going to argue over the telephone because he thought I was being rude and I thought he was being just as rude. When I told him to apologize, he didn't. And then . . . just when I was about to go to market he turned up on the doorstep with that bunch of violets in his hand – don't they smell heavenly? He said he was sorry he'd upset me. I had to go to lunch with him then, else it would have been horribly embarrassing and too cruel leaving him standing there on the doorstep with a bunch of flowers in his hand.'

Aunt Es smiled. 'Good job you had your best dress and make-up on then.'

'Yes . . . it was rather. I invited him in because the house looked a bit menacing in the storm and gave me a bit of a shivery feeling, and I didn't want to go in by myself.'

'I know the feeling. I hate going inside by myself now, have done since we were burgled.'

Meggie laid out the ingredients for the crumble and fetched two bottles of preserved cooking apples from the pantry, Bramleys picked from the garden of her mother's house at Eavesham and preserved for winter use. 'Do you think two jars will be enough?'

'It should be.'

She imparted a little confidence to her aunt. 'Rennie kissed me. I was telling him about my father, and he just kissed me. It was rather nice. I was worried in case he might think . . .' She lowered her voice and looked at the door. 'I don't want to give him the impression that I'm . . . *fast*.'

'Be careful, Meggie. He's a nice man, but he's quite a bit

older than you, and I really don't think you should encourage him.

As Esmé was to say to Leo later, when they'd gone to bed. 'Meggie is quite naive. Would you mind if I invited her to stay longer? I'm sure Livia wouldn't mind. She wouldn't be a drain on the finances since she gets a small allowance from her legacy, and she could probably find employment. I might be able to get her a temporary job at the hospital, in administration perhaps.'

'My darling . . . anything that makes you happy makes me happy. Besides, she doesn't cost much to keep, and she's a good cook.'

'Trust you to think of your stomach. You can be awfully mercenary at times.'

'A man needs his nourishment in all matters, if you get my drift.'

'So does a woman.'

He kissed the junction where her neck met her shoulder, making her skin quiver. 'Tell me how can I nourish you then?'

'There's something I want rather badly, Leo.'

He propped himself up on one elbow and gazed into her eyes. 'You only have to name it?'

'A baby.'

The breath left his body in a rush and he gave a rueful smile. 'I didn't see that one coming. Have you thought this through?'

'Yes, and I don't want to leave it for much longer. You do want children don't you?'

A smile touched his mouth and he reached up to turn off the lamp. 'You bet I do. Place your order, my love. Would you prefer a boy or girl.'

'Surprise me?'

He took her in his arms and nuzzled against her ear, 'I love you, Esmé Thornton.'

Two days later a bicycle went along the road, pedalled by a man in a dark postal officer's uniform. He stopped at number forty-three and rang the bell.

Touching his cap when a man answered his ring, he said, 'Parcel for Thornton sir. Sign there if you please.'

Leo scribbled his signature on the paper the man held out, then took the parcel and gazed at the name on it. It was for Esmé.

Curious, he placed it against his ear and shook it. A faint rattle came from inside. There was no return address on it. He placed it on the hall table, looked at the clock and groaned. It was only six o'clock. What sort of hours did the post office keep?

Then he remembered that he and Es had managed to wangle a day off together. He got back in bed and snuggled up against her back, sliding his hands around her waist to her stomach.

She squirmed. 'Your hands are cold.'

'They'll soon warm up.'

'Who was that?' she said, sleepy and receptive to his exploration, despite the coolness of his touch. She made little cooing noises and wriggled at exactly the right times to let him know his attention was definitely being encouraged.

'It was a parcel delivery addressed to you,' he said against her ear.

'What was in it?'

'How would I know? I tried my best, but I couldn't see through the brown paper wrapping. It rattles though. Are you expecting a delivery?'

'Not yet.' She turned in his arms and laughed when he captured a firm buttock in each hand. 'Not of the kind you've been talking about. Besides, it's Saturday and I didn't think the post office delivers parcels today.'

'They just have. Perhaps they didn't have time to deliver them yesterday. He had several packages in his tray.'

He drank her in, her cheeks flushed with sleep and her body relaxed. 'You look gorgeous when you're rumpled, and you have such a lovely bum.'

'So do you.' She moved against him in a sinuous stretch and gently blew a quivering breath into his ear.

'For that alone, I'll make you a cup of tea, fetch your parcel and kiss your feet . . . but not until after.'

'After what?' She placed her hand on him, and caressing his

length with a light fingertip, she laughed. 'Your little Joey
wants to come out and play, I think.'

Her touch had him reacting instantly and he grunted. 'He's
not so little now.'

'I don't know how you get yourself in such predicaments Leo.'

'You don't, hey? How about this for starters.' He turned her
on her back and kissed each swelling nub of her breasts.

Her initial grunt turned into a growl.

When Esmé finally found time to unwrap the parcel, she said,
'Odd. It hasn't got any post office stamps on. Her face paled
as she gazed at the contents and she fell quiet.

Leo, who'd just decided to snatch an extra half-hour in bed
after his exertions, felt the change in atmosphere and opened
his eyes. 'What is it, Es?'

She gazed at him, the expression on her face bewildered.
'It's the money and jewellery that was stolen from us. I don't
understand, Leo . . . This must be some idiot's idea of an April
Fools' joke.'

Six

Rennie had booked a table at a nightclub. Judging by the
number of patrons it was a popular watering hole, crowded
with a mass of people who seemed to be trying to fill every
minute of their evening with enjoyment.

If anyone were looking in from the outside they wouldn't
have considered that Europe might be on the brink of war,
but it didn't escape Meggie's notice that most of the dancing
couples were of an age to kill — or be killed.

The laughter was just a little too forced, the drinking too
hard and the dancing too frenetic. It was one of those instances
when Meggie appreciated being a woman rather than a man.
She wouldn't like someone to place a gun in her hand and
order her to go out and kill, especially if she was disinclined
to do so.

When Leo disappeared on to the dance floor with her aunt, Rennie said, 'You're looking rather serious. What are you thinking about?'

'I'm thinking there's a reckless feeling in the air that's driven by fear, and it's likely my generation will lose its innocence too quickly if there's a war.'

He took her hands in his. 'I'm trying not to think about the war.'

'Somebody has to, especially when we live on such a small island.'

'Somebody does. It's the government. No doubt they have it all organized, and the rest of us will do as we're told. Buck up, Margaret my dear . . . we survived the last war.'

Not everyone, she wanted to say, remembering her father. But she shrugged off her instinct to argue because she remembered that Rennie would be one of the men called on to fight, and besides, it wasn't his fault that her father had died. 'I'm sorry if I'm being a bit of a drag. I won't mention war again, I promise.'

He had quite a delightful smile, one with an endearing sense of shyness to it, so it came and went swiftly, like a mouse popping out of its den for a quick look round. 'I must say I'd appreciate it if you didn't, for tonight, at least. Come on, Margaret . . . let's dance. I've been practising all week so I don't tread all over your toes, and I feel as nimble as Fred Astaire. You look really lovely, by the way.'

'That's sweet of you to say so. It took me three hours to get ready. I tried everything on in my aunt's wardrobe first and ended up in an old dress of my own. Not old as in *old*, you understand. I've only worn it once, but that was when I was sixteen. Fashion changes so quickly, doesn't it?'

'I suppose it does for women.'

'Aunt Es always looks elegant. My maternal grandmother was a dress designer and my mother thinks that Aunt Es has inherited her flair for fashion. She took the frilly bits off this dress, said it looked more sophisticated without them. She gave me these butterfly clips to use, instead.' When he chuckled she gazed at him. 'You're not really interested in my discarded frills are you?'

'I can't pretend that I am, but the butterflies are pretty. Are we going to dance, or not?'

'As long as you're not expecting a Ginger Rogers to partner your acute attack of Fred Astaireness.'

Still, she wasn't too bad at dancing and neither was Rennie. He was light on his feet. They managed a foxtrot without mishap then tripped over each other's feet and laughed when the music turned into a quickstep. Then they began to adjust their dancing styles as they got used to one another.

They gazed at each other, shaking their heads when an elimination tango was announced with a prize of five pounds. It wasn't a dance that could be taken lightly. There was a rush of couples from the floor as the weaker dancers abandoned it, until there were only six left.

Leo and Es were among them.

Rennie raised an eyebrow. 'A tango? They're game. That couple with the woman wearing the black dress usually wins the prize. They go from club to club.'

The couple did look professional, and confident. 'My aunt is a very good ballroom dancer, and so is Leo.'

Her aunt wore a figure-hugging dress of dark rose satin that flared from below the hip and had a scattering of gold sequins. Gold shoes with ankle straps completed her outfit. They stood, quite relaxed, Leo's arm around her aunt's waist, waiting to be issued with a number to be pinned to the back of Leo's evening suit.

When her aunt turned towards him and murmured something, he smiled, and brushed a kiss against her hair.

The lights were lowered, leaving only the dancers illuminated.

Leo was a natural show-off so he didn't mind being in the spotlight. Her aunt was used to it from her experience as a dancer on a cruise ship. She'd taught Leo the various dances in exchange for flying lessons, and both were a regular activity with them.

They were soon absorbed by the throbbing music, and glances joined they concentrated only on each other, while most of the other couples were eliminated, unnoticed by them. The professional couple started to do some fancy leg kicks, and although they were experts, there was something mechanical about them.

Leo handled Esmé as though she was a delicate twist of liquid crystal he was sculpting into an exquisite art form. It was a sensual dance, two lovers becoming familiar with each other's bodies. Meggie's cheeks heated slightly and she stole a glance at Rennie. There was so much she didn't know about that sort of thing.

Neither Aunt Es nor Leo seemed to see the remaining couple beckoned from the floor. Es was completely in Leo's hands as he twisted and turned her, moving her around as though he was stalking her. At the last turn she reclined backwards over his arm in surrender, ankles crossed. He brought her upright.

They smiled at each other, and then, loosening her hands Esmé hugged his leg and slid down it to the floor. Leo pulled her up, set her lightly on her feet and kissed her, to prolonged applause.

They were laughing as they walked back to the table, fiver in hand. Folding it, Leo pushed it through the slit in a wooden box that stood on the bar, designed to collect donations for the Red Cross.

Half an hour later Esmé stated their intention to leave. 'We've both got work in the morning. But you stay and enjoy your-selves Meggie. We'll take a taxi cab. You'll see her safely home, won't you, Rennie?'

'Of course.' Rennie extended a hand to Leo. 'I enjoyed this evening and I hope we'll meet again sometime. Thanks for the dance, Esmé. I hope I didn't ruin your shoes.'

After her aunt and uncle had gone they ran into four of Rennie's friends. They were older than her, more sophisticated – confident.

'Ah, here you are, Rennie, we've been tracking you down,' one of the women said, and threading her arm through his she kissed him gently on the mouth and whispered, 'I've missed you.'

Meggie was out of her depth, and a little embarrassed by the smart talk of who was doing what and with whom.

So this is Pam, Meggie thought. The woman couldn't tear her gaze away from Rennie, who avoided her self-consciously.

Soon the close proximity of the quartet dominated the comfortable space she and Rennie had once occupied, and she felt like a fish out of water. Her head began to ache with the sound of loud laughter and cigarette smoke.

As the evening wore on Rennie lost his initial reticence and his face assumed an animation he didn't bother to disguise. When he danced with Pam there was a barely disguised familiarity between them, and a lot of teasing. Even so, Meggie wondered if it were the done thing to ask an escort to take her home in the middle of a date.

'What's the girl drinking?' Pamela said. 'Give her a gin and tonic, Rennie darling, it might wake her up.' She peered into her face and breathed, 'My God, what perfect skin you have. You look as though you belong in the nursery wing, tucked into a cot. What did Rennie say your name was, darling?'

Meggie's hackles began to rise. 'It's Margaret Elliot, and I'm already wide awake . . . *darling*.'

'Good grief, it bites.' The shrill giggle Pam gave was halted by an attack of hiccups. 'So this is the reason why you lost interest in me, Rennie darling. You've taking up dating children.'

'You know very well it's not.' He ruffled her carefully styled hair as if she were his pet dog. 'Margaret happens to be a valued client.'

And she'd imagined she was his date. Meggie's ears began to burn and her gaze went to him, her mind ticking over in a slow burning count. 'It's getting late, perhaps I'd better be going.'

'Put her in a taxi cab then come back, Rennie . . . the night is young and we're going over to Ernie's place.'

He must have remembered his duty for he said, 'Don't bother waiting, Pam. Enjoy the rest of your evening.' He pulled back Meggie's chair, smiling apologetically down at her after she'd followed him through the patrons. When they reached the cloakroom and the attendant moved away to get their coats, he said, 'Pam is perfectly all right when she's sober.'

Even so, every pore of Meggie's curiosity had its antenna up to catch any whisper of information he offered her. The words were practically wrenched from her gut. 'You don't have to make excuses for her, I could see she was tiddly.'

'I will anyway. Pam and I were engaged to be married until recently.'

'What happened?'

'Nothing.'

'I see.'

He chuckled. 'Congratulations, not many people can see nothing.'

His irony was wounding. 'I see why you told her I was a client. You didn't want to hurt her feelings.'

'You are a client, and Pam's feelings are already hurt. She hit the nail on the head when she asked me if I was dating children. It made me feel as though taking someone of your age out was wrong.'

'Do you think my feelings are untouched. I've been talked down to, or talked about considerably tonight, and forced to sit there like a stuffed dummy. Being patronized in such a way has diminished me in my own eyes. It never entered my head that I was a duty date. I thought you liked me.'

'I do like you . . . and I didn't intend for you to feel that way. The fact is, Margaret, you are a client, and it's a conflict of interest for me to attempt any kind of relationship with you. Is there anything more you want to know?'

She winced at his biting anger. 'Obviously not. I wouldn't dare ask.'

'Good.' He took her coat from the attendant and placed it around her shoulders. It was gone midnight when she arrived home. Her aunt had left both the porch and hall lights on for her.

She didn't wait for him to open the car door, but stalked up the house steps and fiddled with her keys. He followed her.

They'd been quiet in the car, but she turned when she was safely inside, 'Thank you, Rennie. I enjoyed myself tonight . . . mostly.' She wanted to ask him if she would see him again but there was something conventional about him, and he might think it a bit too forward. All the same he'd been pleasant company for the most part, even if Pamela had proved to be a distraction for him.

'I'm sorry Pam spoiled our evening,' he said. 'I'm even sorrier that I did. Can you forgive me?'

To a certain extent Meggie had held on to her temper, and for that she felt proud. 'She didn't spoil it, because I enjoyed tonight, despite her intervention, and your about-turn.'

'I'm willing to take the blame if your feelings are dented because I encouraged you to think there was more to this than there actually is.' He gently kissed her on the forehead. 'I enjoyed myself too. You're an intelligent girl. Think about it, Margaret.'

'Your former fiancée was right about me being too young for you, wasn't she?'

'Yes, she was, and it served as a good reminder for me. You should enjoy the freedom of your youth. Friends, then?'

She nodded.

'Goodnight, my dear.' He turned and headed for the car, which had been left at the kerb with the engine quietly ticking over.

'How old are you?' She said to his back.

'Thirty-two.'

'That's almost an antique. You know something, Rennie Stone, you might think you're old enough to be my grandfather, but you don't fool me. I'm going to grow older and dazzle you, just you wait and see.'

He turned, his smile wide. 'Is that a threat or a promise?'

'Whichever you see it as.'

He made it clear what he thought of her by saying, 'Invite me to your coming-of-age party.'

She closed the front door and bolted it, then turned off the hall light and crept up to her bedroom, wondering if she'd ever see him again. Perhaps it was better for it to end this way, before she fell in love with him. She appreciated the fact that he'd let her down lightly.

Men! They were so complicated, she thought, just before she fell asleep.

All sorts of patriotic things were going on. People flew the Union Jack, and there were noisy meetings everywhere as the latest news from Europe was digested and debated. Generally the tone was pessimistic.

In July, Meggie and her aunt were walking across Hyde

Park when they were drawn into the crowd watching a National Service parade. A small number of WRNS officers were part of the parade. They looked incredibly smart in their uniforms as they marched along, and they wore flattering little hats.

'I'd like to join them.'

'Esmé smiled at her. 'You're always so eager to jump into anything that comes into your mind. I know it's difficult at your age, but you should think things through a bit more carefully.'

'It always seems like the right thing to do the very moment I think of it. When I try it out it's never as good as I initially thought it would be.'

They looked at each other and laughed.

Later, remembering she'd joined the WRNS waiting list, Meggie wrote them a letter, declaring – untruthfully – that she was just about to turn nineteen and enquiring if her earlier application was still valid.

Three weeks later she received a reply that interviews were being arranged and she'd be informed in due course.

Nicholas had no idea of what James Bethuen's portfolio consisted of, and neither, it seemed, as the lunch progressed, did James Bethuen.

The fact that he'd changed the appointment until the following week had not sat well with his father. There was method in his madness though. To start with he didn't intend to dance to James Bethuen's tune. Also, he would compare favourably with Michael Foggerty,

'Lord Cowan,' Bethuen said, his smile almost ingratiating as he'd got to his feet. He offered Nick a limp, damp handshake, one Nick would have wiped on his trouser leg, except the suit had only been delivered the previous day by his tailor, Dege & Skinner. He rather liked the grey double-breasted jacket, and the trousers with their turn-ups. With it he wore a royal blue tie and two-toned brogues. Removing his trilby he placed it on the hatstand along with his raincoat.

'I'm glad you arrived on time since I was just about to order.' His host beckoned to the waiter.

'I'm sorry if I've cut it a bit fine. I've just come from my gym, so had a good workout followed by a Turkish bath and a massage. There was a bit of a rally of some sort going on in Hyde Park and it slowed me down.'

'It was probably some communist scum planning mischief. What this country needs is more people like Oswald Mosley.'

'You don't believe in a fair day's pay for a fair day's work then?' Nick said evenly.

'Of course, but the riff-raff need keeping under control else they'll walk all over the rest of us. You're only a minute late. Would you care for a drink?'

'A dry sherry as an appetizer would be nice.'

'What do you recommend?' Bethuen said to the waiter.

'The steak and kidney pie is good, sir.'

Bethuen's stomach rumbled. 'I'll have that then, and jam roly-poly with custard to follow.'

'A little too heavy for me this time of day, I'm afraid,' and Nick's glance ran down the page. 'I'll have the braised cod with new potatoes, carrots and peas.'

'A pudding sir?' the waiter asked.

'Just the cheese board, and a half bottle of wine; the house white will do fine, and coffee to follow.'

'Yes, sir.'

When James Bethuen patted his paunch it resonated like a drum. 'You young chaps believe in working to stay slim. Still, I suppose it attracts the popsies. Wait till you're married and middle-aged like me. It will soon catch up with you.'

It hadn't caught up with Nick's father, who was disciplined where food was concerned, and was tall, slim and wiry. But then, his father hadn't been married for several years, and was probably still hoping for a suitable mate to come along. Nick hoped he'd take after him for looks. 'Yes, I suppose it will,' he said agreeably.

James Bethuen leaned forward and lowered his voice. 'Now, about this position. I can't tell you much about it except it needs a man with an exceptional brain, fluency in several languages, and the ability to set up and organize a small work-force. It's hush-hush, you see, and attached to the war office. It's an essential service, which means you'll be exempt from doing national service.'

That suited Nick. 'Can you give me some idea of what's required?'

'It will be code-breaking and stuff to start with. Mostly paper-work. You'll be attached to one of the services so will need uniforms, and you'll be required to attend an officer's course. That's about all I can tell you for now . . . except you might be approached from time to time to do outside work, which may or may not be dangerous, and that work of a nature where your own wits and intellect will be called upon, but not officially recognized. Someone will kit you out with a radio for your yacht.'

'Which branch of the services would that be, sir?'

'Oh, it will be the Senior Service I should imagine, dear boy. You'll need uniforms for the sake of appearances, but your tailor will be able to kit you out. Tell them to send the account to me. I'll deal with it.'

'Navy,' Nick thought later. It could have been worse. He just hoped nobody took it into their head to send him to sea.

Seven

September 1939

The talking was over. Hitler's promises had proved to be empty, and Poland had been invaded. The negotiations had been dragged out and prolonged. Now, Neville Chamberlain was addressing the nation, his voice grave to reflect his utter disap-pointment at the outcome of his efforts.

> *'I am speaking to you from the Cabinet room at Ten, Downing Street. This morning the British ambassador in Berlin handed the German government a final note stating that unless we heard from them by eleven o'clock that they were prepared at once to withdraw their troops from Poland, a state of war would exist between us. I have to tell you that no such undertaking has been received, and that consequently this country is at war with Germany . . .'*

'So it's official,' Leo said when the broadcast ended.

'Does this mean we won't be able to return to Australia?' Esmé sounded disappointed.

'We'll have to wait until after the war, my love. They're not going to run cruises . . . all the ships will be converted into troop ships.'

Girton College was off the menu too, deferred by necessity.

As Rennie had indicated before, the Sinclair estate was almost bankrupt. He had encouraging news though. A government department had commandeered Foxglove House and would pay for the refurbishment and any alterations needed.

'If there's anything personal you need from there . . . it will have to be removed by Christmas,' he advised. 'I've sent a letter to that effect to Doctor Elliot. And Margaret . . . as this comes under the Official Secrets Act you must not discuss it with anyone.'

'It sounds very cloak and daggerish?'

He laughed. 'It's a necessary precaution to remind you that there's a war on, and to be careful what you say to strangers, or in public where it can be overheard. You'll have to sign a statement saying you're aware of the Official Secrets Act, and will be advised by it. It will serve to remind you that you're privy to classified material and remind you that the act exists, and can be invoked if need be. Can you come into the office the day after tomorrow at eleven? I'll make sure you understand all the nuances.'

'My first impression is that it involves not being involved. Must I come to the office?'

'Perhaps we could lunch together, after.'

It wasn't a bad sweetener. 'I'd like that, Rennie.'

Meggie's mother surprised her with a phone call the next day. There's a legacy from your father, Richard Sangster. It will be yours to do what you like with when you turn twenty-one, but I'll release it before if you definitely get a place at Girton College. And there's some jewellery that belonged to your Sinclair-Sangster grandmother. I'll never wear it and I don't imagine you will. It could be sold.'

'Oh, we don't have to worry about that now, Mother. I've deferred any further education until after the war.'

'I see, and I'm relieved. It's not a good idea to dispose of your assets when the world is in such turmoil. In the meantime we can't have you living off your uncle and aunt. You must try and find employment and support yourself above and beyond your allowance. It shouldn't be too hard with a war on. Is that clear, Meggie?'

'Yes, Mother. I do have other irons in the fire, and I have an interview in a day or two. You have your lecture voice on. Are you annoyed with me for something?'

'Force of habit, I suppose. Just be careful. You're prone to making important decisions on the spur of the moment. I'm a little disappointed. I thought you might work nearby for a few years, marry, then settle down and have a family, rather than try and compete in a male-dominated profession where proficiency is achieved only after many years' hard work. You could always join the Women's Institute and do volunteer work, or take up nursing like your aunt. Why are you always trying to draw attention to yourself by being *different?*'

The last thing Meggie wanted to do was argue with her mother over this but it was her life. 'Is that what you think I'm doing? All I want is to live my life in a way that suits me. I know I wouldn't make a good nurse. If you're so keen on nursing why didn't you take it up yourself?'

There was a moment of silence. 'I didn't get the chance. Circumstances for me were very different. I had no choice but to work as a maid when I was sixteen. I had Chad and Esmé to raise. Then you. And then the boys came along.'

Meggie was quite aware of the sacrifice her mother had made, and thankful she could make a choice, and didn't have to work at some necessary, but menial task. 'But didn't you do that so we'd all have a good future in front of us?'

'Yes, but—'

'Then you're achieving what you set out to do. Would you rather have been a nurse?'

'Of course not. I loved being a mother.'

'So you did what you wanted to do. It's just that the circumstances were different and you didn't have much choice. That being the case, why should you object to me doing what I want to do? Just for once, could you, at least, credit me with some sense that I actually do know what's best for me. After all, you created me and brought me up, so I am what you made me.'

'Yes . . . I suppose you are. Just remember you're still only seventeen.'

'*Nearly* eighteen.' She felt a little rush of guilt when she remembered lying about her age in her letter to the WRNS.

She could almost hear her mother shrug, and predictably, she did what she usually did when she didn't want to answer Meggie's questions – changed the subject. 'Are you coming down for your Uncle Chad's wedding?'

'Yes of course. We'll probably come by train now petrol is rationed to a quota of miles per month. It will save Leo's allowance. It will be an uncomfortable journey though, with the trains full of refugee children being sent to the country.'

'Yes, I suppose it will . . . we intend to take two girls in. Luke is grumbling because he'll have to move back into the same room with Adam if you return home, but it can't be helped. The children have to go somewhere. They'll be able to help me about the house when they're not at school. I expect Chad and Sylvia will take in a couple of children too, once they're settled.

'Leo and Es can have the couch in the front room while you're here, or you can all sleep at Foxglove House for the night. We can prepare a couple of rooms there.'

'It's hardly worth it for one night.'

Meggie felt like an outsider again. It had always seemed to her that everyone else in the family came before her. Although she loved her mother, and knew that love was reciprocated, they had never really been easy together. Sometimes she thought she'd been born to the wrong mother. She should have been Aunt Esmé's daughter since they got on so well together. She reached for something to say. 'Have you heard that Foxglove House is being let to the government for the duration of the war?'

'Yes, though I don't know what they intend to do with it. Perhaps it's top secret.'

'How can it be when everyone is talking about it? There are rumours of the place becoming an orphanage, a convalescent home, a secret hideaway for the Prime Minister, a place where spies are trained and a prison camp! Oh . . . my goodness. How jolly exciting war is. No wonder we mustn't talk about it.'

'You won't think war is so funny when food and clothes rationing comes in and there are foreign soldiers running all over our fields and smashing our front doors in.'

A shiver ran through Meggie. 'I don't think it's funny now, and I don't think our own soldiers will allow that to happen. But if we're overwhelmed there's nothing I can do to stop it. We'll just have to learn to live with it.'

Her mother gave a bit of a snort. 'I've gone through the place and rescued the good china, the ornaments, silverware, pictures and anything else of value I could find. We've stored it in that brick shed at the back of Nutting Cottage, at least Chad can keep an eye on it there. Then there's the furniture.'

'Make a bonfire with it.'

'Don't be silly, Meggie. It can stay there. Denton has signed an agreement to that effect.'

'Why don't we sell it to a dealer?'

'It's part of the house. You won't be able to afford to refurbish the place in the same style. Besides, your allowance comes out of that house, such as it is. You can't get rid of assets, you never know when you might need them.'

'Look mother . . . Foxglove House is a liability, not an asset. I don't want the place, or anything in it. Can't I just give it to charity, or something.'

'Yes . . . you can, but not until you're of age, and responsible enough to know what you're doing. The furnishings are part of the house. I'm going to see if that storage place will be able to accommodate some of it though.'

Meggie groaned. 'I don't think I'll ever be old enough or responsible enough to do anything in your eyes.'

Her mother gave a light laugh. 'I've never known anyone so eager to give a legacy away. It's always been easy come easy go with you.'

'I think you're just as eager to get it off your hands.'

'Yes, I am. It's been a nuisance all these years having the weight of the Sangster family on my back, and an added responsibility for Denton . . . not that he complains. I wish the Sinclair legacy had died with Richard. Still, at least the house will be occupied now, and the maintenance kept up to date.'

'Would my father have minded me giving it away?'

'Richard? He might have because he grew up there, and was proud of the Sinclair connection and inheritance. But he never had any time for regrets, or self-pity. Life would have been different for all of us if his expectations had been normal, I imagine.'

'In what way?'

'Oh, I don't know . . . still, it's too late to change anything now.'

'Would you want to?'

There was a moment of hesitation as her mother considered it, then said, 'You always ask such odd questions. No, of course I wouldn't want to. To deny Richard would be to deny you. Is that what you wanted to hear?'

It would explain what she felt sometimes . . . that although she was loved, it was because she existed, which didn't disguise the fact that she was a bit of an inconvenience. But even while she thought it, she felt guilty. She'd always dramatized situations.

Her mother hadn't asked her what the interview was for . . . which was just as well, Meggie thought, after they'd run out of things to say. It was one thing saying she was grown up and another actually being grown up. Her heart began to thump at the change she was going to bring about in her life.

For a moment she gave Rennie a thought. Where did he fit into her life? Did he fit in at all? She was too young to be in a serious relationship with anyone, which to her and her family meant courtship, an engagement ring and eventual marriage and children.

She liked Rennie a lot but that didn't mean they couldn't just remain friends. She had the strongest of feeling that they were going to be parted by circumstance anyway. Rennie had made his intentions towards her very clear – in that he had none. Besides she hardly knew him, and it would be stupid to contemplate building a future on two dates.

Now she'd convinced herself of that, she realized she didn't actually want to fall in love yet, so it would be practical to avoid men altogether and just direct her energies towards establishing her career.

The atmosphere of concentration in the room was disturbed now and again by the scratch of pens on paper and the occasional clearing of the throat. Five other women were taking the exam.

It was all straightforward. Meggie answered the questions, checked through them in case she'd missed anything, and then handed her examination papers to a woman sitting at a small desk overseeing proceedings.

The woman scribbled a time at the top of her papers, and raising an eyebrow whispered as she pointed to a door, 'That was quick . . . the galley is through there. Pour yourself a cup of tea and help yourself to biscuits – you might need to make a fresh pot.'

One by one the others began to finish the written exam and their papers were collected. Then the bell was rung to indicate time was up. The remaining two candidates smiled at each other with some relief, and stood around talking, and sipping tea.

One of them, an older woman made a bit of a face. 'I don't think I did too well. You seemed to get through it quickly.'

'I've just finished school so I'm used to taking exams. I answer the questions I know straight away, and then go back to the ones I have to think twice about. It saves wasting time by trying to puzzle them out at the beginning.'

'If I don't get in here I might try for one of the other services, so I'll remember that.'

'Good luck,' they said when Meggie was called in for the interview first.

Through the next door five women in uniform constituted a panel.

One of them had her examination papers spread out. 'You did well in both your IQ test and the written examination.'

Meggie hadn't doubted it, because the questions had been fairly standard. 'Thank you. I'm pleased.'

Paper shuffled. 'I see that both your father and grandfather served in the army in the last war.'

Meggie reminded herself of Leo's advice not to talk too much, and to tell them what they expected to hear. 'My paternal grandfather, Major Sangster did something in London. I don't know what . . . he never told me except to say it was a secret and he wasn't allowed to talk about it. As for my father, he fought in the trenches. Richard Sangster was gassed, and he died before I was born. He was a hero, and so was my stepfather, who served his time as a field surgeon. They were boyhood friends.'

One of the women smiled. 'Why have you chosen to apply to join the Women's Royal Naval Service?'

'I like the uniform. I saw them at the parade in Hyde Park and thought they were very smart.'

When the women looked at each other and smiled Meggie said quickly, 'I know that sounds horribly vain, but no woman likes to look dowdy, does she, and khaki is so dreadfully, well . . . khaki? After that parade I sent you a letter.'

'Ah yes . . . you wrote to remind us that you'd put your name on the waiting list.' She waved a sheet of paper in the air. 'I have it here. Your enthusiasm does you credit.'

Meggie remembered an old recruiting poster from the First World War that she'd found in Foxglove House. It was a picture of a woman standing on a cliff and pointing out to sea, and had belonged to a maid who'd left her job to do her duty in the first war.

She realized that the answer she'd given might have sounded trivial. 'Vanity is not the only reason I want to join, of course. I'm very keen to do something to help my country in its time of need, and I've wanted to join the WRNS since I first heard of the service.'

'It says on your form that flying is one of your interests.'

'Yes . . . though as a passenger so far. My uncle flies a Tiger Moth and he takes me up sometimes. It's a wonderful experience.'

'So you're not afraid of heights?'

She remembered the manner of address she should have remembered earlier. 'Not at all, ma'am.'

'And you have a driving licence?'

'I'm still learning, but should have one in a month or so. I've been practising in city conditions to gain some experience.'

'Very good. I understand you've been accepted for Girton College.'

'Not accepted, but I've passed the entrance exam. I've deferred entrance until after the war. At the moment my intention is to study law eventually.'

There was a heartening exchange of significant looks as though her intention was being approved of.

A woman at the end of the table shuffled through her papers. 'It says here that you own property in Dorset, yet you live with your family. Tell us about that, if you would.'

'Foxglove House is a legacy, and is a small country estate. The legacy is complicated by the conditions attached to it. I can use the income, such as it is, but the depression has reduced that considerably. I'll never live there. It's too big and I won't be able to afford to keep the house staffed, or maintained. Eventually it will be sold and the proceeds donated to charity. At least, that's my plan at the moment, but I'm advised by my stepfather until I'm of age.'

The woman in the middle gazed at the two either side of her and they shook their heads to indicate they had no more questions.

'Thank you, Miss Elliot. 'What happens next will depend on your medical report. You can pop along and see the doctor after you leave here, after which you may return home. We'll be in touch in due course. If you're accepted into the service you'll be measured for your uniform and sent to training school before you're assigned to your duties. Do you have any preferences as to your placement?'

Although in awe of her interviewers, women who looked and sounded profoundly efficient, Meggie answered with a less than humble, 'Apart from lacking the slightest desire to peel onions and potatoes or clean ablutions blocks, I have no preferences ma'am. Perhaps something clerical would suit me best. I'm sure you'll have a better idea than me where I would best be of use. I just want to serve my country in any way I can . . . well in almost every way, as I . . . um demonstrated,' she said, and then bit her tongue in case she began to ramble on.

'I think that's all then, Miss Elliot.'

Meggie wondered if she ought to salute them, but she was already self-conscious about acting the part when she wasn't actually one of them yet. Had she gone too far by lying about her age? She wondered.

Just before she closed the door behind her she heard one of them chuckle, and hesitated.

'The girl recorded her age as seventeen on the initial application, yet she said she was turning nineteen in October in her letter.'

'In which case she wouldn't need parental permission.'

'Quite,' another of them said drily.

Meggie's smile faded when somebody said, 'Close the door behind you please, Miss Elliot.'

Eight

An approach had been made to Leo to give basic training to would-be pilots in Tiger Moths and Avros, a position he accepted, even though he'd not be officially drafted into the Royal Air Force.

He was put through a rigorous two-week flying programme first at the RAF station at Uxbridge, and came out of it familiar with the controls of a fighter aircraft, and able to handle Hurricanes and Spitfires competently.

He was pleased by the offer because his contract at the teaching hospital had come to an end. His replacement was a junior doctor waiting to enhance his skills. Because the airfield was now closed to private traffic, it meant Leo could keep his hand in, and his flying hours up.

As well, he offered his voluntary services on his day off, and free of charge, to a medical centre in one of the poorer areas of London. He could also be called on as a specialist surgeon when needed, both of which would help keep him busy.

Meggie received a letter from the WRNS telling her that her application to join the service at this time would be filed, and it would help her application if she got some experience of being part of the workforce in the meantime. Her application would be reviewed again when she turned eighteen.

She applied for a job at the hospital her aunt worked at, and was offered a job in hospital administration as a junior clerk. Most of the office workforce were old, and disapproved of anyone who hadn't yet grown a set of wrinkles. She made the tea, typed the letters because she was fast, and kept the office tidy. She was bored on the first day.

London changed in small ways. Sandbags guarded the entrances to public buildings. Shop windows were boarded up. Trenches had been dug that zigzagged across the commons and parks so people could hide in them in case of air attack.

Leo and Meggie constructed a bomb shelter in the back garden, to the side of the vegetable patch they'd been trying to cultivate and not far from the privet hedge dividing them from the house next door, to offer them extra protection.

Leo had bought the shelter in kit form. It had been named grandly after the Lord Privy Seal, Sir John Andersen. Bolted at the top, six curves of steel were partly buried in the ground over a hole dug in the earth. Lined with more metal sheets it had sacking covering the doorway, and was covered in earth.

The two of them gazed at it proudly, then Meggie said. 'Won't it fill with water if it rains.' They gazed at each other.

'Better to be damp than have the house fall down on you,' Esmé said, coming up behind them with a mug of tea in both hands.

'Your aunt speaks from experience. As you know, it happened to her in Australia when she climbed on a roof beam full of termites.' His arm went round Esmé and he drew her against his side. 'I thought I'd lost her before I'd really got to know her. How do you like the new home we've built for you, my love?'

'Extremely cosy. I love the front door, and it has food handy if one likes cabbages.'

'Would you like to launch it by officially naming it?'

'Mole-hole Lodge,' Esmé said. 'I'll paint a sign for it tomorrow.'

They were issued with gas masks, and although they smelled rubbery and moulded to the face with claustrophobic tightness, Meggie bore in mind that her father had been gassed in the trenches, and the damage had eaten away his lungs and eventually destroyed him.

When Aunt Es expressed her relief that Leo hadn't joined up, he offered her a couple of grunts and said, 'Don't count your chickens yet, my love. The war has only just started and none of us can see what the future holds.'

Dressed in their best, their gas masks swinging from their shoulders, they travelled by train to Dorset for her uncle Chad's wedding to Sylvia. Even the earliest train was crowded with noisy children, labelled with their names like living parcels being sent to unknown destinations. Babies cried and their harassed minders grumbled from the sheer fatigue of caring for so many at once.

Though they were all dressed in their best for the wedding, Esmé took one of the babies in her arms and comforted the child until it fell into fitful sleep. Meggie wondered how the mothers felt having to send their children away to be looked after by strangers. Some better-off ones had been sent abroad to Canada.

Better this evacuation than send them overseas, she thought. Meggie followed her aunt's example and took a toddler on her lap. But the child took exception to her and grizzled for his mother all the way.

Leo stood in the aisle, his eyes turned towards the passing landscape and with a smile playing around his mouth. She thought he was far away, up in the air somewhere. Then she realized his dreamy gaze was on Esmé's reflection.

It was a perfect autumn day; the leaves falling from the trees were a thousand shades of shaved ochre. But there was a nip in the air, and nobody would have guessed there was a war on – though Leo had told them of an incident where one of their own planes had been shot down by gunners who'd mistaken it as the enemy.

They left the children behind in the aroma of dried pee the

carriage had collected, and headed towards Livia's home on foot. There was a smell of bonfires in the air and the leaves crunched underfoot.

Meggie's legacy was almost the same as she'd left it, except the long grass of Foxglove House had been trimmed back, and there was a man up a ladder removing the shutters from the window. She'd spent hours there by herself in the dusty, shuttered twilight, hiding from the world, making up stories, feeling like an outsider, even though she'd inherited the place.

Now she *would* be an outsider, because once the place became an institution it would be painted in efficient cream and green, and brown linoleum would spread over the floorboards like an expanse of river mud when the tide went out. It would smell of beeswax and perhaps disinfectant, and there would be notice boards screwed to the walls, with red arrows pointing every which way. Gents Lavatory. Adjutant's Office. Mess Deck . . . Spy Training Centre.

Her laughter brought a smile from Leo. 'What's tickled you?'

'My mother thinks they might train spies here.'

'Anything is possible, I suppose.'

Sheets of paper with commands would be attached to corkboards, and smaller, more important memos with exclamation marks would be pierced through their corners with bright brassy pins, so the paper agitated busily in the draughts, as if trying to escape and go about the business of spreading the news it contained.

She felt like a Sinclair Sangster memo, reluctantly pinned to the notice board and trying to escape from its grip.

Then they were past, and nodding to the postman who crossed their path in the opposite direction and ringing his bell, said in his rich, rural burr, 'Good day to you sir, and young ladies. It's a lovely day for a wedding, isn't it? The church looks pretty.'

'It certainly is a lovely day,' Leo said.

'Mrs Elliot, nice lady that she is, has invited me to the reception. I shall enjoy that.' The postman began to whistle; 'Here comes the bride,' as he went past, his bicycle rattling over the potholes.

Aunt Esmé suddenly exclaimed, 'There's Nutting Cottage.

It looks so pretty. They've painted it cream, and I love those cotoneasters, the berries are so red and the leaves so dark and green, and I like the way it spreads and flattens its bracts across the wall. Look, the picket fence has been repaired and painted to match the house.'

Meggie didn't want to look. The shining red berries shone like beads of blood, she thought, and remembered seeing her grandfather dead in his chair on the other side of the window as if it had been yesterday – his mouth hanging open in his grey face. She'd only spoken to him a few minutes before, and he'd told her he was her father. But he'd been old and feeble and his mind wandered. It had been the worst day of her life.

She forced herself to look at the place. Yes, it was pretty, but she didn't want to live there, and she hadn't been inside the cottage since. She felt slightly ill. What if he had been her father? No! That terrible time when she fought her inner demons over that question had been dealt with.

Aunt Esmé took her hand and tucked it in her arm, as though she knew what she was thinking about. Kissing her cheek, Es whispered, 'Try not to allow the past get the better of you, sweetheart,' and Meggie felt like crying.

A car came up the road. Luke gazed at them from the driving seat. 'Does anyone want a lift?'

Meggie took the passenger seat next to him. 'You're not old enough to drive. Does Mummy know you've taken her car?'

'Of course she does. She was in the middle of making some egg and bacon tarts when she suddenly remembered you were catching the early train and panicked, so I said I'd pick you up. She's been teaching me to drive, you see. She said I've got a natural aptitude. How are you, Sis?'

'Terrific. I've got a job at a hospital.'

He clutched at his throat and groaned. 'Not as a nurse, I hope, or worse still . . . a doctor. They must have all run like billy-o when they saw you coming.'

'Don't be such a mongrel, Luke, else I'll beat you up and it will be you needing a doctor.'

Luke's laughter had a quality of awe to it. 'Doctors are ten a penny in our household. I've heard that you plan to become a lawyer.'

'That's right.'

'Mother nearly tore her hair out after you rang her. Grandmother Elliot overheard, and had her thruppence worth of say about it . . . though it went on a bit and was more like ten shillings' worth. In the end Mother politely told Grandmother Elliot that it wasn't really her business, and would she kindly not listen in to her private phone calls. So Gran went off in a frightful sulk.'

Meggie was impressed that her mother had taken on Grandmother Elliot, and had won.

Luke turned to Leo and Esmé, who had slid into the back seat with the bags. 'It's nice to see you again, sir, and you, Aunt Es. Mother's in a panic I'm afraid. You know what she's like when she has to cater. Dad and Adam have disappeared up into the attic to play with the train set. We've got an electric one now . . . with two engines, passenger and goods trains. We've got quite a clubhouse up there too. You must come up to see it, Leo.'

Meggie sighed. 'Let's get going then, so we can help sort Mummy out. Put your foot down, Luke.'

He did put it down. The car lunged forward a couple of times, and then stalled. '*Donner und Blitzen,*' Luke said under his breath.

'What's that supposed to mean?'

'It's German. It means thunder and lightning.'

'Well, why don't you just say it in English, then everyone can understand it?'

'Because it's a rude expression in German.'

'It doesn't sound very rude to me. Besides, if somebody hears you spouting German they'll probably shoot you. A natural aptitude, did you say? If we stay here much longer it will be quicker to walk home.'

In the back seat, Es got a fit of the giggles and Leo began to laugh unrestrainedly.

Luke turned red. 'A chap can make a mistake, can't he? You're putting me off my driving, Meggie.'

'How can you be driving when the engine isn't running?'

She kissed her brother on the cheek. 'Stop complaining you dolt, I was only teasing. You'll never know how much I missed you.'

'Welcome to the Elliot household,' Es said under her breath.

They made it to Eavesham House without incident. Livia Elliot was in a right royal flap when they got there. Relief filled her eyes when she saw them. 'Thank goodness you're here. The service is at one o'clock, and I'm never going to have everything ready in time.' She gave their outfits a quick perusal. 'You look good, Es. Isn't that suit and hat a bit grown up for you, Meggie?'

'Goodness, Mother . . . how many times do I have to tell you. I *am* grown up. I even have a responsible job, though it's totally boring.'

They shed their coats and hats, and went back to the kitchen, Meggie feeling as though she'd shrunk to half her age and had never been away. Her mother took her duties seriously, to the point of smothering.

'That's good . . . you must tell me about it sometime, but not now . . . pass that mustard would you,' she said and surveyed the messy table vaguely. 'Oh dear . . . I should have got the caterers in. Now . . . where did I put my list?'

'I've got it.' Meggie exchanged a grin with her aunt. Taking a clean white apron down from a peg she tied it around her waist and said to her mother,' Go and have a soak in the bath, it will help you to relax. Your hair looks pretty in that style.'

Livia patted her hair. 'Do you think so? Denton liked it too. Can you manage in the kitchen by yourself, Meggie? Of course you can. You were always so capable in the kitchen. You'll make a good wife for some lucky man before too long.'

Meggie grimaced and counted loudly to ten.

Tossing her a grin, Leo gave her mother a hug and gently redirected her train of thought. 'Where's the bridegroom?'

'Chad's at Nutting Cottage. You're his best man, aren't you, Leo? I'm surprised Luke didn't drop you off there.'

'He probably forgot. He was concentrating on his driving.'

'Yes . . . well, Luke's sensible about such things. I taught him to drive myself . . . Meggie as well, so they're both safe drivers. Why don't you take the car, Leo.'

'We have to economize. Besides, I need the walk and it's not far. We'll get to the church in Chad's car.'

'Be a love and flush Denton out of his hidey-hole first. Ask him to see to the drinks. There's bottled beer and wine, and champagne for the toasts. Tell him to remember the bottle openers. We don't want to have to look for everything when we get back from the church.'

'Tell him I've brought his favourite humbugs with me and he can't have them until he's finished all his tasks. That will dig him out of his hole,' Esmé added.

Leo winked at Esmé. 'What are you going to do, my love?'

'I'm going to make a cup of tea, and then act as ladies' maid to Livia and kitchen assistant to Meggie. I'll make sure the reception room is ready, too. I imagine it's going to be a buffet lunch.'

Gradually everything was sorted out, and before long they were in the church. Chad offered them all a smile as he waited calmly with Leo at his side, for his bride to arrive. He was dressed in a grey suit with striped waistcoat. The congregation was sprinkled with men in uniform, standing tall and proud in a field of fluttering flowers, as though the responsibility of war had revealed the adventure of it to the congregation, but not its deadliness.

They wouldn't have to look far for reminders of it, a list of names of men from the village that had lost their lives in the Great War was on the War Memorial. For the most part they were heartbreakingly young.

Meggie had read her father's diaries of the last war, and now her heart quaked for those who were going into the unknown. She looked at her two brothers, who were not old enough, thank goodness. She must try and be nicer to them, she thought, overwhelmed by love for them.

Her stepfather cruised up and down the aisle, stopping to exchange pleasantries with the guests and keeping an eye out for the bride and her father through the open church door.

Her mother fretted over whether everyone would fit in the house every time he came their way.

Denton dismissed her worries with a grin. 'Shall I dash home and build an extension?'

Her mother's giggle bordered on hysteria. 'Don't you dare make me laugh, Denton Elliot.'

Meggie smiled at her. 'We've opened the folding glass doors to the dining room, so stop worrying about it, Mummy, and we've turned the radiators on to warm the place up a bit.'

Even that innocuous remark produced a fret. 'I do hope the icing on the wedding cake doesn't melt. Sylvia's family provided the cake, so I don't know exactly what's in it.'

'Plaster of Paris, I expect. We won't be able to get our teeth through it.'

'Behave yourself, Denton. You do look pretty, Meggie. No wonder that man over there is trying to catch your attention? Is he one of ours or one of theirs?'

'Which man is that?' She turned to gaze to where her mother had indicated and received the spontaneous smile he curved her way. Her heart did a bit of a dance around her chest, and blood rushed to her face. She hadn't seen Rennie for quite a while. 'It's Rainard Stone. He's my solicitor, and manages the Sinclair estate. Did you invite him, Daddy? If we'd known he was coming he could have travelled down with us.'

Livia said in dismay, 'Gracious, I shall have to find him somewhere to sleep. You must tell me all about him, Meggie.'

'I will not. If you want to know anything about him, you must ask him yourself.' A man at the other end of the aisle signalled to Denton, who in turn gave a wave to the organist, who began to softly play Mendelssohn's wedding march. Meggie grinned. She did like family get-togethers. There were so many oddments in the family, and they all fitted together and expanded like pieces of the same jigsaw puzzle. Sylvia's family would just add more pieces.

'Sylvia must be on her way, I'm dying to see her dress.'

Livia sighed. 'I'm not. It took me hours to stitch round the hem. Girls these days should be taught more domestic skills. They all want careers. You forgot to tell me you'd invited a man called Rainard Stone, Denton. What an odd name.'

Meggie told her, 'He told me he was born in a deluge, so his mother called him Rainard. Not that I believe him, since his mother doesn't look like the type who would possess that ironic sort of wit. She's sort of vague, with a sinister undertone.'

Livia shrugged. 'None of that helps me to find him

somewhere to sleep. There isn't an inch of spare room left in the house.'

Denton chuckled. 'What about the hen house.'

'Denton Elliot, it's you who'll be sleeping in the hen house if you're not careful.'

'Don't worry, my love. He's going home on the evening train. I intend to show him round Foxglove House later. Meggie, you can come with us if you like, so you'll know what's happening with your legacy. He hasn't seen what he's been lumbered with yet. Here comes Sylvia, doesn't she look lovely?'

Preceded by two young nieces dressed in pink velvet with white fur trim, Sylvia looked sweet in a simple white damask gown with a pleated yoke and sweetheart neckline with pearl buttons. A shoulder length veil with pink embroidered rosebuds scattered on it was attached to a flower-filled wreath and matched a spray of pink carnations.

Meggie's Uncle Chad had a tender smile on his face as he watched his bride approach, and there was a collective smile and exclamations from the congregation when he took her white, gloved hand in his and kissed it in rather a romantic fashion.

But then, she wouldn't have thought her rather ordinary Uncle Chad would fall in love. And although he was Aunt Esmé's twin, and although his sister had inherited all the elegance and beauty of the pairing, there was an air of quiet dependability to him that brought tears to Meggie's eyes.

Beside her, Aunt Es gave a barely repressed sort of sniff that was stirred into a giggle when Chad turned to catch her eye and winked at her. Es blew her brother a kiss and Meggie took her hand.

'*We are gathered together in the sight of God to join this man and this woman in holy matrimony . . .*'

When the jollity was over and the couple had left for a week's honeymoon in Cornwall, which was all the time Chad could afford to take off from his practice, Meggie accompanied her stepfather to Foxglove House and they wandered from room to room.

'There's just enough light to show you around, Rennie,' he said. 'My wife has been busy organizing the clearing out of the cupboards, and everything will be placed in storage until after the war.'

Meggie had her say. 'I told Mummy she should make a bonfire of it, except for the grand piano. I'd like to have kept that, but it's too big to put in a suitcase and carry from place to place.'

'Not everything is rubbish. Some of it is family history and might be worth keeping for when you have children, Meggie, especially if you decide to write a book, as you once mentioned you might. There is quite a lot of your grandmother's stuff here too. Richard loved this place, and I don't think he'd like you to treat it with less than the respect it deserves.'

'I do understand that, Daddy, but I'm not Richard Sangster. I feel like an alien, rather than part of his family, and an alien in my own family because of the connection.'

'You'll never be that to me, Poppet.'

'But don't you see, Daddy. This house anchors me to a life I don't want to live, and keeps me there. I don't want to be responsible for it, and I'm truly sorry that you and Rennie have wasted your time trying to keep it viable, when I intend to give it to charity as soon as I'm able.'

'Don't be too hasty,' Rennie said. 'There were new laws passed regarding entailed estates, like yours. I'm making enquiries.'

'Who did that Sinclair ancestor think he was, insisting the legacy be passed down from Sinclair to Sinclair, as though we had no free will of our own? How dare a man who died a couple of hundred years ago try and inflict his will over his descendants?'

Denton shrugged. 'God help anyone who tries to inflict their will over yours, Meggie.'

Rennie chuckled. 'You needn't feel sorry for me, Margaret. My firm gets paid a fee from the estate.'

'Which is more than I get,' Denton said with a grin.

'And probably more than the allowance I get as well. But you got me to raise instead, Dr Denton, so you got the best of the bargain.' She gave him a fierce hug. 'And so did I. I'd rather have you for a father than Richard Sangster, or a dusty old heap of bricks full of someone else's memories. You know, I think the heart left Foxglove House with my father.'

'You could be right.'

Rennie laughed. 'I'm glad you sorted that out. Thanks for showing the place to me . . . it does give me a better idea of what I'm dealing with. Now I must go because the light's beginning to fail.'

Meggie glanced at her watch. 'I'll walk with you to the train station, just in case you miss the train. Though we can fit you in somewhere, I'm sure, even if it's in a sleeping bag in the attic.'

Rennie nodded. 'Good . . . because I've got a favour to ask you, Mags.'

They'd been striding – for that's how Rennie walked – for only a few seconds when he took her hand is his and said. 'I've enlisted in the army.'

'Slow down Rennie,' she said, almost breathless from the exercise. 'I can't keep up with you in these shoes.'

'Sorry.' Bringing her to a stop he gazed at her and smiled. 'I'd forgotten how lovely you were until I saw you at the church.'

Her heart seemed to cease its beating, and there was an extraordinary quietness inside her, as though she no longer existed, except as a beautiful spirit twisting and turning in the currents of air. She wanted to cry, but knew she mustn't, at least, not in front of him, so she pulled on a smile.

'You're prone to exaggeration, and rather abrupt, Rennie. But thank you for the compliment. I'll treasure it. And I'll miss you.'

He gave a faint smile. 'You didn't strike me as a sentimental sort of girl who would have a treasure box. The compliment will probably have to last you until the war is over.'

'Not if you put it in writing. And I shall start a treasure box just to keep it in. What will happen to your legal firm while you're away?'

'There is a cousin on my mother's side available. He's too young for retirement and too old to go to war. He's a barrister. Mother will take up practice again.'

'It was your mother working in reception that day I called on you, wasn't it?'

'Yes . . . but she's qualified to practice law. Didn't I tell you? The thing is, Margaret, I thought you might like to work for the firm in reception, and doing secretarial tasks.'

'But I'll be going in the WRNS before too long. I want to do my bit, as well.'

'Not before you're eighteen. Even a month or two in a law office will give you some valuable experience of how things work in the legal world. You'll be able to gain experience, and our law books will be a valuable reference for your legal studies as well as your grading, should you join the WRNS. What do you think?'

She smiled. 'I think I'm going to give you the biggest hug you've ever had, and don't resist.'

He didn't, just hugged her back, her head folded into his shoulder and his breath warm against her back. Then he gently made a space between them and their eyes met, his were a foxy amber in the gloaming light.

'Kiss me goodbye,' she said.

He smiled. 'Are you intent on turning this into a romantic ending to put in your treasure box?'

'Yes . . . but not an ending . . . a treasured memory that will always be remembered. Please kiss me. I'm going to feel a fool if you walk away leaving me standing here with my lips pursed, a rejected old maid, and at my young age.'

'That would be cruel,' he said, his voice quite serious. So he did kiss her, and his lips were warm and teasing, but disappointingly, pressed against her forehead in a very circumspect manner.

Somewhere in the distance the train whistled.

'I'll wait for you,' she said.

'No, don't wait, Mags. I don't want you to make a decision you'd come to regret, and I don't want the responsibility of knowing you have. Be young and carefree while you can, and know that I'll always be your friend.' He placed a small flat box in her hand. 'An early birthday present. Give my mother a ring in a day or two and discuss the position with her, but don't leave it too long.'

Then he was gone, striding through the gloom towards the station, which was in darkness. The windows of the houses of England were all dressed in depressing black, not even a chink of candlelight shone through the blackout curtains hanging in the cottage windows. In the sky, the stars seemed to weep tears. She wished one would drop into her hand. She could do with some reassurance that eventually the world would be right again.

A cold wind circled her legs and body with a whiplash rattle of fallen leaves. The world seemed to shiver . . . and had an air of waiting.

Because she was curious as to what a man like Rennie would give a girl like her as a birthday present, she opened the little box and aimed the thin gleam of her torch on it for a moment. She smiled. She'd got her star – in the form of a small twinkly diamond that dangled from a mother of pearl, crescent moon brooch set in silver. It was so very pretty.

Meggie made her first wish on them both. 'Bring Rennie back safely. And when you do, make him realize I'm not too young for him, unless you think I am, I suppose.'

She heard the clank of metal bones and the breathless chuff of the train as it pulled out with Rennie on board, taking him to God-only-knew what hellhole he was destined for. 'Just make sure you look after him,' she said.

She jumped when a wet nose touched her knee. It was the black curly-coated retriever who owned the Elliot family. 'Shadow, what are you doing here? Did you follow after me?'

'No, but Luke and I did.' It was Adam's voice. 'We didn't want you to have to walk home alone in the dark all by yourself.'

'Thank you, that's thoughtful of you . . . I appreciate it.' Though she'd rather have been left with her solitude and the soft blanket of night sky after the busy clamour of the day. She wondered if they'd overheard her conversation with Rennie, or had seen him kissing her. Either way it didn't matter. She was grown up, and at last she felt grown up.

She would take the job with Andersen and Stone. Rennie was right. It would give her an insight into the business, and was an opportunity not to be missed. And if it turned out that Rennie would never be more than a friend, so be it.

Nine

Meggie was glad to leave the hospital with its air of emergency, where everyone walked the corridors at a hundred miles an hour, and telephones constantly rang. Stretchers rushed here and there with squeaking wheels, and with patients hidden under bloodstained sheets.

Everybody except herself was so efficient, and looked it. In her element, Meggie's aunt was every inch the authoritative ward sister in her starched apron, cuffs and hat with its knife-edged creases. Very different from the ethereal figure she presented at home.

Meggie had been slapped down on the very first day by a woman nearing retirement age. 'Don't leave the files there, put them in the cabinet as soon as they come back. You do know your alphabet, don't you? Dearie me . . . what are we being sent these days. Schoolgirls?'

'Every problem is practical by nature and nothing is left for the imagination of a lowly clerk to wrestle with, unless I happened to book two patients into the same bed,' Meggie told her aunt, thankful that she hadn't.

Leaving had been a relief.

She felt more comfortable here at the legal office. They recognized and respected her intelligence, and that she needn't be told twice what to do.

Meggie eyed her territory with proprietorial interest. She buffed the desk with beeswax until it resembled polished toffee and installed her own aspidistra in a brass pot she'd found in the yard and polished to a gleaming shine. Soon the waiting room looked professional and welcoming.

Within a week she'd sorted out the files, mastered the type-writer, ordered some office supplies, and discovered where the law books were kept.

She took to the job in the legal office like a duck to water, and ran around being indispensable to everybody.

It began to occur to her that Constance Stone's impression of vagueness was a front for a mind that was as sharp as a recently honed carving knife. Mostly she did the desk work and research.

When she'd been interviewed by Constance, Meggie had received a look that had peeled off any pretensions she might have absorbed about legal work in general, taking in everything about her from her head to her shoes. 'Rennie told me you intend to study at Girton College, Margaret.'

'I can afford the first year, I think, thanks to a legacy.'

'And then?'

'If I can't afford a second year I shall have to cram everything into my one year. It will be hard, I imagine, but I learn quickly.'

Constance's nod was accompanied by a little grin, but not one of disbelief. 'I trod that path myself. I'm sure you'll find a way if you want it enough, though you'll have to sacrifice a large part of your youth, when you should be married and laying down the foundations of a family . . . then it's all put aside.'

'Yes . . . I've thought of that, of course.'

'This will be the first time we've had a client as an employee working here, you know. It will not, of course, negate the administration fee. I will be handling your estate in conjunction with your guardian. Have you met Rennie's father?' She turned when Meggie shook her head and called out, 'Come out of your cave and meet Margaret Elliot, Robert. You as well Cousin Ambrose.'

There was an air of combined intellectualism lingering about them, like the smell of oregano, parchment and mahogany stirred into one brew. Their eyes were astute, spotlighting her in their collective gaze. The stare was prolonged, as though they were examining a new specimen of humankind, and she did her own examination of them, wondering if cultivating a legal-type stare would get her anywhere.

'Hmmm,' they both said together.

'Hmmm,' she said back.

Constance gave a dry and dusty laugh. 'Gentlemen, you won't stare her down so you can abandon the double act. I've already tried it. Now, hasn't anyone got something more sensible to say besides hmmm?'

One of them cleared his throat, which was a signal for the other one to say, 'Hello, my dear.'

Robert Stone displayed a marked resemblance to his son, and was just as straightforward in nature, she thought. Rennie would look like Robert when he was older – neat, upright and gruff. His hair was iron grey with lighter streaks, and his smile was cautious until she said, 'Rennie looks a lot like you,' and then it came out like the sun, so she couldn't help but respond with a smile of her own. 'He has your smile, as well.'

Robert made a courtly bow over her hand and kissed it. 'Good looks have always run in the Stone family.'

'They didn't reach me.'

Cousin Ambrose was long-faced and silver-haired, and wore side whiskers. He looked as though he might be part of a barbershop quartet, for he was flamboyant for a man leaving middle-age behind, dressed as he was in checked trousers, yellow shirt and a pale jacket over a waistcoat the colour of a billiard table. He wore a cravat with a gold horseshoe pin, and had cat hairs on his jacket. Introduced as Cousin Ambrose, that's all anyone ever called him, except when he was with a client.

Both men were silks; which meant they were KCs; which in its turn meant they were King's Counsel. They took precedence in the office hierarchy.

'You're Rennie's girl, the one with a good mind he told us about?'

Constance interjected. 'No, Cousin Ambrose. Margaret is one of our clients, and because he knew we needed someone for the office, Rennie asked us to accommodate her. She's with us to gain experience in legal office work. Pamela is Rennie's girl.'

'Oh, I thought that affair was over.' His eyes twinkled. 'Going to be a lawyer, are you? It will be nice to have a pretty little filly frisking about the office. It will brighten up the day.'

Meggie tried not to roll her eyes. 'I'm not Rennie's girl but we're friends. And I don't frisk, I'm afraid. I'm much too young for Rennie, in fact, he's already said so.'

'Then he's a fool.'

Constance chuckled. 'Rennie was always sensible about such matters. He can be a stuffed shirt at times, also like his father. Now gentlemen, we must get Margaret an assistant who can answer the phone and see to the files. If Margaret is going to learn anything useful in her time here we need someone to do the less important tasks while she assists us.'

Along came Ella Richards, middle-aged and no-nonsense, who rearranged the working space to suit herself and took the most comfortable chair as her own by right of age. She moved Meggie's pot plant to the corner where it immediately became the depository for the clients' cigarette butts. Neglected and forgotten, it eventually died and was thrown out into the yard, again by Ella, who muttered, 'I'm not paid to be a gardener or keep that ruddy great lump of brass clean.'

Ella was very efficient and brisk on the telephone, and she bossed the cleaner around so the corners were kept clean and the window sills free of dust. Ella provided everyone with tea twice a day, and the occasional biscuit when the black market allowed.

Constance Stone worked mostly on matters that could be settled out of court, so was usually at hand, if needed. Rennie had handled the solicitor's duties and his mother had stepped into his shoes.

Meggie was appreciative of the fact that the woman shared Rennie's news with her, and his occasional enquiry as to her own progress. His love always went to Pamela, and Constance made sure she knew that. He always hoped that little Miss Elliot was proving useful.

As for Meggie herself, she looked up references in the library, attended meetings in the conference room, sat in on the conferences and meetings with clients – where she was able to take notes in shorthand – and generally impressed herself and her lawyers with her efficiency and her ability to soak up knowledge like a sponge.

She made good use of the library of law books.

Sometimes she went to court with the two barristers, loaded

down with files and trying to keep up as they strode through the street, wigs askew and robes ballooning behind them, as if about to launch themselves into the air like a couple of wizards on broomsticks. They certainly put on the style. She wondered if Rennie would do the same when he became a barrister. Would she?

She loved the cleverness and the cut and thrust of the court work, but woe betide her if their papers weren't in the proper order when they were needed, or she kept them waiting. The barristers were indeed an arrogant pair, who thought nothing of giving her a dressing down in public. But far from letting it crush her, she learned to live with it.

Leo and Aunt Es helped her celebrate her eighteenth birthday with a fruitcake her mother had sent in a parcel, and which had disintegrated into crumb-coated sultanas and currants en route.

The three of them stared at the brown mess that emerged from the parcel. 'Only my sister could have managed to cook something like that,' Esmé said, as they all stared at the heap of crumbs.

Meggie giggled. 'She didn't leave it in the oven long enough to cook in the middle. Honestly . . . I'm surprised my step-father has survived all these years on Mummy's cooking. He's a saint.'

'It smells delicious, and doctors usually develop a cast iron stomach,' Leo said. 'What are you going to do with it, Meggie?'

'It would be a shame to throw it away. I'll bind it together with a couple of eggs and some milk and re-bake it. We'll call it something else and have it with custard for pudding over the next few days.'

'Flatulence pudding sounds more lively than calling it "something else",' Leo suggested, his juvenile humour earning him a pinch on the rear from Aunt Es.

There were birthday cards in the parcel with notes from her brothers and stepfather, and a long letter from her mother. It contained all the local gossip. She told them that Sylvia and Chad were expecting a baby, and begged them all to be careful. It made Meggie feel quite homesick.

Her aunt went a bit quiet at the news of the coming baby,

and then, when Meggie hugged her, she kissed her cheek and said, 'We must send Sylvia and Chad a congratulations card.'

At the office there was a distraction when Rennie came home on leave, in early Decmber.

The day had been unusually quiet and Meggie was alone. The lawyers had gone to their favourite Friday haunts, and Constance Stone had used the free time to catch up on her home affairs.

Meggie had sent Ella home early, and had stayed behind to catch up on her typing, so she wouldn't be overwhelmed by it the following week. When she heard the street door open she went through to the front office, and then stood stock still, though she wanted to leap across the room and hug Rennie tight. He looked smart in his peaked cap and uniform, and said, 'Captain Stone at your service.'

'Rennie? How wonderful to see you. Nobody is here, I'm afraid.'

'You are.'

She took a step towards him. 'Did your parents know you were coming home?'

He nodded. 'I wanted to surprise you. I'm going to see my father and Cousin Ambrose at their club. I'm taking you out dancing tonight if you've got nothing else on. You won't mind if Pamela and her friends come with us will you?'

She'd rather have Rennie all to herself, but realized his time was limited. She'd met Pamela a few times since their first meeting, mostly when she came into the office to visit Constance Stone. Expensively dressed, Pamela always sniffed when she saw her and said something meaningful and obvious, like, 'You're still here then?' or 'Still hanging on?'

'Don't you work?' Meggie asked her once, to which Pamela answered, 'I don't need to. Daddy pays me an adequate allowance.'

Meggie suspected Rennie had been posted abroad and would be leaving soon, but she wouldn't tell Pamela or Constance that.

'I can pick you up at seven and we'll go to one of the services clubs.' His smile sent her heart thudding. 'Aren't you going to give me a hug, Mags?'

He made it easier for her to overcome her sudden shyness by holding out his arms. Two steps forward and she was in them, her cheek against the rough material of his greatcoat, his breath sifting through her hair.

'How are you getting on in the job?' he asked the top of her head.

Tilting her head back she gazed up at him. 'It's a mad scramble, but the silks are terribly awe-inspiring, and sometimes they're mean to me, but I love it. I'm learning such a lot.'

He laughed. 'My mother seems impressed by your intellect. She said that anyone who can handle the silks like you do, gets her vote.'

'I'm being voted on?'

'I'm her only son . . . of course you are. She thinks there's something going on between us. They all do. On that my parents disapprove.'

She gave an exasperated little whuffle. 'I told them we're just friends on the day I started work here. *Honestly!*' Her face heated a little. 'Actually I like your mother a lot, and your father. You're very much like him . . . a bit on the serious side but with a soft centre. Besides, you've made it clear that you're not on the menu so I've reinforced your belief that I'm too young for you by falling in love with Cousin Ambrose instead.'

He laughed. 'Don't tell him because he can be incredibly conceited at times.'

'That's half his charm.'

He kissed the end of her nose then let her go. 'I'll walk you to the bus stop? I'm going that way.'

'Thanks, Rennie. Just let me put these papers next to the filing cabinet for Ella and get my coat. You can lock the back door if you would. Remind your father that he's due at the Bailey early on Monday. Tell him to go straight there and I'll meet him there with everything he needs.'

'Goodness, you are efficient.'

They talked until the bus came, skirting around the subject of the war, though the havoc it caused was plain to see all around them. 'I'll see you later,' he said, when the bus rumbled to a stop.

I could easily love you because you're kind and nice, even if you are a bit boring, she thought, and smiled at him. 'I'm looking forward to it.'

'Hey Juliet . . . are you getting on the bus or waiting for it to turn into a balcony so Romeo can propose?'

'Sorry.' Meggie leaped on to the platform when the bell pinged for the driver to carry on. She hung on to the pole and waved to Rennie, who blew her a kiss.

'Gentleman friend, is he?' the conductor chatted while Meggie took her seat.

'Not yet. He's waiting for me to grow up.'

'The very idea. Tell him from me that if he waits too long someone else will snatch you from the cradle . . . and then he'll be sorry. He's not a bad looking sort, at that. A bit old for you though I would have thought, love.' She moved up the aisle of the bus with a cackle of laughter.

Would Rennie be sorry? Meggie wondered, and then she grinned. Nobody was twisting his arm to take her out . . . certainly not her.

When she arrived home the house was still empty, and it was almost dark. She still got a jittery nervous feeling entering the house when it was unoccupied, and she knew her aunt did. It was as if someone was lurking there watching them.

But then, if she couldn't see who that someone was, then they certainly couldn't see her either. Such reasoning failed to reassure her imagination that her logic took precedence.

She reached for the torch they kept on the hall table and followed its thin beam, skittering across the hall into the kitchen, where she drew the blackout curtains across and switched the light on with a sigh of relief.

There was a menu on the table for first in. *Toad in the hole. Cabbage, two carrots and mashed potato. Boil enough cabbage and potato for bubble and squeak tomorrow. Bread pudding with an apple and a handful of sultanas sliced in, and Ideal milk, for pudding.*

She set the table, prepared the batter and cut up three sausages for the toad-in-the-hole. Cabbage was plentiful in the garden at the moment.

Putting sixpence in the gas meter slot she ran herself a

shallow bath; knelt in the warm water and washed her hair before sponging herself all over.

She was in her dressing gown when Leo and Esmé came home.

'Rennie's coming for me at seven. We're going dancing at a services club. You can come as well if you like.'

Esmé grimaced. 'My feet are killing me. I've delivered three babies, all boys, and they all decided to arrive one after the other.'

'I'll swap your aching feet for my rump,' Leo said. 'I had a couple of heavy landings today. All I want to do is lie on the settee in front of the fire and listen to some nice soothing music. That's all the dancing I'm doing.'

'I'll do your hair for you after dinner, Meggie Moo,' Esmé said. 'Dinner smells nice. You must have got home early.'

'It was a quiet day. You look tired, Es.'

'I'll be all right as soon as I've had a cup of tea. After dinner I'm going to rest and allow Leo to give me a foot massage.'

Leo grinned at that. 'My pleasure, madam.'

Meggie wore a blue satin blouse borrowed from her aunt, with a pleated navy skirt. She pinned the brooch Rennie had given her to the shoulder. Her hair fell in soft curls after Esmé had used the heated tongs on it.

Rennie arrived on time. He helped her into her overcoat, saying, 'I'm afraid we'll have to walk, unless we can find a cab. It's not far, about half an hour.'

The services club was packed, but Pamela and her companions had got there early and had a table. The merriment was in full swing with the band playing the latest tune and everyone dancing. Pamela's escort was a man of about forty, a bank manager. They bickered with each other a lot, which was a bit uncomfortable for the rest of them, but they were otherwise friendly.

It was nearing eleven when the sirens began to sound a warning. There was a scramble to get into their coats and hurry to the nearest air raid shelter. Some went down to the cellars, while others hurried on to the street, heading for the nearest underground station, where a warden blew his whistle and shepherded the crowds inside with some urgency. Pamela and her escort had gone in the opposite direction after bidding them a hasty goodnight.

The first crump of the bombs exploding in the distance, the throbbing of the bombers and the searchlights piercing the night sky with their beams was heart-stopping. They went down into the station. It was crowded with families, children asleep, head to toe, guarded by parents who, rightly of wrongly, couldn't bear to be parted from their offspring in the early push for evacuation.

They found a clear space in a shadowy corner, where Rennie folded his greatcoat. They sat on it, their arms around each other while they waited it out. Further along the platform a man was playing 'I'll get by', on a harmonica.

Rennie sang the words softly against her ear. He had a pleasant voice and sang in tune.

'I didn't know you could sing,' she said when he finished.

'Neither did I.'

She jumped, burying her face in his chest when there was an extra loud, but muffled explosion. Dust drifted down on them and the lights flickered off, and then came on again. What if they took a direct hit and were buried down here, slowly suffocating as they ran out of air? She began to feel claustrophobic. 'Let's get out of here, Rennie.'

'Not until it's over. You're scared, aren't you?'

'A little bit . . . no, quite a lot. I keep thinking—'

His finger covered her lips. 'Don't keep thinking anything.'

A few feet away from them a baby began to cry, and its mother hushed it with a soft lullaby.

Meggie felt comforted by Rennie's arms while the world crashed around them. 'Aren't you scared?'

'Not for myself.'

'You're going overseas soon, aren't you?'

He nodded. 'I'll be back . . . and don't forget, you're going to dazzle me.'

She chuckled through her tears. 'I won't forget.'

'I'm counting on it.' He kissed her mouth, a tender sort of kiss that gave more than it took and left a memory printed on her mouth. He glanced at his watch afterwards. 'I can hear the all clear. I'd better get you home, your uncle and aunt will be worried sick about you.'

There was a fiery glow to the sky on the other side of the river. 'It looks as if the docklands copped most of it, poor sods,' he said.

'Thank you for tonight, Rennie.'

They didn't need the torch, for the moon was full, providing illumination for the bombers, even while it lit the streets and gave them a safe journey home. There were tiles blown off roofs and broken glass everywhere. Rennie stopped to help a man board up a broken shop window.

Leo must have been keeping a look out for her, because he called softly from the bedroom window when they reached the house. 'I'll let you in, love. Es is asleep and I want her to stay that way till morning. She's a bit under the weather.'

He came down fully dressed. 'I've been called out. There are civilian casualties, too many to handle. They're sending transport and it should arrive any minute. We can give you a lift most of the way home, Rennie, that's if we can avoid the rubble. I imagine we're going in the same direction.'

'I'd appreciate it. I've been danced off my feet tonight.' He kissed her hand and whispered. 'Until next time then, Margaret.'

No sooner had he finished speaking when there came the sound of a motorbike. The two men arranged themselves around the driver, Leo folding himself into the sidecar. They putted off into the night.

Taking off her shoes, Meggie tiptoed up the stairs by the light of the torch, trying to avoid the creaks.

'I'm awake, Meggie,' her aunt called.

'I'm sorry if I woke you. Leo said you were unwell and he wants you to sleep.'

'It's nothing, I'm tired that's all. I'll be all right in the morning. Your mother rang earlier. I told Livia you'd give her a ring tomorrow. Don't forget.'

There was an edge of excitement in her aunt's voice and Meggie smiled. 'There must be a reason why you're tired. Come on, out with it.'

'I haven't told Leo yet, because I'm not sure myself yet, and the last time this happened it came to nothing. My period is overdue, and I think, and hope, that I might be pregnant. I'll see my doctor if needed next month. And I'll tell Leo when I'm sure.'

'Isn't there a test?'

'Yes . . . the Hogben test, where they inject urine into the back glands of a frog. If it ovulates it means that you're positive. I don't see the point. There are other signs beside a missed period, morning sickness to start with. You won't tell anyone will you? Not even your mother. I want to be the first to tell Leo when I'm sure.'

'I'll keep quiet about it. I'll also keep my fingers crossed.'

'It's cold out there. Get in bed with me so we can talk. Leo won't be back until morning and you can tell me all about your evening.'

They didn't talk for long before her aunt felt sleepy. Yawning, Meggie turned on her side. She couldn't be bothered to go to her own bed, and there was only three hours of darkness left.

'The doctor has prescribed an iron tonic. I used to like it when I was a kid. I had chronic bronchitis and was iron deficient from poor nutrition in the orphanage. I'll be all right in a couple of days when this starts to take effect. I have the day off today, thank goodness.'

'Leo is worried about you. I'm surprised he hasn't put two and two together.'

'He's been disappointed in the past too, so he probably doesn't want to think along those lines at the moment. He's working round the clock, poor love. Besides I've seen my doctor and there's no need for him to worry.'

'Then you can stay in bed and rest. I'll wait on you hand and foot. Now, go to sleep.'

Esmé did.

Several months into 1940, an official-looking letter arrived for Meggie telling her to report for another interview for the WRNS if she was still interested.

She arrived at a heavily sandbagged building, wearing her work suit of sober grey with a pretty blue blouse, to be directed by the doorman to an office. There, she was seated in an armchair in a small sitting room. She stood when two officers came in to occupy chairs on the other side of a small table. One of them she recognized from the last board.

'Good morning, ma'am . . . and ma'am,' she said.

She sat when indicated and the older of the two women engaged her eyes. 'Miss Elliot, we have asked you to return for an interview, to ascertain if you're still of the mind to become one of us. The fact that you're here suggests you are.'

'Yes, ma'am.'

'Your examination results were exemplary and the medical report tells us you're quite healthy.' The woman moved the paper around with a fingertip, topped by sensible short, squared-off nails. 'It was thought at the last interview that, at that time, you were a little too young in your ways to take on the responsibility that comes with being a Wren. As well as being underage, and lying about it to the board, your mother was not forthcoming with her permission, when contacted. Mrs Elliot felt, as did we at the time, that we should wait until you'd matured, both in years and attitude. Do you have anything to say to that?'

Her mother hadn't told her that she'd been approached for her permission, and had refused it. She supposed it was no more than she deserved, since she hadn't told her about her application to join up in the first place.

'Yes, ma'am. I apologize for lying about my age. It was a spur of the moment decision, made on the spot when I realized I wasn't quite old enough. I knew my mother wouldn't give her permission.'

'I see. As a matter of interest, young lady, would you lie again to get your way? Bear in mind that the Wrens only take the best into their ranks.'

Meggie slanted her head to one side as she thought about it for a couple of seconds, and then nodded. 'It would depend on the circumstance. To be honest, I'm sorry I was caught out the first time. But since then I've learned not to be quite so impulsive. With hindsight, if I could relive that moment again I'd probably think things through longer, since I've learned a lot through my employment. I'm pleased I didn't miss the opportunity it offered me though. It never hurts to have an extra string to your bow, does it?'

One of the two officers leaned forward. 'Now you have me intrigued. What have you been up to in the meantime, Miss Elliot?'

Meggie had come prepared. 'I've been working in a legal office. My employers have been aware of my plans to join the Wrens from the beginning, and have furnished me with practical experience for which I'm grateful. They've also provided me with a reference, signed by all the partners.' She placed their card on top of the envelope and slid it across the table. 'I've gained valuable experience and insight with their guidance.'

The reference was read and added to her file.

'Very good, Miss Elliot. You will receive official notification of your acceptance in due course. In the meantime, you may go and get yourself measured up for your uniform. Wear it with pride, and report to the officers' training unit in Greenwich in four weeks' time. It's a two-week course, after which you will be given weekend leave, so you can go and visit your family. Then you will be given your posting.'

'May I ask where that will be, ma'am?'

'We'll probably move you around a bit so you can gain experience. You're young to be accepted into the rank of officer, but the best way to gain respect from the ranks is to know what you're doing.'

She had not told her mother that she'd finally been accepted into the WRNS, or that she was spending the weekend.

Bidding a tearful farewell to her lawyers, who'd already found a suitable replacement for her, she left their employ with their best wishes ringing hollowly in her ears, and a vague promise to contact her when they had news of Rennie. She didn't expect them to call.

Now she was on her way home to Dorset, courtesy of a free railway warrant. The sky was a wash of silver from a fitful sun, the air smelled like rain and newly ploughed earth, and the fields were brown crumbly furrows waiting to cradle and nurture the seeds. The tiny pods would be turned into grain and vegetables to feed the troops. The logistics of such an exercise was totally baffling, and it made her feel humble, for she'd grown from a tiny fertilized egg herself and was part of the process.

She passed Foxglove House. A high brick wall had been

built, with thick shards of broken glass stuck into the cement capping. Looping along it, coils of barbed wire exposed its shining new surface to the weather. Beyond the wall the grass had been removed, the exposed earth replaced by a spread of black tarmac that curved through the gates and flared out both sides to the edges of the land boundaries. A small hut sheltered a soldier who operated the boom that served as a gate.

What a boring job, she thought when he saluted her uniform. Her father's beloved home looked impersonal and official – not like a proper home should look but a determined, standing-to-attention-and-doing-my-bit sort of look. It was hard to believe she'd hidden herself inside its dusty corners and told it her secrets. The house had always seemed to reject her, and it still did.

The short slab of tarmac was a road that started nowhere and ended nowhere else, whichever direction you came from. At a pinch, it could have served as a runway for a Tiger Moth, except the telephone and electricity cables that looped from one rustic pole to the next, and onward, didn't allow room for the wings. The tarmac disturbed the village of Eavesham's previous air of bucolic timelessness, like a thick black line underlining Foxglove House's sudden elevation to importance.

When she reached her mother's house she let herself in without knocking, disturbing her stepfather, who'd obviously been taking a nap in front of the fire while he had the house to himself.

Denton smiled at her when she handed him a packet of humbugs from Esmé. 'Aunt Es said you're to make them last, because they're becoming hard to get.'

'Your mother is at the church, dusting the pews or doing some other equally useless activity, since all churches have dust. I often wonder if it's the same dust that was there hundreds of years ago, and it just flies up in the air, then lands again when you're not looking.'

She kissed the top of his head. 'I imagine that's exactly what happens.'

'Why don't you surprise Livia? She'll be glad to see you; she misses you, you know.'

Meggie found her mother in the graveyard. She was wearing a jacket that had seen better days, and was weeding Richard Sangster's grave. A beam of sunlight stroked against her hair now and then, revealing a lightening streak of grey at her temples. How old was her mother? About forty-four Meggie thought. She was still slim, still lovely, with barely a line.

She glanced up at Meggie's footfall, smiling when she saw the uniform. 'I've been expecting this since you turned eighteen. You look so grown up.' She held up a hand, laughing, when Meggie sighed and was about to protest. 'I know . . . I know, you are all grown up. Your father would be proud of you.'

'Are you proud of me, Mother?'

'That's an odd question. I suppose it's because I refused to sign your papers last year. I didn't think you were old enough or responsible enough then. If you had been you would have paid me the courtesy of approaching me first.'

Meggie hadn't expected her mother to go straight into the attack, and she knew she'd hurt her. 'Yes, I know, and you were right. I thought I was clever enough to outwit everyone, but I discovered I couldn't. I didn't deliberately set out to hurt you. I just wasn't old enough to know I had.'

Her mother looked surprised for a moment, then she grinned. 'You mean I actually did something right?'

'I wouldn't have thought so then, had I'd known, but time has changed my perspective on things. You allowed me to stay in London. Why?'

'Esmé said you needed friends and activities to keep you busy. She offered to take responsibility for you if I allowed you to stay. You always got on better with Esmé than you did with me.'

'Now you're making me feel guilty. Was I much of a brat?'

'At times you were precocious, and I found it hard to cope with you. I didn't realize then that you were one of those children who were born gifted. Everything came easily to you and you became impatient with those of lesser intellect.' Her mother stood and, placing a hand either side of her face she gently kissed her forehead, as though she was bestowing a blessing on her. 'Just so you understand, Meggie. I am proud of you. You'll never know how proud, or how much I love you . . . not until you've got children of your own.'

'You're going to make me cry if you keep that up.'

'I know you think I loved the boys more than I loved you, but it's not true. They just needed me more. You were so independent and self-contained, and would never let me in.'

Now Meggie did weep, a pair of tears making a wet track down her cheeks. Even as she controlled it, she wondered why the twin displays of physical emotion had arrived in unison, rather than one measured tear on one side.

Her mother dabbed them away and filled in the moment with: 'Did my cake arrive in one piece? I had the feeling it was still a little bit damp in the middle. You know what my cooker's like. It never gets anything right. One of these days I'll get a new one installed.'

Meggie hid her grin. 'Yes, it arrived in perfect shape, and it was delicious. I thought I told you that on the telephone. But you mustn't do it again, d'you hear? You need those dried fruits for your own use.'

'Be careful, my dear, won't you? Where will you be posted?'

'I'm afraid I wouldn't be able to tell you even if I knew. I had to sign the Official Secrets Act. I won't be at the front with a rifle though, Mummy. Just stuck in some boring office somewhere typing blisters on to the ends of my fingers. And it's only for the duration of the war. It might be over by next week.'

'Yes . . . I suppose it might.'

Her glance went to Major Henry Sangster's neglected grave, situated next to his son's. Taking off her gloves she picked up her mother's trowel and began to tease out the weeds. 'Major Henry did something hush-hush in the last war, didn't he? Perhaps I take after him.' Her mother didn't answer, and when she finished her task, Meggie offered, 'He was sorry about what happened, you know. Can't you forgive him just a little after all this time.'[1]

'Is it important to you, Meggie? I really don't know if I can. There's something very satisfying about anger.'

---

1. See *Secrets and Lies*

'I don't like to think of you feeling bitter and sad about something that can't be changed. It will also make me feel better about myself. I know I disobeyed you about seeing him, but I liked him, and he made me feel special to him. I can't say I'm sorry I did that. I've always hoped my visits made up in some small way for him losing his only child. I was the only family he had left.'

'I don't know if I'm entirely comfortable with the concept of sins being washed away by death, but I'll try, since I'm not his only victim. You were one as well. I don't think I'll ever forgive him for having the last word and dying in front of you though. For months afterwards you were a nervous wreck, and I couldn't get it out of you what was wrong, until Es figured it out.'

Meggie gave a little shiver. 'I don't suppose he died in front of me on purpose.'

'It does seem a little stupid to waste one's anger on a man who is dead and buried. I suppose I could unbend a little and weed him too . . . not that he'll notice.'

'Neither will Richard Sangster. Why don't we let the grass grow over both of them?'

'D'you know something, Meggie, I really think you might be right.' Linking arms they strolled towards the gate.

'What's in the parcel?' her mother said when they got home.

'Nothing very exciting, I thought you might like to look after it for me.' She handed it over and watched her mother unwrap the framed letter.

> *To Margaret Eloise Elliot*
> *You are hereby appointed as*
> *Third Officer*
> *of the*
> *Women's Royal Naval Service*

Smiling a little, her mother read the rest then gazed at her, surprise in her eyes. 'You've left out the Sinclair Sangster names.'

'Deliberately . . . I don't seem to need them any more. Having so many names sounded pretentious and there's never enough room to write them all on one line.'

'I'm glad you kept Denton's name.'

'He gave it to me as a gift eighteen years ago and because he's the only father I've ever known and loved, of course I kept it. It will be the only name I'll ever use from now on.'

'I'll place this letter on the sideboard in the sitting room. We have our Women's Institute meetings there and I'll be able to show you off. Most of them have sons serving in the forces. Mine are too young, thank goodness, but I can be proud that my daughter is being of use to the country.'

'And Mummy . . .?' Meggie took the brooch Rennie had given her from her pocket and handed it to her. 'Look after this. It was a birthday present and is precious to me.'

'From Rennie Stone?'

She nodded.

Meggie was the recipient of a searching glance, but her mother's only comment was, 'I would have thought him to be a little too old for you. I don't want you to be hurt. Is your heart involved? Is his?'

If Rennie had a heart he hid it well, Meggie thought with a wry grin, and knowing she was being unfair to him. But she hoped there was some truth in her mother's words as she answered, 'I don't know, but you'll be the first person I'll tell if I discover that it is.'

Ten

Nick Cowan was settled into his small department, with an assistant who was second-in-command, and reasonably intelligent.

If asked what it was he did, Nick would have been pushed for any answer other than, 'Very little.'

What he did do was everything that seemed a bit shady, sometimes shoddy. He decoded messages and he found messages where there shouldn't have been any, disguised in newspaper articles and magazines. He had a small team of men in the field, unknown to each other, who were loosely described as field operatives. He used them for surveillance. He kept the files – with TOP SECRET stamped importantly on them in red – locked away in a sturdy grey filing cabinet for when and if they were needed. He added to them now and again.

And he went abroad, despite the danger, using his own yacht to cross the Channel. He kept away from the main shipping channels in case he ran into a ship or a submarine. That would cause a bit of consternation in Bethuen's department, he thought.

Nick already had many social contacts on the Continent, including some influential Germans, and he sailed along the coast. He smuggled goods, bringing back to England gold, jewellery and paintings that would otherwise have fallen into German hands . . . and he made money doing it. He also smuggled people back and forth from time to time, sometimes people who were not influential, but who needed a safe harbour because of race or religion.

Everything was cloak and daggerish, like living inside the pages of a work of fiction. The intrigue of being Nicholas Cowan appealed to him.

There was someone controlling him though, someone above Bethuen. He didn't know who that someone was. He probably acted as a subordinate to Bethuen, one of his aides, perhaps. Nick would have liked to know who it was. Nevertheless, he found some satisfaction in what he was doing. Bethuen rarely interfered and Nick liked the thought that nobody really trusted anyone else while everyone pretended to know more than everyone else did. It added a twist of spice to the brew.

He had a dangerous feeling of euphoria, as though he was invisible. He walked abroad in the air raids without fear, feeling as though he was in Dante's *Inferno*, and knowing the bombs wouldn't touch him, or if they did he would be released from the mortal coils without knowing much about it.

When Bethuen requested a meeting it caused Nick a flicker of unease. He didn't like explaining the unexplainable. He sat when invited, crossing one leg over the other at the ankles in a relaxed manner.

Bethuen smiled his greasy smile, the one that told Nick

that he might be his superior where class was concerned, but Nick was a subordinate in the office. 'How are you getting on, Nicholas?'

'Fine thanks. The job's not all that taxing. It's like juggling balls.'

'You're doing well. You've already dug one or two flies out of the ointment. The PM was pleased. How's that waterfront thing coming along? Your man's still on it, I suppose.'

Waterfront thing? Man? Though taken by surprise Nick managed a credible shrug. 'You know, sir . . . these things take time and usually solve themselves. I'll let you know when I've got anything concrete to report.'

'Quite. Keep them coming. I shouldn't be surprised if there wasn't a gong in it for you, and a knighthood for me once the war is over. Your father hinted at it a while back. A favour for a favour, he said. Any complaints young man? Have you got everything you need?'

Nick's eyes sharpened at the mention of his father. 'As I said before, I could do with another assistant.'

Bethuen poured them both a whisky. 'And you shall have one . . . Soda?'

'Just a little, thanks.' Nick sighed with pleasure when he took a sip. It was double malt and as smooth as honey. 'A nice drop, sir.'

'It came from a cellar in a chateau in France. If you need any, just let me know. By the way, I've got an order for you. Our ground forces are in a bit of a fix, and there's a push on to repatriate them from the beaches at Dunkirk to Dover otherwise they'll be massacred. The estimate is about ten days, and the exercise is not without risk. You do still have a boat, don't you?'

'A small yacht.'

'Everyone rescued is a life saved. There's a flotilla going over of everything that floats. I thought the hands-on approach of it would be just up your street, dear boy. At least it will get you out of the office, and I'm sure Goggles will manage without you for a while.'

'Yes, I suppose he can. I'd be obliged if you didn't tell my father when you see him. He worries, you see, since I'm his

only heir. By the way, he controls the family cellars, so you
should ask him about the whisky.'

'Ah, yes. How is the earl?'

'He's well, as usual . . . robust in fact. He's in the country
for the duration. He's wearing his farmer's hat, and his contri-
bution to the war effort is geared towards growing food. They've
allocated him some women from the land army. I'm surprised
you haven't been down there. He entertains now and again at
weekends.' His mouth twitched as he tried to suppress his grin.
Knowing he hadn't been invited would crap Bethuen off no
end. 'As for myself, I manage in the London house with a
couple of live-in servants.'

Bethuen sniggered, though his eyes were mean. 'Young ones,
I hope.'

'Not at all.' Nick took out his pitchfork and began to prod
Bethuen. 'One of them used to be my nanny. She still has a
tendency to treat me like an infant. The other one is a house-
maid, and both are a little past middle-aged, like yourself. Then
there's my valet, William. He doubles as my social secretary. I
also have a cleaning woman who comes in during the week.
Most of the rooms are in mothballs for the duration, but one
must keep standards up.'

Bethuen was hardly able to hide his ire as he leaned forward
and slid a couple of files across the desk. 'I've been offered a
couple of secretarial types from the new flock of Wren officers.
Whitehall is usually offered the best, and these are the cream
of the crop, apparently.' He took a handful of files from the
drawer and threw them on the desk. 'Take your pick. I rather
like the look of the chubby one. Judith Scott, her name is.'

Judith Scott could hardly be described as chubby, but her
breasts were well developed and her face on the round side.
She didn't lack secretarial skills, because that had been her job
before she'd signed on, and she was happy to remain a secretary
who'd fetch and carry for her boss. Nick wanted more than
that in an assistant. He wanted a woman who could think for
herself.

Flicking open another file Nick's eyes centred in on the
photograph of the second girl. She was a stunner. 'I'll be
damned,' he breathed. She appeared to have emerged from her

teenage gaucherie, and was quite lovely. Clear-skinned and bright-eyed she gazed into the camera, a wry quirk stitching the left-hand corner of her mouth.

He called on his memory. Queen's Road, Finsbury Park. Margaret, Eloise, Sinclair, Sangster, Elliot. 'Meggie for short,' he whispered.

Bethuen's eyes narrowed in on him. 'You said something that sounded like a name. Do you know her?'

'I said Margaret Elliot was a pretty sort.' His eyes skimmed down her record. She'd gained top marks in the written exam and had done extremely well in the intelligence test. Her references and ambition were solid gold. Two barristers, both silks, and a solicitor had signed her letter of reference. She aspired to go to university and become a lawyer.

'I'll be happy to take this one on.'

'Yes . . . . I dare say you would. She's an attractive little piece, isn't she? And as clever as a monkey. Her paternal grandfather was an intelligence officer in the last war. He tried to shoot himself and failed. Her other one was a bit of a political hack.'

'She seems to have a good brain, as well as looks.'

'You do understand the department has a hands-off policy when it comes to hanky-panky between staff members, so if you've got any thoughts in that direction, forget them, or play away from home. I know of places where one's urges can be catered for, whatever they are.'

Places Nick had avoided in the past, and would continue to do so. He was filled with distaste that this slimy excuse for a man would frequent them. 'Margaret Elliot looks too young and innocent—'

'Girls are never too young or too innocent . . . or boys come to that.' Bethuen gave a schoolboyish snigger, then said hurriedly when there was no reaction from Nick as to his own preferences, 'Oh, come on, surely you have some red blood in your veins. We both attended boarding school, and know what goes on when the lights go out. Where's your sense of humour, man? It was a joke, not a proposition.'

But it *had* been a proposition. God knew, Nick had never been perfect but there were lines he wouldn't cross. Bethuen had the sort of dirty mind that would make an average man puke, and Nick wondered how far he took his perversions. He shrugged, ignoring the remains of his whisky as he stood. He no longer felt like drinking with this man, but it might be worth the effort to keep an eye on him.

Yes, Nick had plenty of red blood in his veins – among the blue, and despite his own foibles he liked to think he had some decency left in him. He'd certainly never deliberately hurt anyone, unless he had to. And yes . . . he remembered boarding school, and overfed bullies like Bethuen. Anger radiated a sour sort of warmth in his stomach as he walked through the dusty corridors to the small stronghold that was his domain. He wanted more than this. He wanted Bethuen's job, and his heart on a platter. And he intended to get both.

Going into his office, a small partitioned section of a larger room – he gazed morosely down at the road through windows sectioned with crosses of packing tape, which was there to prevent the windows from shattering in a raid. The traffic was heavy at this time of the afternoon.

He remembered another woman who'd lived at the same house as Meggie Elliot did. The aunt's name had been Esmé Thornton. On his second visit he'd met her husband, tall, loose-limbed and muscled. He had an Australian accent. He was a good-looking chap, his manner happy and relaxed as though he enjoyed his lot in life. And why wouldn't the man feel good with the luscious Esmé for a wife and the equally lovely Meggie as a boarder?

He called for his assistant and placed the Elliot girl's file in his hands. Gordon Frapp was supposed to be a bit of a boffin, though Nick hadn't seen anything spectacular in him yet. He'd attended the same school as Bethuen, so was probably there to keep his eye on Nick, and report back.

'We're getting a new assistant – a Wren. She'll be coming in on Friday to get the feel of the place.'

Frapp didn't seem surprised. 'I'll get in touch with supplies and see if I can get her a desk and a typewriter.'

'Find her something to do besides typing, would you? After that weekend I'll be going away for a week or so.'

Frapp gazed at him, his brown eyes magnified by his reading glasses so they looked like aniseed balls. His sight hadn't been good enough to support his application to join any of the service branches on active duty, and he resented not being able to wear a uniform. Bethuen called him Goggles, something Frapp detested. A lock of lank brown hair fell over his forehead. 'What would you suggest?'

'Use your imagination, Gordon. God knows we have enough bits of paper floating around the place. Give her some messages to decode. Mix in some cryptic crosswords with messages embedded in them. Let's find out what she's made of.'

'Where will you be if I need you, sir?'

'Unobtainable. Operations, you know. You'll be answering to Bethuen until I'm back, but unless it's urgent . . . well, you know the score.'

'Anything special, sir?'

'You should know better than to ask, but I expect you'll hear in good time. He hesitated, then smiled and took a shot in the dark. 'How's that waterfront affair coming along . . . the one you didn't tell me about?'

The aniseed balls flicked sideways in guilty unison, and then came back to him. 'It was nothing to do with our department, so I shuffled the problem over to Customs and Excise.'

'Good. Keep me informed of everything that comes in from now on, would you. As head of department decisions like that should be left up to me, don't you think?'

'Yes, sir. It won't happen again.'

'If it does I'll look on it as a disloyal act. You can't serve two masters. It's just not done.' Besides which Frapp wasn't clever enough. 'I think I might have something that would be right up your street? It will get you out of the office from time to time, but you might have to do some of it in your own time, and of course, you wouldn't be able to tell your wife what it is.'

'I'm not married, I live with my mother.'

'Ah, yes, so you do . . . let me think a minute. It will be quite a test for your detecting skills, you know.' Not to mention his loyalty.

There was a doggy enthusiasm about Frapp now, like a bloodhound waiting to explode in a ball of energy from its leash and get on the scent. 'I won't let you down, sir. I promise.'

'I wouldn't expect you to, and you will have my absolute trust.' He decided to give the pot of intrigue a bit of a stir. 'Very well then, the subject is . . . James Bethuen.'

When Frapp began to splutter, Nick smiled, then went to the door and made sure it was closed. He lowered his voice. 'This comes right from the very top, Gordon, so be careful. I recommended you because you attended school with Bethuen, and know him better than any of us. Give the file a code name . . . Maggot would be appropriate, I think.'

Frapp's smile exposed a row of slightly crooked teeth. He was a nondescript sort of chap who bit his fingernails, but otherwise had clean habits, and was neat and thorough. Lies didn't sit easily on him, and that sort of inner self-righteousness was an arrogance that could be fed and used. 'You know, Gordon, once this stoush with the Jerry is over I'm going to set up my own investigative department. I'll need an assistant who is both discreet and skilled. If you bring this off satisfactorily, and you're interested, I'll keep you in mind.'

'Thank you, sir. I imagine I will be.'

'Now – this Bethuen thing. It's no big deal. I expect there are dossiers on all of us in various offices. My superiors especially want to know what he does after hours. Do you think you can manage it? I shouldn't have to remind you that you've sworn an oath under the Official Secrets Act?'

'Of course I can.'

He looked so eager to set about the task of helping Nick bring Bethuen down that Nick wondered what Frapp had against the man.

Meggie presented herself to her new workplace on the dot. Shown to a small office she was told to wait. There was another young woman there. She had blue eyes, light brown hair and a ready smile, and Meggie liked her on sight. They wore matching uniforms, though the other woman was a few years older than Meggie. 'Third officer Margaret Elliot,' Meggie said with a smile, trying to sound efficient.

'I'm third officer Judith Scott. I think I saw you at a couple of the officer training sessions. Is this your first posting? It is mine.'

'Yes it is.'

'Perhaps we could get together later and swap notes. And if you hear of a room going begging let me know. I'm crammed in an attic with several other girls. It's the size of a dog kennel and we're sleeping head to tail, like sardines.'

The door opened and Meggie's glance travelled up a long pair of legs, picked up speed and tangled with a pair of eyes that had stolen their colour from the silvery grey of unfurling bracken. There was something familiar about him that was instant recognition, but totally elusive.

'Margaret Elliot?' he said, his smile shadowed by charm.

Meggie stood. Lor, but he was handsome, and in a well-bred sort of way that could only be enhanced by his uniform – especially one so obviously made to measure.

'Yes, sir.'

In a voice like smoked silk, he said, 'I'm Lord Cowan. I believe you might belong to me.'

He had an intimate, possessive way of introducing himself and claiming her – too intimate. He was also too sure of himself, and the hairs on her arms were beginning to prickle with an instinctive unease. 'How would you prefer to be addressed, my lord?'

'Just sir will do.' He then looked at Judith who was gazing at him through wide eyes. With looks like his, he probably got a lot of that, Meggie thought, tearing her gaze away from him with difficulty. 'You must be third officer Judith Scott. I'll take you on a tour with us before I introduce you to James Bethuen, who runs the department. He's busy at a meeting at the moment. You'll be working as his private secretary.'

'Won't he need me at the meeting then?'

He gave a lazy sort of smile. 'Probably, but he won't be expecting you because I told him you wouldn't be here until ten.'

Meggie's attempt to stifle a giggle, earned her an assessing look and a faint grin. 'Miss Elliot, I'll leave you with my second-in-charge Gordon Frapp. He's not as amusing as I am, but he's very thorough. He'll give you something to do, though we're still waiting for your desk to arrive. The office closes for lunch between one and two p.m. The tea trolley comes round three times a day, with sandwiches at lunchtime. I've ordered a round of egg and cress for you both for today, but you must put in an advance order for next week. Gordon will walk you through it.'

One delicate female shaped eyebrow arched. 'I think I'm capable of ordering a week's supply of sandwiches.'

'I'm sure you are. Look on it as an intelligence test.'

An exasperated intake of breath was a just reward for his remark.

They walked after him as he pointed out the various features, such as the supplies room, where everything had to be signed for. Then there was the files room, and a common room, where they could eat their lunch if they wished, and the washrooms.

Handing her over to Gordon Frapp, Lord Cowan disappeared with Judith in tow. They didn't see him for the rest of the morning.

'Sometimes he goes off for days,' Gordon said with a smile.

'What is my actual job description?' she asked.

'It's hard to say, really. We do anything that comes in. You can describe yourself as a writer or a secretary if you want a label and anybody thinks to ask, but generally we don't talk about the department, or what we do outside these four walls. If you find anything that seems suspicious tell me and I'll phone it through to the correct department who will follow it up.'

She was handed some cryptic crosswords, obviously doctored to contain a message, though she enjoyed doing them anyway. Then a magnifying glass was placed in her hand and some photographs taken from the air over the continent that came in pairs and had different dates on them.

'Familiarize yourself with any features, and see if you can find anything that looks strange and out of place,' Gordon said. 'We inform the air force if we see anything that resembles guns, or any sudden density of foliage that might conceal a build up of weapons or troops.'

Meggie began to feel as though she was a tangible part of the war effort.

'Is this what I'll be doing all day?'

'We do all sorts of things, usually what we're asked to do. You might be given files to collate. Just remember that everything we do is top secret, even if it seems trivial. At the moment I'm trying to find out your strengths and weaknesses. We don't ask questions.'

By that he meant she shouldn't ask any either.

Time went quickly, and her boss came back. 'Still no desk, Gordon?'

Gordon shook his head, then rose and went into the filing room.

Lord Cowan went into his office, shut the door and dialled a number. Meggie could still hear his voice. 'Where's that desk and chair I requisitioned for my department. You promised we could have it today. Where d'you expect my new assistant to sit . . . on my lap? And don't forget the typewriter. A new one would be appreciated. I don't want some worn out old banger with half the letters missing that clatters, and keeps me awake when I'm supposed to be asleep at my desk.'

Meggie giggled when he laughed and purred silkily into the receiver, 'Who am I? I'm Viscount Cowan. You may address me as My Lord. Who are you? No . . . don't tell me. You're that cute young lady with baby blue eyes and dark hair that I pass every day in the lobby. Of course I noticed you, my dear. Now, about that desk . . .'

On the way home Meggie wondered if Leo and her aunt would have room for Judith. She shook her head. They'd been wonderful making room for her, but she couldn't expect them to accommodate a complete stranger. All the same, it was a big house.

The basement came into her mind, as it had on a couple of occasions before when she'd gone to bed early because she knew that her aunt and uncle needed privacy. If the rubbish was thrown away and the other stuff down there stored in one of the spare upstairs rooms she could live there and not be a bother to anyone. There was enough furniture for their needs in the house, too.

The old-fashioned cooking range in the basement would heat the place as well. There was no bathroom, but a small laundry by the back door that could be screened off, and the housekeeper's room used as a bedroom. They could wash in a tin bath there, and there was a necessary at the end of the garden that she could clean the cobwebs from so they wouldn't disturb the upstairs occupants. It would be fun to have her own flat, and she could invite friends to visit if she ever made any.

She raised the subject with her aunt and uncle over dinner.

'Are you sure, Meggie? The basement will take a lot of cleaning.'

'Not once I've got rid of the rubbish. There's a girl I met who's looking for somewhere to live, and we could both pay rent. Also, we'd have our own street entrance to the house. You and I can visit each other for a chat via the inside stairs if we get lonely.'

Leo huffed with laughter. 'With the navy living downstairs, we'd better have a periscope and intercom installed. What's the girl like?'

'I've only just met her, but I like her, and I think you'll both like her too. Her father's a greengrocer in Bury St Edmunds.'

'And the job? Will you enjoy it as much as your legal office?'

'I expect so. To be honest, it was such a scramble there, and fun, but I'd rather be using my own brain than type up the results of another's reasonings. The silks were such prima donnas. Sometimes I got the impression that they didn't really approve of me. I don't know exactly what I'm doing at the moment, but at least I'm doing my bit. I'll get into some sort of routine eventually, I expect.'

'And your commanding officer?'

'My immediate boss is quite nice, from what I've seen of him. He's on operations at the moment.'

'It's not common knowledge, but rumour, so let's keep this inside these four walls. I heard it from one of the other doctors. The ground troops are trapped, and being evacuated through Dunkirk. Apparently we're using every boat that can float to bring them home, including civilian pleasure craft. What's your boss's name?'

'He's an aristocrat called Viscount Cowan, and is quite suave and handsome, a bit like the film star Stewart Granger. We get free sandwiches for lunch, and tea. That's a bonus.'

Aunt Es smiled. 'I would have thought having a boss who resembled Stewart Granger would have been the bonus.'

Leo snorted. 'I'll deal with you later for that remark, woman.'

'And the basement?'

'Get it cleaned up first and then we'll see what we can make of it. You need to mix with people of your own age. And at least I can still keep an eye on you for your mother.'

Meggie rolled her eyes and gave an exaggerated sigh.

Leo ignored it. 'We can have a bonfire with the rubbish, as long as it's during the day. We'll start on it tomorrow. If you still want to ask that girl, and she wants to come here, tell her she can come and help clean the place. We won't charge you any rent, but you can pay half the utility bills between you.'

'What about the landlord . . . will he mind?'

'The rental agent said the owner is overseas, and has no intention of turning the place into bed-sitters. Anyway, I don't see why he should mind, since you're already living here. It's not as though the place is going to be altered. We're just using the space we already rent.'

'I'm going to miss your cooking.'

'We can leave that arrangement as it is. I can cook for both of us, and deliver it via the dumb waiter if need be.'

The cleaning of the place didn't take as long as Meggie had expected, and they found enough oddments of kitchenware, china, cutlery and bed linen to keep them going. Judith set to work with a will. When they finished dragging a pair of beds down the stairs between them, they gazed at their domain with pride.

Leo came down to fix the blackout curtains in place later.

'What do you think of the place now, Leo?'

'I especially like those white tiles on the wall, it reminds me of an operating theatre. The pair of you have excellent design skills. The copper pot looks pretty, it would hold a gallon of stew.'

'Except it's got a hole in it and the handle is loose. But other than that . . . how does it look?'

'I don't know what effect you were trying to achieve, but

it looks exactly like a cleaned-up kitchen. You'll be able to sleep on top of the stove in the winter to keep warm. Don't the Nepalese do that? And they bring their donkeys, sheep and oxen inside so they don't freeze to death. I'll keep a look out for a couple of oxen as a house-warming gift.'

Meggie exchanged a glance with Judith and grinned. She'd warned her new friend to expect only honesty from Leo, but that didn't mean she couldn't tell a small, white lie. 'Wonderful, because that's the effect we were aiming for. By the way, the couch has only got three legs. Can you fix it for us?'

'I'm a doctor not a carpenter. I suppose I can find a brick to prop it up with from somewhere.' And he did.

Gradually they got used to their odd accommodation, and added a few small comforts, such as a rug, a plant in a pot, and a ginger kitten that someone left at the door in the middle of the night. They called him Jack Frost because he was frozen half to death.

When the kitten recovered from his ordeal, Leo announced his intention to fix him. 'We don't want him to spray everywhere, or wander off and add to the stray cat population. He'll feel sorry for himself for a couple of days, but if you make a fuss over him he'll soon get over it.'

And so it was done, and Jack Frost became a lap cat, though his hunting instincts remained.

Judith came home with bits and pieces of greenery and planted them in pots. Soon they had a flourishing herb garden on the window sill. Meggie got on well with Judith. She was quiet and thoughtful, and had a sense of humour, so was pleasant company.

One morning Leo sought Meggie out and said casually to her, 'I've joined the RAF.'

'As a pilot?'

He nodded.

'I can't say I'm surprised. How does Esmé feel about it?'

'I haven't told her yet. I'm going to tonight, before dinner. I wanted to see you first though, because I won't be home much from now on. Could you be there when I tell her? She might get upset.'

Meggie nodded, thinking that it might be an understatement. She gave him a hug.

It turned out not to be as bad as Leo had been expecting, though Esmé gave a little cry. 'Why you, Leo? The hospitals need doctors as well, and you're one of the best.'

'Why me? Because I'm a pilot as well, and because the kids I train only get the minimum of flying hours before they go off to defend the country; to defend us . . . you . . . me . . . Meggie, and all the people we love. You should see them, Es . . . young men who've just got their wings and are full of spit and vigour and heroic deeds. They're just babies. Many of them don't make it back, and those who do are quickly disillusioned. For every one of those brave boys who don't return, I've died a thousand deaths for them when I check the lists.'

'You got that little speech from that film we saw the other evening.' It seemed to Meggie that her aunt mentally stamped her foot, but the heat had gone from her voice when she said, 'And don't you dare talk patriotic sense to me when I'm trying to be angry with you.'

Leo spread his hands and offered her a little grin. 'It was because you cried throughout the speech. Don't be angry my love. We all have to do our bit in the best way we can. I need to set them an example. First I've got to do a couple of weeks training at Uxbridge.'

The fight went out of her and tears filled her eyes. 'Why didn't you tell me what you intended to do before?'

'Because I knew you'd try and stop me, and besides, I couldn't bear to see you cry, my darling girl, which is why I've brought Meggie up to mop up after you. The bombing raids are only going to get worse and I want you to go to Dorset and stay with Livia till the war is over.'

When Leo took her in his arms, Esmé scolded, 'Absolutely not! If you think you can butter me up, think again, because you haven't got a cockroach's chance in a lava flow of succeeding. I'm going to stay right here in this house so you've got someone to come home to when you can make it. Besides, I promised Livia I'd look after Meggie.' A pale smile came her way, but Esmé's cheeks were flagged with patches of colour that told Meggie her aunt was gathering her resources together. 'Not that you need babysitting, but we'll look after each other, won't we, Meggie?'

Her nod brought a dirty look from Leo, who was still stating his case. 'You know this is the right thing for me to do, Es.'

Esmé's voice softened. 'Leo, darling . . . right or wrong I know your heart's in the right place, and it's typical to your way of thinking. So go and do it. There's nothing I can do to prevent it, now.' She reached up and touched his face. 'Listen now . . . I've got something damned important to tell you, and I'd planned to have a candlelit dinner to go with it.'

'I haven't forgotten our anniversary, have I?'

'No, and I'd still love you even if you had, since you've forgotten the previous ones. We're going to have a baby in a few months and I want it to grow up with a father and mother in Australia, like you promised. So you'd damned well better be careful.'

'A baby . . .? Jeez, Es. You certainly know when to hang an anchor on a man! Did anyone ever tell you that your timing is total crap? No wonder you've been looking a bit fragile lately. I had suspected.'

'*My timing?* What a cheek. I didn't create the situation all by myself, you know.'

A smile edged across his mouth. 'No, you didn't. When was the last time I told you how much I adored you?'

'I told you not to butter me up, Leo Thornton . . . I think it was this morning . . .' She gave up trying to dodge a swarm of small kisses with a sigh of defeat.

Meggie grinned. 'I think I'll go and start on the dinner. It's rabbit casserole.'

Her aunt had stars in her eyes, and as she didn't think that either of them had heard her Meggie turned and left them to it, thinking that Leo could charm the warts off a dog's tail if he felt like it, and without even trying.

Eleven

The Atlantic convoys were being increasingly harried by German U-boats and the loss of life was heartbreaking. It seemed as though Meggie and Judith were being called on to attend memorial services at Westminster Abbey every other Sunday. The whole of England knew that something was in the offing and there was a general uneasiness in the air.

Early in June, the prime minister, Winston Churchill, inspired everyone with his speech to the nation. Afterwards, every man, woman and child in the street felt like a hero who could stand against the foe.

The amount of suspicious messages coming through the office increased, hidden in newspaper articles, crosswords and radio broadcasts . . . even music. Once solved, they were sent for further analysis to Bletchley Park, the central code-breaking unit. Photographs were minutely examined. Meggie was especially vigilant now Leo had taken to the air as a fighter pilot.

Her boss spent less time in his office and more time in helping to decipher messages. Meggie was very aware of him, and it was a relief when another assistant was taken on, a rather taciturn man called Joseph Bruch, who spoke with an accent and was endearing, but in an old-fashioned scholarly way. He arrived and left on the dot, shuffling off towards his one-room flat.

One day he didn't turn up, and Judith told her he'd been killed in a raid. He wasn't replaced.

By July the sky was so full of aircraft they resembled a swarm of flies, so if that hadn't alerted them before, everyone now knew something was going on. The fat barrage balloons, designed to prevent enemy aircraft coming in low were a comforting sight.

Leo was lucky if he got home at all. On those rare occasions when he did, he fell into bed and slept heavily. Casualties were heavy, and Esmé lived in dread of receiving a telephone call from Biggin Hill, or a telegram.

They used the upstairs gas for cooking while Meggie and Judith hoarded their coal ration to keep for the stove in winter, for they'd discovered that the water it heated circulated through the radiators and provided the house with warmth. They also bought bundles of wood collected from bombed houses by enterprising children.

Lord Cowan, who'd previously had very little to say to her, and spent more time out of the office than he did in, cornered her one day. 'How are you getting along, Margaret?'

'I find the work a little . . . well, different to what I expected, I suppose. I worked in a legal office before, and it was so varied, and there was always something going on.'

'I expect there was.' He shrugged. 'Believe it or not, what we do here is a small, but useful part of a cog.'

'Yes . . . I suppose it must be, else we wouldn't be doing it.'

'Does Judith enjoy her job?'

'Yes . . . I think so. We tend not to talk about work when we're at home.'

His expression became one of approval. 'It's best not to get involved in office politics. I understand you're renting a flat with her.'

'My aunt and uncle have allowed us to live in the basement flat of the home they rent. We just help pay for the utilities.'

He picked up a pencil and gazed over her shoulder at the crossword she was working on. She was aware of him and because of it, stiff and uncomfortable. He smelled of expensive, sandalwood soap, and his nails were manicured. His breath tickled her ear as he murmured, 'A weaver tells a story? The obvious answer is?'

'Spins a yarn.'

He filled it in, his letters backward sloping. 'What can we make out of that, Margaret?'

'That someone with the code name of spider has been telling lies.'

'Or the Bayeux tapestry is embroidered from wool on linen, not woven. Did you know that?'

'No, but that will give someone a headache,' she said and laughed. 'What about, my stockings have a ladder in and need darning?'

'I'll get you some new ones. Perhaps you'd like some French perfume, as well.'

'I don't think so, sir. It's not my birthday. Besides, the navy provides stockings.'

'In fifteen denier nylon? I can lay my hands on practically

anything I want, including your stockings. I know a lot of people who have many fingers in many pies.'

He grinned when she gave him a surprised look, and said, 'Unless you want a good slap, you'd better keep both your fingers and hands off my stockings.'

'Miss Elliot, I'm surprised at you.'

'I doubt it.' She hoped he didn't seriously want to lay hands on her, not because the thought didn't appeal, but because she wouldn't know how to handle it.

Much to her relief he threw the pencil down and straightened up, laughing. 'I wonder what it will take for me to tempt you.'

'Why should you want to? You're left-handed, aren't you?'

She remembered the crossword on her bed, and the burglar who'd completed the last clue. The handwriting had been that of a left-handed person. A shiver ran through her and she gazed at Nicholas Cowan's feet. His shoes were black. How silly to imagine this perfectly decent and normal person, who was not only a peer, but also held a responsible position in the war office, was a burglar. To start with, he wouldn't need the money, and there were many left-handed people around.

'Yes, I've always been left-handed.'

She laughed. 'I imagine you have.'

'I've got a proposition for you, Margaret, something you might like. My father is sending me half a sheep from the farm tomorrow. It will be much too much for one man and a couple of servants. I'd hate for it to go off, and I thought you and Judith might like to have the leg. My maid will be picking it up from the station Saturday morning, and she can deliver it to your door.'

A whole leg of lamb! 'Now that would be wonderful.'

'There's a condition. Perhaps you'd invite a lonely man to Sunday dinner. Your aunt and uncle are welcome to join us, of course.'

'I don't know about my uncle. He's working round the clock.'

'He's a doctor, isn't he?'

How had he known that? 'He's also a pilot in the RAF for the duration.'

'Well . . . I have no objection to having dinner with two lovely ladies.'

'Three. Judith will be there, as well. The four of us share our food rations, and the cooking. It cuts down on fuel. We can't really afford to entertain.'

'How stupid of me not to think of that. Not to worry, my dear. I'll make sure you don't have cause to make inroads on your rations.'

Meggie would rather not have dinner with him on her day off, despite the thought of a delicious joint of lamb sizzling in the oven. However, she couldn't really turn him down without creating an atmosphere. And she couldn't help wondering why he didn't simply invite them to dinner at his house. 'I'll have to ask my aunt if she'll mind.'

Nicholas Cowan's eyes glinted when he said coolly, 'I've never known anyone turn their noses up at a leg of lamb before. I'll give you my phone number. Perhaps you could let me know if it's convenient.'

The conversation came to an end when Gordon came in. Lord Cowan went to his office and closed the door rather loudly.

Without looking up from what he was doing, Gordon said softly, 'I don't want to pry, but is Lord Cowan making a nuisance of himself?'

'Not at all. His father is sending him a side of lamb and he offered me a leg, as long as I cooked it and invited him to dinner. I don't really want to socialize with him on my day off, but I could see no way of refusing. Judith and my aunt will be there, so at least there will be safety in numbers. At a pinch, my uncle might even get home for dinner.'

'Most women would fall into the lap of a man like him. What don't you like about him?'

'I don't dislike him, Gordon. It's just . . .' She shrugged, knowing she liked him too much to imagine he'd be interested in her other than in a shallow way. 'I don't know. I just feel uneasy when I'm around him.'

'I expect Cowan has opened a file on you, and is information-gathering. Be careful, Margaret, he can be a slippery customer. Listen to your instinct and don't tell him anything he could use against you – nothing concrete, but just to be on the safe side.'

'Thanks for the advice, Gordon.'

Meggie had not counted on Judith offering a verbal reference for him with her aunt. 'Lord Cowan is so sweet and polite. I wish he was my boss.'

Esmé raised an eyebrow. 'I'll take your word for it. I can't resist the thought of a leg of lamb, though I do have some scruples about profiteering on the black market.'

'It's not profiteering. It's from his father's estate and he's not selling it to us, it's a . . . well, it's a donation towards dinner,' Meggie said, a trifle reluctantly.

'That settles it then. Phone him and tell him that both he and his leg of lamb are welcome.'

Early on Saturday morning Meggie took delivery of a hamper of meat and vegetables delivered to the basement flat. It was a fine day and she and Judith had already done all the washing and hung it out on the line.

Judith had gone off to market with a shopping list for the week.

Meggie had expected the food to be delivered by a maid, but there was a pair of long, trousered legs beneath the box, and a two-seater convertible sports car at the kerb, level with her line of sight. Perhaps Lord Cowan's valet had delivered it.

'Would you be kind enough to bring it in and place it on the table.'

'Certainly.'

She knew that voice. 'Oh . . . it's you, Lord Cowan. I thought you said a maid was going to deliver it?'

'It was too heavy for her to walk all this way with it so I thought I'd make a personal delivery.'

'Where did you get the petrol from? I thought it was banned for private use.'

'It is . . . but this is pre-war petrol that I managed to siphon out of my father's Rolls Royce.'

He had an answer for everything, she thought.

'Are you very cross with me?'

'A little, but I don't know why.'

'Perhaps it's because you're wearing that ghastly pinny and you haven't brushed your hair. You simply feel at a disadvantage.'

She investigated her hair, and then she laughed. 'I have brushed it.'

'You look a little dishevelled.'

'If I may be frank, we can't all afford servants. I've just finished hanging the washing out, and I'm in the middle of doing the housework. You, on the other hand, probably had a valet to iron your socks before you got out of bed . . . and to fasten your buttons in case the action spoiled your manicure.'

He began to laugh. 'Ouch! and ouch again. I'm wounded to the very core, you sarcastic creature. See if everything you need is in the box before I leave. I'm dying for an excuse to return and continue the jousting.'

There was asparagus, baby carrots, potatoes and spinach, and a can of baby peas. Strawberries blushed invitingly in their punnets and Scottish shortbread smelled all buttery and melt-in-the-mouth. She remembered a jelly in the pantry and instantly thought, strawberry shortcake. The leg of lamb was wrapped in greaseproof paper. She gazed at the garlic cloves. She would create a herb and garlic crust for the lamb.

There was also a bottle of wine, a Cabernet Sauvignon. She expected it would be perfect to accompany the meat, since Lord Cowan would know about such things. Her mouth began to water as she gazed at the extra goodies – cheeses and wafers and after-dinner mints. She was sure her smile informed him he'd gone up in her estimation.

A paper bag contained two pairs of nylon stockings. Not so good because they spoke of a relationship that wasn't there. But she couldn't very well accept the food and throw the stockings back at him, so she lessened the intimacy of them with, 'Oh, that's kind of you. I'll give one pair to Judith.'

'Oh, that's kind of you . . . I'll give a pair to Judith,' he teased. 'If it will put your mind at ease and help you relax when you're around me, Meggie Elliot please do. What if I told you that you don't attract me in any shape or form?'

There was something not quite right about what he'd just said, but she didn't have time to wonder about it before she shot back, 'Good, because you don't attract me either.'

He took her by the upper arms and swung her round. 'We both know we're telling lies. What have I done to annoy you?'

'You're hurting my arms.'

'No I'm not, I'd never physically hurt a woman unless she was about to strangle me, and you could easily move from my grasp.' He removed his hands anyway. 'Can we stop all this nonsense and behave in a civilized manner? It's the Germans we're fighting, not each other. I've been thinking seriously of having you posted. On the other hand you're good at your job and there's nothing in the rule book that says you must be friends with your superior officer.'

Alarm filled her. She didn't want to leave her aunt at this last stage of her pregnancy. 'Please don't.'

He smiled. 'All right, let's start again. You could introduce me to your aunt and uncle if they're home. You seem very attached to them. Once their approval is gained perhaps you'll relax a little in my company'

She hesitated for just a moment. 'My aunt might be resting . . . I'll see if it's convenient.'

A dark eyebrow rose. 'At this time of morning?'

To hide her blush at being at the cutting end of his irony, she washed two luscious strawberries and placed them on a plate with a shortbread finger. 'A treat for my aunt.'

'My father grows them in the conservatory.'

She realized she hadn't thanked him. Her mother would have been furious over her lack of manners, but what was it about this man that caused such a reaction inside her. 'It all looks so marvellous it's going to be a shame to eat it. Thank you so much.'

He obviously didn't hold on to a grudge because he smiled and said, 'It's my pleasure.'

Meggie found her aunt listening to the radio in the sitting room. She was crocheting a square for a cot rug made from a variety of colours. Livia had sent her a bag of leftover wools she'd collected over the years, for she rarely threw anything away. At seven months into her pregnancy Esmé had gained a little weight and her stomach was nicely rounded.

She held out the plate. 'Look what I've got. A strawberry for you and one for the baby, and a shortbread between you.'

'Oh, that's such a treat. My mouth is watering already. Where did you get it from?'

'It was in the hamper Lord Cowan brought over. He'd like to meet you and Leo so I said I'd see if it was convenient.'

'He can't meet Leo because he's not here. But yes . . . do bring him up since I'm dying of curiosity. Just give me time to tidy myself up.'

'I'll make some tea for us. When she went down Lord Cowan was fiddling with the door to the outside steps. He gazed up at her. 'The lock was a bit loose and the door came open.' He slid a small screwdriver into a small leather case and placed it his pocket. 'You can never be too careful, so I've just tightened it.'

'Do you always carry a set of tools in your pocket?'

'It's hardly that.' Pulling out a little crested leather case he handed it to her. His initials were tooled in gold. Apart from the screwdriver, it contained a small pair of scissors, a nail file, a magnifying glass with a fold-down handle and a pair of tweezers. 'It's handy to carry, since it doesn't take up much room. You could have it for your handbag if you'd like it.'

She handed it back to him. 'No thanks.'

He put it back in his pocket. 'I've got a machine gun strapped inside my trouser leg. You could have that and kill me with it, if you'd like that better.'

'I wouldn't like. You're welcome to come and meet my aunt. I'll just make her some tea while she tidies herself up.' She tried not to sound too reluctant when she offered, 'Would you like one?'

'At the risk of irritating you further, thank you, that would be pleasant. I'm sorry I was rough.'

'You weren't rough. I just wanted to complain. Also I wanted you to know that you might be my superior in the office, but when you're in my home the reverse applies.'

'Ah . . . I see. Are we going to be friends now? If so,

out of the office you may call me Nick, and I'll call you Margaret.'

She set the tray, trying to match saucer pattern to cup without success. She was still reluctant, but told herself that all he'd done was give her a meal to share. She'd done nothing but pick at him since.

The kettle lid was rattling and as she filled the teapot with boiling water she considered that it was probably a kindness on his part rather than an ulterior motive, and he hadn't deserved her scorn. 'Yes, of course . . .'

He looked dashing in a charcoal suit with a matching waist-coat over a maroon shirt with silk cravat, both enhanced by a gold pin and cufflinks. She automatically glanced down at his shoes. Black! There was a vague sense of disappointment in her. It was silly looking at everyone's shoes, when there were thousands of brown Oxford brogues walking thousands of miles on thousands of feet.

To compensate, she retreated back into her habit of thought meandering. Her mind painted a pair of horns and a tail on Nick, and surrounded him with a cloud of sulphurous smoke. The image took on a satisfying air of truth as she slotted it into place and said, '*Nick . . . as in devilish?*'

He chuckled. 'As you wish. Be careful . . . I might be recruiting souls today.'

'Are you?'

His eyes seemed to take on a darkness to match his suit and she shivered when he said in a low voice that seemed to be full of smoke, 'Anything is possible. Aren't you having a short-bread, too?'

'I'm going to make a strawberry shortcake with them for pudding tomorrow, so if I start eating them now I'll never stop.'

'That sounds divinely mouth-watering. He pulled a bar of Nestlé Crunch from his pocket and placed it on the tray. We'll share this between the three of us instead. Allow me to carry the tray up for you.'

Esmé could understand why her niece was cautious where Lord Cowan was concerned. He was too much of everything

– handsome, wealthy, clever – a magnet with a great deal of attraction. And like Meggie had said before, there seemed to be something familiar about him.

Meggie introduced him, stumbling over the title.

He laughed when she finished, saying, 'Now I've tortured your niece with my title, please call me Nick,' something that earned the man a glare from Meggie and a smile from herself.

He took the only armchair, a sagging creature well past middle age. It accepted his elegant aristocratic rear as if he was the king settling on his throne.

His eyes widened a little when his glance fell on her swelling stomach. He turned to Meggie, saying almost reproachfully, 'You didn't tell me your aunt was expecting a baby.'

Meggie's instincts would be telling her to shoot from the hip now, but Esmé could see she was struggling to find a retort that would neither subjugate her, nor put her at odds with her boss. Feeling sorry for her, since Lord Cowan gave every appearance of being able to run rings around her niece, she gave her a hand. 'It's not something I'd expect my niece to discuss with those outside the immediate family circle.'

He smiled, saying with practised ease and no hint of embarrassment at all, 'Of course not, except I wouldn't have disturbed you had I known of your delicate condition. Congratulations Mrs Thornton, and to your husband as well. If you need anything extra, please let me know.'

Smooth – very smooth. 'That's kind of you. We do try to manage on our rations by pooling them and working to a menu planned in advance, the same as everyone else has too. My husband said it's character building with a vengeance.'

'You're making me feel ashamed.'

'Quite unintentionally.' She gazed at her empty plate and smiled. 'If it makes you feel any better, I scoffed the strawberries and shortbread like a ravenous dog. I do get a little extra on my rations, but I'm certainly looking forward to dinner tomorrow. My niece is an excellent cook.'

'I'm sure she is. She's also a clever young woman. I consider myself fortunate to be her superior officer . . .' He sent her a grin. 'In the workplace, at least.'

Esmé didn't want to eat the chocolate so soon after the shortbread. Nick ate a small square and left the remainder of it on the plate. Shortly after drinking his tea, he rose. 'I mustn't outstay my welcome. Thank you for your hospitality. Look after yourself, Mrs Thornton . . . or should I call you Esmé now we've formed a social connection?'

'Please do.' Put like that, she couldn't really refuse, though she didn't equate one morning tea with establishing a social connection.

Nick Cowan rose like an elegant cat, so Esmé almost expected him to stretch his lean body and sharpen his claws on the furniture before moving any further.

'I'll see you out,' Meggie said, the air of relief about her almost visible to Esmé. 'Mind you don't shoot yourself in the foot.'

'I could think of more unfortunate places to get shot. No need to disturb yourself. I'm sure I can find my way, since I've been in several of these houses before and they're all similar in layout.'

A few minutes later and the front door clicked behind him.

The two women gazed at each other, then Esmé laughed. 'Now . . . there's a man and a half for you. He just oozes sex appeal.'

'He can ooze it all over somebody else . . . I don't want him.'

'Still hankering after that lawyer, are you?'

'I'm trying not to. He doesn't give me any encouragement by writing to me though. Rennie doesn't want to be anything but friends.'

'That's a typical male defensive position. Perhaps you should give him some encouragement the next time he's home on leave. If you allow men to become too noble another woman will settle for their less noble side, and snatch them from under your nose.'

'If that happens it just proves he wasn't worth waiting for. There's a woman called Pamela that he was engaged to marry. She kept dropping into the office for a tête-à-tête with his mother when I worked there.'

'That's not right, Meggie. Love doesn't come with a book of checks and balances. Some men need encouragement, and you might have to get the timing right. Other men know exactly what they want when they see it, and they go after it until the end of time.'

'Was that what happened with Leo?'

'Ah Leo, now there's a technique for you . . . pure caveman. He thumped me over the head then dragged me off to his cave, shouting in triumph. "Me Jungle Jim and you a tabby cat."'

When she'd finished laughing, Meggie said, 'I don't think Rennie's family think I'm suitable for him, especially where age is concerned. Anyway, I haven't seen him for a long time.'

Esmé's baby began to kick. She took Meggie's hand in hers and placed it on the gently heaving stomach under her paisley smock, moving the hand around. 'That's its little arms. It's in a curled up sort of position with its knees out, and feet curled into the tummy. Down here is its bum, and this more solid bit here is its head. It's in the breech position at the moment, but in about a month or so it will turn and the head will come down and engage in the pelvis. At least, I hope it does.'

With some alarm in her voice, Meggie asked, 'What if it doesn't?'

'It will either be delivered as a breech birth, or a Caesarean section will be needed.'

'A Caesarean is when they cut you open, isn't it? I won't have to be there for that, will I? I'd probably faint, or be sick, or perhaps both at the same time.'

'Certainly not . . . the surgeon wouldn't allow it.'

Esmé had gradually introduced the subject of maternity to Meggie, because if things didn't go to plan, she didn't want the girl to panic, but to do exactly as she told her. 'Don't forget there will be a midwife here to help me deliver the baby. She'll be in charge and will get me to hospital if need be.'

The sound of voices came to them and Meggie moved to the window and gave a running commentary. 'He's carried the shopping basket down for her.' Obviously Judith arriving home coincided with Nick Cowan's departure. Three minutes passed. 'Here he comes.'

Meggie waited until the car drove off, then frowned. 'I wonder what took him so long.'

'I expect he stayed as long as was socially acceptable. After carrying heavy shopping baskets for young ladies into basement flats, he couldn't just run off, he would have made some small talk. He has good manners bred into him.'

Meggie gave an unmannerly snort. 'That must be it. Would you like another cup of tea before I take the tray away, wise auntie of mine?'

'You could leave some of that chocolate, just in case Leo makes it home. It was nice of Nick to think of us. There's something very likeable and attractive about that man, you know.'

'I can't think what it is,' she said.

'Then why are you fighting it? What was that about him shooting himself in the foot?'

'Oh, nothing . . . we were having an argument, and he said he had a machine gun strapped to his leg and I could shoot him with it if that's what I wanted. I don't know what he meant by more unfortunate places.'

Chuckling, Esmé said, 'That rather depends on which way the muzzle is pointing, I suppose.'

Her niece turned a rosy shade of red and said in a satisfyingly scandalized manner, 'Aunt Esmé. Do behave yourself.'

They dissolved into girlish giggles at the thought of such a fate befalling Nick.

Twelve

Meggie enjoyed her dinner the next evening. The lamb was delicious and it cooked to perfection in the old-fashioned stove. Jack Frost wove around her ankles, and then left her, to settle on what was left of Esmé's lap. He began to purr loudly when she petted him, and kneaded her stomach, as though he was massaging the baby inside.

Nick was wonderful company. They sat round the big kitchen

table, laughing and chatting about anything that came into their heads, discussing books they'd read and poetry. She fell in love with Nick a little bit.

Upstairs in the hall the telephone rang.

Meggie rose. 'I'll get it. I'll call you if it's Leo the Magnificent, and you can waddle up.'

'I'll waddle up after you anyway. I hope you'll forgive me, Nick, but I'm tired, and I fancy an early night. I enjoyed your company, and it was a pity that Leo couldn't make it.'

'We must do it again sometime,' Meggie heard him say, and with enough sincerity in his voice to let her know that he meant it.

Meggie took the stairs two at a time, hoping it was Rennie on the other end of the line. It was neither of the two men. It was her mother.

'Hello, Meggie, my dear.'

'Mummy . . . is everything all right?'

'Of course it is. I just rang to tell you that Chad and Sylvia have a sweet little daughter. They've named her Patricia Anne, though they're already calling her Patsy.'

'That's wonderful. Give them all my love.'

'How is Esmé keeping?'

'You can ask her yourself if you like. She's just coming, leaping up the stairs like an inflated duck trying to be Margot Fonteyn in Swan Lake.'

'Don't make me laugh, it makes me want to pee,' Esmé said, laughing anyway.

Meggie vacated the chair and pushed it towards Esmé with her foot.

Her mother was saying, 'I thought the phone was in the hall.'

'It is . . . but I haven't had time to tell you I've got my own flat in the basement now. I share it with another Wren, and I've just held . . . am holding my first dinner party.'

'A dinner party, on rations . . . how did you manage that? You must tell me all about it. How many guests attended?'

'Only three. Aunt Es, my flatmate and my boss. Leo couldn't make it. It was a sort of practise dinner. With the rationing it's hard to entertain, but my boss provided us with a leg of lamb.'

She didn't want to say too much about Nick, lest her mother got the wrong idea about him. 'His father has an estate in the country and he brought some other food too. They have glasshouses.'

'Ah, yes . . . Denton grew some Cos lettuces in a glass frame last year, but he left the lid off just as they were ready, and the rabbits came in from the fields overnight and ate them. It's a pity we couldn't have utilized Foxglove House to produce food. After all that intrigue that went on, it's become a convalescent home for soldiers. Most unexciting, but the grounds look nice and neat, or so Chad tells me. The staff call him in from time to time.'

'At least it's being useful, at last. Anyway, I must get back to my guests. I'll try and get down to Dorset after Aunt Esmé has delivered her addition to the human race. Or you could visit us, if you like. We have the room.'

'With those bombs dropping all over the place I'd be too frightened. We're worried sick about you.'

'I know. Here's Aunt Es. You can talk about the gory bits of childbirth to her if you like. Goodnight and God bless, Mummy.' She handed the receiver to her aunt.

When she went back down Nick was standing at the sink doing the washing up. There was no sign of Judith.

'Your flatmate has gone to bed. She said she's going to start on the book you loaned her, and read for a while. Which book was that?'

'*How Green Was My Valley.*'

'Ah yes . . . Richard Llewellyn wrote it, didn't he? I enjoyed it too, so we have something in common.'

She didn't want to have anything in common with him at all, but deep in her heart she knew there were probably many things they had in common, and she wasn't being practical. 'You shouldn't be doing the washing up.'

'I know . . . I'm your guest and it's beneath me.'

'At least protect your suit.' She took an apron from the hook and handed it to him. He held it up and gazed at it. 'Which bit goes where?'

Giving an exasperated sigh she shook it out and held it up. 'Put your head through this collar.'

Ducking his head, he did as ordered. She was flattening it tidily on to his shoulders when she found herself looking straight into the dark blossoming heart of his grey eyes.

'You have a lovely mouth, like a crushed rose,' he said.

She was about to withdraw her hands in alarm when his fingers and thumbs closed around her wrists and drew her hands down and behind him. Pulling her close against the length of his body his mouth touched against hers with an incredibly tender caress. The alarm intensified when she realized she was experiencing a strong urge to go to bed with Nick Cowan, and do whatever it took to satisfy the urges that spread a tingling awareness along each nerve. It was like lightning.

The sexual urge had a strong pull to it, and although she was a little bit scared of it, she was now filled with curiosity.

'Heavens, that wasn't fair,' she said, which was the opposite of the sinful feelings fermenting inside her. In fact, she could almost smell her flesh singe from the heat he'd generated in her.

'What wasn't fair about it; didn't you like being kissed? I'd say we were at flashpoint.'

'I'm not going to answer that.' For the sake of her own salvation she whispered, 'Please don't do it again, Nick Cowan. There are workplace rules in place.'

He laughed. 'We're not in the workplace now, and besides, I live by my own rules. It's so much more exciting.' He trailed a finger gently over her lips. 'Your mouth is as soft and downy as a bumble bee to kiss.'

He kissed her again . . . as she knew he would and a swarm of imaginary bumble bees droned around her. Had he ever kissed a bee? She doubted it. He would have his own sting though, she thought, and sighed when the kissing came to an end.

They finished the cleaning up between them, her mind dreamily absorbed by the way of bees, with an occasional bird of paradise thrown into the mix, when the warning siren sounded. The drone of bees became the throb of bombers in the distance.

Esmé came down the stairs, a blanket wrapped round her. Judith emerged from her room in her dressing gown. They had recently begun using the space under the stairs, especially when it was cold or wet outside, but there wasn't space for four of them.

'You two use it. I'll share the Andersen shelter with Nick.' After all, she couldn't leave a guest to fend for himself, and liked the unpredictability of him.

Halfway down the garden, Nick said, 'Have you ever been caught out in the open in a raid?'

'Never. I always head to the nearest shelter, though the bombers usually leave our patch of London alone.'

'They probably know that all the prettiest girls live here.' He took her by the hand. 'Come with me if you want an adventure.'

Her interest piqued, she went. They turned about and headed through the gate into the lane and made for the expanse of green that passed as a park in the nearest square. Already they were being pursued by the noise of the approaching bombers with their lethal loads and fierce growls.

Nick spread his coat on the grass and they lay on their backs and gazed up at the sky.

They came like roaring monsters, the noise throbbing heavily, so it reverberated up from the ground and into her spine to compress her heart, causing its beat to swish an alarm against her eardrums. Her tongue tasted of the salt created by fear, and of the fuel exhaust drifting down from the dragons flying above.

The bombers flew between the earth and the moon, deadly black crosses creating their own graves to mark. Meggie wasn't afraid, but she'd never felt such exhilaration in the face of danger, though she'd never faced such danger before.

'All that death flying over us, hundreds of pounds of high explosives,' Nick said. 'One bomb, and our bodies would disintegrate into the sum of its parts. No more breath except the ruby bubbles escaping to turn the moon red . . . no more words with which to lie to each other. No more partings with no endings, or making love and dying a thousand small deaths in the almost unbearable climax of it.'

'Hush, Nick,' she said, and although she'd never experienced a climax of a thousand small deaths, she could imagine what

it would feel like because sometimes she thought she experienced a small percentage when she had to part with his
company.

But he didn't hush. 'Your breasts would never know the
feverish homage of a man who'd lost the love of his mother,
or a child who was born in the image of his father, because
the need to carry on a name was more overwhelming than to
love the child who bore it.'

He was talking about himself.

Opening her blouse he captured her hands against the cool
grass and stooped to kiss each nipple through the barrier of
her cotton bra. She sucked in an audible breath. The night air
cooled them so the nubs were sensitive, hard and thrusting to
the point of wanting to experience again the rough rasp of his
tongue against them, and her breasts were prickled with a fine
scattering of goose bumps.

She hugged him tight, not knowing how to handle this
sweetness of touch that made her body so strangely agitated
and receptive.

'If we die this night, your loins will never know or accept
the touch of a man or have him fill your soft moistness with
the hard, thrusting knowledge of his love and lust.'

He edged up her skirt and he scratched gently on the divide
of her sensible white knickers, making her moist with need,
as though he was a knight home from the crusades, trying to
rouse the keeper of the drawbridge so he could gain admit-
tance and unlock his lady's chastity belt. When he located the
most sensitive spot, the need to scream with the aching joy of
his touch and to open her thighs to the intimate stroke of his
touch was almost overwhelming.

'Dearest girl in her lisle stockings and passion-killer knickers,
all tied up in elastic. Would you let the devil in, I wonder.'

'I don't believe in the devil.' She kissed him to stop the
darkness of his words. 'And please stop spouting speeches, as
though you're a ham actor in a tragic drama.'

'What's going on around us is a tragic drama. You understand
me, don't you, angel? We're a bit old for these fumbling advances
in the dark, and I've got a hard-on as big as a fireman's hose.'

She didn't misread the meaning of his words. 'Yes, I do

understand you.' And she did, for his hurt had touched a chord in her. He needed her as much as she needed him. 'Do you have one of those rubber protective thingamajigs with you?' she lobbed into the depths of his passion, then giggled as what he'd said sunk in. 'Do they sell them that size or are you just showing off?'

Unexpectedly, he began to roar with laughter. 'Where did that basin of cold water come from? What does a girl like you know of such sensible precautions as rubber thingamajigs? I don't carry them around, just in case.'

'My aunt is a nurse. She runs classes on birth control and advised me to ask the man if it appeared that intercourse was to take place.'

'A lovely, and decent woman, your aunt is, but her lecture sounds rather clinical for this occasion. It would be a shame to ruin her trust in me now, though.'

She fell quiet and waited, not knowing whether to laugh of cry while he did her buttons up, his fingers fumbling to find the buttonholes in the dark.

The night's bombing run had begun. Over near St Paul's Cathedral a dull red began to make the sky glow like a shepherd's warning. There was a crump, crump, crump of the explosives hitting their targets, filling the air with smoke and fury and a fiery eruption of sparks. She imagined men, women and children, cowering from the heated metal, slashed into strips by an inferno of metal and shattered glass.

'How useless it all is; I wish the war would end.' Tears in her eyes she pressed her face against his chest. 'Why did you stop?'

'Because you don't deserve to be taken furtively in the dark on your first time, but royally, in a four-poster bed spread with satin sheets, and me ravishing you in fine style for half the night beforehand, so you don't know whether you're coming or going.' Pulling her to her feet he tipped her face up and kissed her; then picked up his coat and shook the plant debris from it. 'I won't allow anyone to hurt you . . . not even me.'

She believed him.

As they walked back to the house a plane with a trail of smoke and flames cartwheeled silently across the sky and disappeared behind some buildings. There was a huge roar and flames shot into the air.

'How many air crew would that have been carrying?'

'I'm not sure, seven or eight as a guess.' And then he added as though he'd read her mind, 'I imagine they used their parachutes and all got out.'

Fire engines clanged everywhere. A warden came out of the darkness, swearing as he shouted at them to get under cover and calling them bloody fools.

Beside her, Nick stiffened. 'We're British. Stiff upper lip and all that.'

'You'd better be, else you'll get a bullet up your Khyber Pass.'

The warden was a short, podgy man of middle years. Nick placed a hand on his shoulder and warned gently, 'Try not to be so coarse, there's a young lady present.'

''Ere, who do you think you're talking to . . . what's your bleedin' name?'

'In answer to your first question, perhaps you'd care to advise me as to that. Nicholas Cowan to the second.' He handed the man a card. 'If you wish to take this further please feel free to present yourself at my office. I work for the Admiralty. In the meantime I'd be obliged if you'd apologize to my companion.'

A straw of torchlight flickered over the card and was quickly switched off. 'Sorry miss . . . sir,' he said, and Nick let him go.

'Thanks for not taking it further. He was only doing his job. He probably fought in the last war.'

'Actually, he was right and I was wrong. He was being heroic in the only way he knew how. I just didn't like our adventure being spoiled by something so mundane as a warden telling me off.'

'Don't be so haughty. He might be a professor of theology in his day job. The man was concerned because we were behaving like idiots. I didn't like your adventure much. You scare me.'

'I admit, it didn't end as happily as it should have. Didn't the danger make you feel gloriously alive though?'

She supposed it had, but it was a double-edged sword. 'It also made me think about the dead, the dying and the maimed.'

'Their lives are the price we pay for war.'

She refrained from stamping her foot. 'The only price we pay is inconvenience in our daily lives. The dead pay the ultimate price for all of us. It's easy to dismiss life when you're an onlooker and death is faceless.'

'I know. I also know that it's the industrial area that's being targeted. We were not in any real danger.'

They went into the Andersen shelter, where she turned her back on him.

'Don't shut me out. Come here. There must be something you like about me.'

Everything, she admitted to herself.

Placing an arm around her he pulled her against his shoulder and she relaxed. He was always so neat and clean. Tonight the soft covering of skin on his neck smelled of sandalwood soap. The small pink lobe of his ear was in reach of her tongue, should she care to extend it. She wondered what it would taste like. She was too aware of him . . . of herself. She spent a pleasant twenty minutes imagining almost every inch of him under her exploring hands. Her body was in a feverish turmoil from his closeness, though she kept her hands tightly fisted in case they wandered.

Before too long the planes flew back from where they'd unleashed their cargo of death, but they were bloodied. Engines coughed and spluttered and missed their beats, like failing hearts. Some trailed smoke. There were a couple of explosions as they released the leftover bombs, dropping them like sizzling dumplings into a seething stew. The act was indiscriminate and anonymous, so the pilots wouldn't feel the guilt of seeing a face twisted with pain, or hear the cries of a mother being carried on a stretcher, away from the side of her terrified children. They didn't watch a man trapped in his fireside chair, legs crushed, and listening to the rest of his life ticking away while hearing the cry of his first grandchild who'd been born without medical help in the stair cavity to a terrified woman with nowhere else to go.

'Don't be cross with me. I didn't start the war.'

'I know you didn't.'

When she ran a finger gently down his face he took her hand in his and placed a kiss in the palm. 'I think I'm falling in love with you, Miss Margaret Elliot.'

Everything inside her churned at his declaration. She didn't know whether to laugh or cry at the thought of him being in love with her. 'You can't do that to me . . . I like someone else.'

'Tell me about him.'

'He's in the army, fighting at the front, and he's a lawyer.'

'And a hero, and you're waiting for him to return home.'

'Yes to both . . . they're all heroes.'

'And you're wondering what an able-bodied upper-class twit like myself is doing behind a desk.' He had that teasing note in his voice again. 'If I were a hero instead of a coward would you wait for me?'

'Nick . . . I don't think you're a coward. Don't talk like that. Somebody might hear you and report it.'

'What's his name, this hero of yours?'

'Rainard Stone. He's an army captain. I worked for his parents before I became a Wren.'

'Rainard? What sort of name is that?'

'People call him Rennie.'

'Does this Rennie love you in return?'

'I don't know, really. He hasn't said. I think he might do . . . he said I'm too young.'

He sighed. 'He's a lost cause who doesn't want a child bride because he knows he's too dull and you'd leave him eventually. You're waiting on the off chance that he might change his mind about that. So what were you doing with me tonight? It's a big responsibility for a man to have a young woman in love with them. Having one love requires fidelity, which is a sacrifice on the man's part. To start with, they have to stop whoring around.'

'Rennie wouldn't do anything like that. Besides, I didn't say I loved him, just that I like him . . . quite a lot.'

'Are you sure about that? The sexual act means very little to a man except to provide a need to satisfy his urges.' Picking up her hand he ran his thumb across the fingers. 'Where is your engagement ring?'

'Oh, we're not engaged or anything. Rennie is much too sensible to commit himself during the war. He was engaged once, to Pamela. She still loves him, I think.'

'He should be getting all he can of you, while he can. You didn't act as though you were serious about someone else, earlier.'

Her ears heated even though her blood ran cold at the thought of anything happening to Rennie. 'Oh . . . I didn't do anything with you.'

'But you would have done if I'd had some protection in my pocket, admit it.'

'Well . . .' a blush spread into her cheeks and she was glad it was dark so he couldn't see it. 'I was curious, and got carried away by the moment.'

'You found me irresistible, did you?'

'Yes, Nick . . . I did just at that moment. Wasn't that the outcome you were trying to achieve?'

'You could quite as easily say I was just a man who came to dinner, one who saw an opportunity for a pleasant and sensual interlude to round the evening off with – and forgot the basic precaution. Next time, if there is one, I'll come prepared and try not to disappoint your maidenly heart. That's if your heart was involved.'

'You could also say . . . in fact, I think you *did* say – and she deepened her voice. 'I think I'm falling in love with you, Margaret Elliot.'

'Stop making a mockery of me. I've never loved anybody except myself before. It makes me feel self-sacrificial.'

'Woe is you, my lord, for you were nearly undone.'

The burst of laughter he gave was self-deprecating. 'I'd say it was nearly the other way round. I might have been lying when I said that.'

'I considered that at the time. Now I'll say that my maidenly heart wasn't involved, and you didn't disappoint me. You would have done if you'd been less considerate though. I shall wait for the four-poster bed and the satin sheets.'

'Ouch! I'll have you know it was more selfishness than consideration on my part. I didn't want to be responsible for either the loss of your virginity, or the creation of an unloved child.'

'I reserve the right to hold myself responsible for the loss of my virginity.'

'And what about the child?'

'Who said it would be unloved, though it would be better off with the love of two parents.'

The all-clear siren began its banshee wail, like the curtain coming down at the end of a Shakespeare play, though whether farce or tragedy, she couldn't tell. She only knew it had been magnificent in one way, and tragic in another.

Taking her face between his hands Nick kissed her. It was a long and lingering kiss . . . loving almost – an enigma, like him. 'I don't think I can win this debate I'm having with myself,' he said when he finished with her.

'Neither can I.'

'And I doubt if there are any satin sheets to be found. We're down to practicalities.'

Now it was her turn to laugh. 'If nothing else this little episode poses the question: If you don't want me and I don't want you, what the hell are we doing here with each other wanting each other like crazy?'

Nick could find no answer for that. All he knew was the girl had managed to get under his skin without even trying, and was fast becoming an obsession.

When he arrived home Nick went into his father's study, picked up the receiver and gave the operator a number.

'Do we have a file on a Captain Rainard Stone?' he asked the man who eventually picked up the receiver.

Thirteen

9 July 1940

Leo managed to snatch a few hours at home. He took a bath and then fell asleep, waking to find his pot-bellied woman watching over him.

He'd stolen a red rose he'd seen blossoming in a cottage garden, and although it was only half open and hardly more than a bud, it was in a small crystal vase on Esmé's dressing table.

He smiled at her. 'I've missed you, my sweet. Come here and lay down beside me.'

When she joined him, he gently palpated her stomach, and then he placed his ear against it. There was a fast, steady tick of the baby's heart among the gurgles of the fluid sac. The infant . . . *their* infant was of a fair size. He kissed her swollen midriff then looked up at her. 'The head's engaged.'

'You don't have to worry, Leo. Everything's proceeding as it should.'

'BP?'

'Blood pressure is perfectly all right. I've kept a diary. If you want to read it then it's on the dressing table. But may I remind you that you're not my doctor, even if you are my doctor . . . Doctor.'

He chuckled. 'You're looking a bit pale. Have your iron levels been checked lately?'

'I'm taking iron pills.'

'I wish you'd go and stay with Livia. I'm sure she'd love to have you there.'

She sighed. 'You're worrying unnecessarily. I've got a midwife on call and I've got Meggie and Judith.'

'I can't see Meggie doing much. She faints at the thought of pricking her finger.'

'You'd be surprised at how grown up and capable Meggie's becoming, and haven't you forgotten one thing?'

'What's that?'

'I've delivered lots of babies for other women, so I don't see why I can't deliver our own if need be.'

'I love you, Mrs Thornton.'

Tears touched her eyes.

'Why are you crying, my darling girl?'

'It's because I love you too, and I miss you. I'm feeling a bit weepy now the baby is almost here . . . something to do with the imbalance of the hormones, I expect.'

But that wasn't the reason. She was crying because of what

must stay unsaid between them – the reason why he wanted her to go and stay with Livia. If something happened to him she would need someone strong to support her. And if anything happened to her he knew he wouldn't want to live.

So he took her in his arms, spooned her into his body and held her gently, loving her and feeling contented, even though they feared for each other and lied while the clock ticked away each second. Soon, she slept, the rise and fall of her chest and the steady pulse of her heart against his, reassuring him.

His precious few hours of normal life were used up too soon, but not wasted, he thought, as he quietly dressed, and drew the quilt up over her.

He gazed down at her, kissed her mouth and whispered words of love against her ear. He left her in the early hours of the morning – left her with the responsibility of their unborn infant, both of them pretending she was asleep to make the parting easier.

He stood outside waiting for Derek Smithson to arrive on the squadron's shared Triumph 100 motorcycle. None of them knew who actually owned it.

One of the engineers had found it in a hedge, bent and battered, and after a while had adopted it as a squadron mascot, and had fixed it up. Leo's car was languishing in a garage that had access to the lane at the back.

The air had a damp coolness to it. The moon had travelled on, the sky was dark, and rain showers pattered against the dark, sightless windows. There was a hint of orange in the sky to the west, but whether first light or fire Leo couldn't tell. Both perhaps.

Smithy arrived, the bike growling, but with an occasional wounded cough thrown in. Leo took the pillion seat and they were off, the rain bouncing off their helmets and shoulders. He began to wonder what the day would bring.

For the last couple of weeks the airmen had snatched what rest and sustenance they could. Air raids had been constant and fairly predictable, but mostly they were confined to the industrial and dockyard areas. They slept in their clothes.

When they weren't flying they used the accommodation

on the base, for sleeping, writing letters or playing chess. Today they were home in time for breakfast. Clattering into the engineers' workshop they abandoned the bike and followed their noses to the mess.

A battered Spitfire had just hopped over a line of trees and Leo's eyes narrowed in on it as it skewed sideways to come into land.

Most of the flyers were awake, responding to the smell of breakfast.

'G'day, Doc,' they began to call out when they spotted him, and he grinned when someone began to whistle 'Waltzing Matilda'. They were an unruly and disrespectful bunch of buggers, but he wouldn't have them any different.

He slapped several strips of bacon and an egg between two pieces of toast, savoured every morsel then washed it down with a mug of tea.

The door opened and a young man entered. He stood there, looking as nervous as a fish on Friday. His face was familiar and Leo sifted through the dregs of his memory.

He was young, but not too young to have seen some action, for he walked with a limp. Approaching him, Leo held out hand. 'Squadron Leader Leo Thornton.'

'If I'm not mistaken, you're Edwin Richards.'

The lad looked pleased at being remembered. 'Yes, sir. I'd prefer being called Eddie though.'

'How did you come by the limp?'

Richards' flushed. 'I had a bit of a prang, and broke it. That was three months ago.'

'What were you flying at the time?'

Richards looked even more embarrassed and lowered his voice. 'Actually, I wasn't flying anything. I was on my brother's go-cart when the front end parted from the back. When the leg healed it was shorter than the other.'

'Either it wasn't stretched into position correctly before it was splinted or you tried to walk on it prematurely and moved it out of place. I can see the lump from here where it healed and the bone is overgrown. I'm surprised they allowed you to fly.'

'I'd applied to become a pilot long before the accident and

I was able to report to training school. I told them I'd pulled a muscle to explain the limp, and nobody looked too closely at it. It doesn't hurt. A couple of days ago I was given instructions to report to you.'

'Have you trained on Spits?'

'I brought one with me,' he said with schoolboyish pride.

'Ah . . . is that what that aircraft is? How many flying hours have you put in since school cadet training?'

Richards shrugged as he admitted. 'Twelve . . . six with the RAF.'

'Let me see your log book.'

At least he hadn't lied about the six. 'Collins . . .' Leo bawled across the room. 'This is Eddie Richards. He's yours, so take him up and give him a workout for half an hour.'

'Have you seen what he arrived in, skipper? It's patched up with corned beef tins and one wing is higher than the other. She drags her arse along the ground like a dog with worms.'

Eddie was as hot in defence of his ungainly first aircraft as a mother was of her infant. 'She's a bit of an antique and she rattles like hell, but she flies straight if you compensate for the wing. Her frame is twisted by hard landings, and she's been pancaked a couple of times. As long as you put the tail down gently she doesn't scrape.'

'No wonder they got rid of her. She's expendable. However, they should remember that pilots aren't. But if it's capable of being flown, we have to fly it. I'll put you on the list for something more serviceable. You can have some breakfast when you come back and we'll get an engineer to look her over.'

'Thank you, sir.'

Leo laughed. 'You won't thank me when you're up there. Off you go then. Follow Collins and stick to him like glue.'

Surprisingly, both Eddie and his craft made it back, her faulty wing causing the craft to flap along the runway like an injured duck, her tail wagging from side to side. The watching pilots set up a cheer.

'If he can fly that thing he can fly anything,' Collins said when they walked into the ops room. 'Well done, Eddie my boy. Go and get yourself some breakfast if there's any left.'

The mechanics scratched their heads and gazed with pity upon Eddie's ugly aircraft.

It was half past seven the next morning, when the telephone in the office rang.

Somebody cracked, 'If that's Hitler tell him to call back next month, I intend to sleep until then.'

'Good luck to you?'

'What day is it?' someone else said through an extended yawn.

'Wednesday.'

'Dash it all . . . I hate Wednesdays.'

'Scramble! Scramble!'

Pulling on life preservers, helmets and goggles, and grabbing up a parachute as they went, four of the pilots raced towards their orderly row of serviced Spitfires, their propellers just visible against a false dawn. Adrenalin gave their feet wings. Leo was one of them.

Engines coughed, fired, coughed again and fired up. Soon they began to peel off the rank and roar along the runway, water spitting from their tyres.

The sky was overcast, the land and sky sandwiched together with a smear of inky clouds.

Leo flew automatically, breaking free of earth and taking his plane up through the cloud and through a saturation of water that scrubbed over his craft's metal skin. With nowhere else to go it shattered into droplets at the edge of the wing, and was scattered back into the vapour it had just left.

He broke through the cloud cover at 10,000 feet, and the sudden burst into a blaze of dazzling sunshine and azure sky reminded him for a moment of his Australian homeland.

But he had no room for nostalgia – no time to ponder on the welfare of his family – on his mother, father, and his brother, Alex, who'd married Esmé's best friend, Minnie. They were safe unless, or until, the Asian countries became involved.

His companions were still with him; at the same time he was given a bearing of where the enemy had been spotted on the radar.

It was not long before the intruder was within their sights.

It was a lone, twin-engined Dornier bomber, probably checking the coast for weather conditions or looking for convoys.

The Spitfires attacked one by one, and though the Dornier put up a fight it was soon banking in a cloud of smoke. It fell into the sea off Yarmouth and sank. There were no survivors.

There were other German planes on reconnaissance, guarded by numerous single-engined Messerschmitts.

Something was brewing . . .

The raids that day had a different pattern to them and were more numerous. The pilots began to show their exhaustion, and that was reflected in the losses.

The German aircraft kept coming in hundreds, and they were unrelenting. The squadron was kept busy.

In Whitehall Meggie was trawling through recent For Sale notices in newspapers when she came across the words *sea* and *lion*, either grouped together or mentioned separately in the same sentence. She crossed referenced them with a couple of editorial letters, but could make nothing sensible from the anagram.

The fact that sea was mentioned might be related to a convoy. The lion could be referring to the British coat of arms. Where else were there lions? Piccadilly circus . . . a zoo – Leo – Africa – golden syrup tins.

She hesitated. There was a biblical quote on the tin. 'Out of the strong came forth sweetness.' The legend was that Samson had slaughtered a lion. Later he discovered that bees had taken up residence in the lion's body. Samson had tasted the honey and from that the adage of sweetness from strength had arisen.

So many mentions were too much of a coincidence.

With Nick having been out of the office for several days, supposedly visiting his ailing father in the country, she typed up her report and placed a sealed carbon copy in Gordon Frapp's in-tray, along with her list of sources.

The original, she placed on Nick's desk. It was gone the next morning, along with a couple of less urgent reports. She said nothing in case it caused gossip.

Gordon Frapp knew office protocol as well as she did, and could have noticed for himself if he'd bothered to look.

Frapp's eyes gleamed when he read his copy.

'Excellent, my dear. I was working on that one myself. We should have synchronized our findings. Is Lord Cowan not back yet?' It was said too casually.

Truthfully, she said, 'He may be, but I haven't seen him.'

Frapp picked up the telephone and said he needed to see Bethuen urgently. He came back from the meeting with a pleased look on his face.

Bethuen called her into the office and leaned back in his chair. 'I believe you helped Mr Frapp collate that sea lion information. Well done, young lady. That information is now on its way to Bletchley Park. It will be a feather in our departmental caps.'

Judith winked at her when she left, both of them knowing that only one person was likely to receive a feather, Bethuen himself.

'I'll be home a bit late tonight,' Judith said when the door closed on her boss. 'I'm going to have a drink with Alan Gibbs before he rejoins his ship. I'll warm my dinner up when I get home.'

Later that day Frapp approached her and grumbled, 'Bethuen has just given me a dressing down. He said he came out of it with egg on his face. Apparently, intelligence about Operation Sea Lion was delivered the night before. He said to be sure of our facts next time, and to do things through Lord Cowan. How can we when he's absent all the time? Are you sure you haven't seen him?'

'Of course I'm sure. I don't suppose we're the only people doing this sort of work, do you?'

Nick turned up two days later in the afternoon. He looked pale and drawn.

Waiting until Gordon had left for the day he came to her desk, where she was busy covering up her typewriter.'

'I have a bullet in my arm and it needs to be dug out. No questions asked. Can you do it?'

Her blood ran cold. 'I haven't got the stomach for that sort of thing. I could ask my aunt. She's a nurse. But I know that she'd tell me to take you to outpatients.'

'Who would be duty bound to report it to the authorities. I don't want to involve her.'

'What if I faint?'

He grinned. 'I'll faint with you, so you'll have company.'

'Be serious Nick.'

'I am being serious. I would have dug it out myself if I could reach. But it's in my left arm, and I'm left-handed and can't manage it with my right. When we leave here follow me down to the river. My boat's moored there and it has a first aid kit. The boat's called *Petite Coccinelle*.'

Little Ladybird. What a pretty name to give a boat, she thought, dreading what lay ahead. 'Give me time to lock this file in the cabinet first and tidy up.'

She reached the boat fifteen minutes later.

The boat was a small yacht with a navy-blue hull and her name painted in gold in an oblong of paler blue. The decks were varnished, though scuffed in places. It was the size of boat that could be managed by one person, and just the thing a navy man would own for his pleasure. That's if he was a navy man. She had the feeling his uniform was one of convenience. Despite his unpredictable nature, there was a conventionality about Nick that was part of his upbringing, mostly kept for public display.

She stepped aboard and down the couple of steps into the small cabin. He'd changed from his uniform trousers into casual grey ones. His feet were clad only in grey socks. Obviously, he kept a change of clothes on his boat, as he was half out of his shirt.

'Good . . . it didn't take you long to get here.'

He had everything laid out ready on a padded sheet, a scalpel and hook, a bottle of iodine and some cotton wool, a pad of lint and a bandage. There was also a bowl of water and some soap to wash her hands in.

She blanched, and sucked in a breath when he pulled his shirt half off and the sleeve from his arm. The sight of the angry red lumps made her feel queasy.

He said, 'It's gone through the side and is lodged just under the skin at the back. It's only a small bullet, little more than an air pistol. All you have to do is make a cut over the lump and hook the bullet out. Not too deep.'

'I . . . I don't know if I can.'

'Let me assure you that you can. It will be like lifting an almond from its shell. Do it now, Margaret. The sooner it's out the sooner it will heal.'

'It will hurt you.'

'No more than it's hurting me now; I didn't pick you for a coward. Get on with it . . . I can stand the pain and I'll talk you through it.'

His tone of voice was scathing. Reluctantly she washed her hands and picked up the scalpel.

'Use the iodine first. Saturate the cotton wool and swab both wounds. They're fairly clean, but a bit more won't hurt.'

Her hands were shaking when she approach the swelling with the scalpel.

'Take the bullet firmly between your finger and thumb. Then when the skin is taut, run the blade of the scalpel gently over it. Mind you don't cut yourself at the same time.'

'Eeeeek!' She made the noise along with the cut. There was a small release of blood and she gulped back an urge to turn and run.

'Pull yourself together. Use the hook and pull the bullet from the percussion cap end.'

'What's a percussion cap?'

'The flat end. You won't have to probe very far. If it won't come out you'll have to use your fingers and go a little deeper.'

'I'd prefer it if you were willing to die of blood poisoning.'

He laughed. 'I dare say you would, but I wouldn't prefer to.'

With a bit of persuasion and a couple of intakes of breath from Nick, the bullet came out.

'Thank goodness,' she exclaimed, almost to herself. Making a pad with the lint she pressed it against the wound, then firmly bandaged it. Washing her hands she gazed at him. His face was bathed in sweat, and so was hers. 'Are you all right, Nick?'

He nodded. 'You?'

'I can't really tell, though I'm trembling.'

'There's half a bottle of brandy and a couple of glasses in that locker. Pour us a nip each while I get my spare shirt out from under the bench.'

'I'll get it, it will be quicker.'

He tore the dirty shirt from his body and threw it in a bloodied heap.

She could feel his glance on her as she got his clean shirt on and buttoned it. He slid his feet into a pair of brown Oxfords. 'Don't bother with the tie.'

He was tautly muscled and strong. 'Your other shirt is ruined.'

'It doesn't matter. Help me on with that roll-necked sweater, if you would.'

She glanced up at him, her eyes tangling with the smoky grey of his. A chuckle escaped from him. 'Go on then, ask me.'

'I have no intention of asking you how you happened to get shot, if that's what you're talking about.'

He stopped, allowing his beautiful mouth to engage hers in a moment or two of sublime pleasure. She was growing used to his kisses, looking forward to them. 'That's good because I've got no intention of telling you.'

She reached for the brandy and glasses, handing them to him. His hands shook as he poured a small amount into each glass.

'You're suffering from shock.'

'It will go in a minute or two.'

'I'll just get rid of this,' she said, picking up the bowl of bloodied water.

Making her way up the ladder she tipped it over the side and lay on her front to rinse the bowl in the river. Her head felt swimmy when she went below again. The first thing she saw was Nick's discarded shirt, which he'd picked up and thrown into a waste paper basket. Although the blood was dried, it served to remind her that she couldn't stomach blood.

She smiled at his fading image, said weakly, 'I can't believe I dug a bullet out of your arm. Remember I told you the sight of blood often made me . . . feel . . . faint . . .'

He caught her before her knees completely buckled, drawing her down on to the bench and against his shoulder. 'Here, drink this, it will help.'

The brandy fumes brought her round quickly. She spluttered

and coughed when the liquor hit her stomach like a firebolt. Crossly, she said. 'They might have killed you.'

'Who might have?'

'The person who shot you.'

'Why should you care?'

'I don't . . . what have you been up to, Nick Cowan?'

He laughed. 'If I told you I doubt if you'd believe it.'

'Try me.'

'I was shot while exiting a lady's boudoir through her bedroom window.'

She didn't know whether to believe him or not and stared at him. The disgruntled innocence in his expression would have disarmed her if it were not for the devilment lurking in his eyes. 'Are you disappointed?'

'Why should I be disappointed?'

'Because you'd rather I was shot leaving *your* boudoir.'

Her mind scrambled with the accuracy of that thought. 'Hah! I would have shot you before you got in. It would have served you right if her husband had killed you.'

'It was her mother who shot me . . . she was jealous and trying to stop me from escaping her clutches.'

Meggie burst into laughter, knowing she would never get at the truth about what had happened. Feeling stronger, she straightened. 'I'm going home. I like to spend as much time as I can with my aunt, and Judith won't be there until later.'

His glance took her in and he made a humming noise in his throat. 'I'll take you.'

'Thanks, Nick, but you should rest.'

'I'll take you. Well done on the sea lion thing, by the way. I bet Bethuen was fuming when he found out.'

'Nobody likes being made a fool of. He gave Gordon Frapp a dressing down, and told him to go through you from now on. Had Gordon checked your desk he would have known you were around, but he preferred to blame it on me, rather than act on it earlier.'

'And you didn't tell him.'

'I'm not going to help either of you score points off each other, especially when the security of the country is at stake.

I don't want to be part of your games. I've got enough to worry about.'

She picked up her bag. 'Goodnight, Nick, I'm going. I don't want to be caught in an air raid.' Leaving, she jumped ashore and walked rapidly away.

He caught her up five minutes later, and placed a paper carrier bag in her hands. This is a gift for your Aunt Esmé. No doubt she'll share it with you.'

'What is it?'

'This-and-that. Some smoked bacon . . . gooseberries and asparagus, cheese. Biscuits . . . a bar of chocolate perhaps. Everything that's bad for you.'

'You're bad for me.'

'Taking her hand in his he kissed her palm, and then smiled. 'You were brave to remove that bullet.'

'You were braver for bullying me into doing it.'

'Aren't you going to ask me if what I said was true?'

'No.'

'Aren't you even curious?'

'I'm not in the least bit interested.'

'You're a liar.'

'I know . . . and you're acting like a child, playing games. If you're going to tell me, then do. If you're not, well . . . that's fine.'

Taking her by the shoulders he turned her round to face him. 'Except this game is too real and deadly for children to play, Meggie. You know I can't discuss what I do. I can't trust anyone.'

'I'm well aware of that.' She touched his cheek and softened her voice. 'There's someone you can trust in case you ever feel the need. I'm going. There will be a bus along the Strand in a minute and I'll take that, since it will get me nearer to where I'm going. Look after your arm.'

Meggie, he'd called her, but not for the first time. He'd called her Meggie Elliot when he'd delivered the food hamper to the flat, and at that stage he hadn't met any of the people who did call her that. No wonder she'd thought it odd when he'd first used it. He couldn't have known her family nickname was Meggie then.

He sighed. 'You certainly know how to stonewall people. I'll make sure you get on the bus safely.'

'As you wish.'

She really wanted to be alone, to think. Her mind was already a jumble of questions and answers.

He was left-handed. He solved cryptic crosswords. She gazed at his shoes. Oxford brogues. Brown! What more proof did she need? Her heart began to thump erratically, and then a little niggle of common sense stamped its foot. She was constructing a scenario out of something too flimsy to be true.

'Are you sure you're all right?' he said.

'Of course I am.' But she remembered the burglar, and felt herself falling into a deep, dark hole. She was tempted to leave it alone. What mattered was that the burglar had returned the goods he'd stolen. It showed that he had a conscience.

But no, it wasn't all that mattered, it was the fact that he'd frightened both herself and her aunt, and just for the heck of it. She must find a way to bring this out into the open, and without involving her aunt and uncle.

He was involved in something far deeper than she'd expected if people were shooting at him. Perhaps she'd got it all wrong. 'What if it was all a coincidence!' she said out loud.

'If what was a coincidence?'

She blinked. 'Sorry, I was thinking of something else.'

'Allow me bring your mind back to me.' He tipped up her chin and kissed her, feathering her mouth with his so the thought of him making love to her sent darts of desire into all her most sensitive places.

Please don't let him be the burglar, she thought.

On Monday she opened a new file. Inside, she placed the crossword and a list of what the man had taken, and when. What he'd worn. She put the date of when they were returned and the method. Also the newspaper cuttings, and copies of the statements she and Esmé had made to Constable Duffy.

She wrote a small passage to describe the effects the burglary had on herself and especially her aunt – but using different names.

Police Sergeant Benjamin Blessing, she named the file.

Nick's filing cabinet was the only one kept locked. She

found a bunch of keys in his drawer and tried each one. When none of them worked she inserted the flat blade of a penknife into the lock and juggled it around until something gave. The drawer opened an inch before it stopped, but that was enough room to slide the file inside.

She pushed the drawer shut again.

Fourteen

Everyone knew that the pilots of the Royal Air Force had a fight on their hands in defence of England.

The day raids increased, and it seemed that if it were not for the need to refuel, the pilots would have stayed in the air permanently.

Day after day people went to the coast to watch the battle unfold. It seemed like a high wire trapeze act. Planes fell from the sky in scribbles of vapour and exploded into the sea. Parachutes floated across the sky like mushrooms, their flimsy silk sometimes tangled in the strings, so the first instant of safety offered, sometimes degenerated into a swift, deadly plunge. Some half open, made it to earth and bumped their occupants along the ground like puppets on strings. Some stood upright afterwards. Others were driven away in ambulances, glad to be offered a rest, however short.

The Germans had a bigger air force, and it seemed that they were going to win the battle, except the British, with their facility to land, refuel and take off again almost immediately, managed to shoot more of the German planes down.

The battle was taking its toll of the pilots. Deprived of sleep they were totally exhausted . . . yet still they carried on. Planes rolled off the assembly line and young, hardly trained pilots walked out of wrecks on the runway and took to the skies in the next available aircraft. Many lost their lives.

At forty-three Queen Street, Esmé waited for her precious baby to arrive. She scanned the casualty list every day, trying to remain hopeful when she didn't see Leo's name there. She kept herself busy stitching small garments.

She was in the middle of reading the latest casualty list when the telephone rang. It was Leo. 'I've just called to tell you that I love you.'

She burst into tears, mostly from the relief of hearing his voice.

'Hush, my love,' he said. 'Everything will be all right . . . I promise.'

She sniffed back her tears. 'I'm sorry, darling. I'm a bit emotional at the moment. I seem to cry at the slightest thing and I feel horribly hormonal. All that practical training in midwifery and the advice I dish out, and I've just discovered I know nothing about being the broody hen.'

'You'll do wonderfully well at hatching the egg. Did we decide on a name yet?'

She knew he'd said it to take her mind off the negative and give her hope for a future together. Leo was so brave, and it was agony trying to imagine what he was going through. 'I thought Lydia Jane would be pretty for a girl.'

'Lydia Jane Thornton it is then.'

'You can choose a boy's name if you like.'

'What about John Oliver? We could call him Johnno.'

'Perfect. He sounds like a member of parliament already.'

'The prime minister at the very least.'

She managed a watery giggle. 'One thing . . . he couldn't be mistaken for anything but an Australian with a nickname like that.'

The phone call was too short, and she knew others were waiting to use the telephone so as to reassure their loved ones. She sent him a kiss down the phone. 'Lots of love Leo, and from Meggie as well. She's looking after me, and is turning out to be a treasure. Her superior officer said that if I need her, to phone him and he'll send her home and she can have a few days off. He's very nice.'

'I'm relieved.'

They said goodbye and she put the receiver down and had a prowl round. She felt restless. Meggie usually came home straight from work. Today she was late . . . half an hour late.

She went back to the paper, and with the cat balanced on the portion of lap she had left, she went down the casualty lists in the paper. She found names of people she had known on the pleasure cruisers, who'd joined the navy and been torpedoed and drowned. How long ago that time seemed now. Sadness crept over her. Leo had advised her not to read the casualty lists.

Meggie usually attended the navy memorial services, which were happening more and more. Her natural ebullience seemed to desert her on those occasions. She was far more unselfish and thoughtful. The destruction going on had a profound effect on her, though the changes had been gradual.

Esmé hadn't heard from her friend Minnie since before the war. Married to Leo's brother, her best friend had achieved all she'd ever wanted in life . . . a family who loved and appreciated her. And she'd found it in Australia, as had Esmé.

Her finger hovered over a name and shock filled her. *William Denison (corporal).* Her eyes filled with tears again as she remembered the man she'd almost married and she whispered, 'Poor Liam.'

She'd been luckier than either Liam or Minnie, having a loving family to turn to for most of her life, if the need arose.

She heard a key in the lock. Jack Frost's ears pricked up and he gave an imperious meow, just in case she hadn't heard. She called out, 'I'm in the kitchen, Meggie.'

Meggie's arms came around her from behind and she kissed her cheek before placing the carrier bag she held, on the table. 'Why are you crying?' Then with more alarm, 'Everything's all right, isn't it?'

'Leo rang, and I felt lonely and missed him, and I didn't feel like being brave about it so decided to be miserable instead. We've decided on baby names. It will be Lydia Jane for a girl.'

'That's very pretty.'

'Leo wants John Oliver if it's a boy. He intends to call him Johnno.'

Meggie laughed. 'I like that. They're both nice names.'

'Do you remember Liam Denison? I found his name in the lists, and got a little melancholy when I read that he'd died on active service.'

'That's the man who used to be your dancing partner on the *Horizon Queen*, isn't it? I'm so sorry to hear it. He taught me the Charleston once. He was terribly good. Didn't he go to Hollywood to try his luck? And didn't he give you that engagement ring you gave to me.'

'That's him. We were engaged for only a short time. He got into the chorus line in a couple of films. Poor Liam. He wasn't content with who he was, as though he'd lost himself on the way to becoming a man. He wanted so much to be somebody. Even though he appeared confident he didn't have much confidence in himself. He didn't like responsibility.'

Meggie reminded her, 'He did become somebody . . . a war hero, like my father. But that doesn't count unless there is someone left who remembers them and can feel proud enough of them to bask in their glory. I still remember the Charleston Liam taught me, but nobody does it any more.' Meggie went into the dance routine, kicking her legs about and singing. When she tried to cross her hands on her knees in unison her knees knocked together. 'Ouch!'

'Liam wouldn't have taught you that move.' Esmé stood, spilling the cat to the floor. Holding her stomach she crossed her legs and began to giggle. 'Don't make me laugh . . . you know it makes me run to the lavvy . . .'

'Better out than in,' Meggie said when Esmé was moving towards the door.

Esmé stopped and turned. 'Tell that to the baby.'

'Be patient. It's not due for a couple more weeks. I'm going downstairs to change into civvies, and then I'll get on with dinner. Judith won't be in until later. She's got herself another boyfriend. She said she's going to enjoy herself while she can.'

'Good for her. I quite like her, and it's nice that you've got someone nearer your age to talk to. Now . . . what do we have for dinner?'

'We've got a proper potato each, though we'll have to have the reconstituted stuff if you want more. There are carrots, turnip and two slices of corned beef each. We'll have to have tapioca pudding and bottled rhubarb.'

'Ug!'

'Don't be a baby, Es. It's good for you, and the rhubarb has medicinal properties.'

'Stop lecturing me, Meggie Moo. You're just repeating back what I said to you in the first place. By the way you'd better put that blouse into soak in cold water. It's got blood on the cuffs. What have you been up to? You didn't kill someone by any chance, did you?'

Meggie thought fast because there were more bloodspots further up the arm and a splash of iodine on the front in the shape of an octopus. She didn't even want to think about what she'd done . . . something she was proud of, now it was over. 'Would you believe I was shaking a bottle to get the sauce to run and the top flew off and splotched me? Or would you prefer it if I told you that I changed into a vampire on the way home and had to find a quick snack.'

Nick's blue blood came to mind. It hadn't looked any different, or any tastier than hers. Baring her teeth at the cat, who had leaped on the table to investigate the carrier bag, she hissed at him. Jack Frost shot to the floor and gave her such a look of surprised disdain that she laughed.

Esmé laughed even more at the thought of her having vampire tendencies. 'That would have been something to see. I thought you'd abandoned fiction in favour of presenting the facts . . . studying law, that is.'

'I knew you wouldn't believe me.' Meggie had counted on it. 'Go and have a wee before you do it on the floor. You look undignified standing there with your legs crossed.'

'What's in the carrier bag? I thought I smelled chocolate earlier.'

'So did the cat, obviously. It's a gift for you, from Nick Cowan. You can open it when you come back.'

'What a splendid creature that man is. I used to be all prissy in case it was black market . . . my holier-than-thou attitude has fallen by the wayside now you've met him.'

So had Meggie's. 'Creature being the operative word,' was all she could manage to say.

21 August

'Never in the field of human conflict was so much owed by so many to so few.'

The speech by Winston Churchill to the House of Commons was published in the morning paper and like most of the prime minister's speeches they were designed to inspire.

It reminded Leo of school, of the St Crispin's Day speech from Shakespeare's *Henry V* that he'd had to learn by heart. He'd solemnly recited it at assembly, his heart throbbing like a drum.

> *'From this day to the ending of the world.*
> *But we in it shall be remembered –*
> *We few, we happy few, we band of brothers,*
> *For he today who sheds his blood with me*
> *Shall be my brother . . .'*

He gazed around at his companions and felt a strong connection to them that he knew would last for as long, or as short, as he lived. It was almost like they'd become one.

They were fighting for everything Britain represented . . . for the lives of the wives, their way of life and a future of freedom for their children. Despite the danger . . . or perhaps because of it, Leo enjoyed what he was doing. At the back of his mind he worried about Esmé. But there was nothing he could do about the situation. He wished she'd gone to stay with her sister Livia when he'd asked. London was an obvious target, and the raids were increasing day by day.

Over the past few days the German long-range bombers had been busy. The raids had been heavy and had extended to Liverpool. They had also begun to target RAF airfields. Several aircraft on the ground had been destroyed, and personnel killed or injured.

Then there was the safety of their baby to consider. He didn't have the faith in Meggie that Esmé had. She didn't like the sight of blood and would probably fall to pieces in the face of an emergency.

On the other hand, his Es was in good health and there

had been no problems during the pregnancy, except for the occasion when her iron levels had plunged, but iron pills had restored the balance. But like she said, she could deliver it herself if she had too. Perhaps he could persuade her to move out of London after their child was born.

Once inside the mess the smell of food made everything else fade from his mind. Placing a fried egg and some bacon between two slabs of bread, he considered that he was probably worrying unnecessarily. He ate the doorstop sandwich quickly, and lifted a mug of tea to his mouth, taking great gulps.

'Scramble! Scramble!'

A chorus of groans went up. Not surprising when they'd not long ago got down. Today, the enemy was using a new tactic, prowling along the coast in small groups. They attacked one of the airfields, destroying a hangar and planes in Cornwall.

Eddie Richards got to his feet and followed after Leo through a summer rainstorm. Leo smiled to himself. Eddie was an old hand now, and the proud possessor of a brand new aircraft. He'd earned every rivet in it. Leo supposed he looked equally tired, though he seemed to have gone past tiredness and into an automatic state.

He was still drinking the remnants of tea that had managed to stay in the cup, and when he reached his aircraft, which was already armed and ticking over, he dashed the dregs to the ground and tossed the mug to the engineer, who grinned at him and said, 'She's full and flirty, Doc . . . raring to go. See you when you get down.'

The ground crews as well as the pilots had the scramble down to a fine art now.

Then it was chocks away and he was off, racing down the runway with Eddie on his wing, having lost Collins a couple of sorties ago. But upstairs, it was mostly every man for himself.

He nearly gasped when he saw what they were about to take on. About eighty aircraft belonging to the Luftwaffe were up there.

But the Spits were above them, so had the element of surprise. Saying a short prayer he gave the thumbs up to Eddie, then put the nose of his craft down and began the dive down among them.

Two bombers and a Messerschmitt were downed before the Luftwaffe was turned back and encouraged to go home.

The next day the raids were light but well spaced, as if the object of the exercise was to prevent the pilots from resting.

He managed to telephone Es again, grinning like a shot fox when he heard her voice.

'How are you, my lovely girl?'

'Stuffed to the gills . . . Meggie's been rubbing olive oil on my belly. She read it in a magazine and said it will prevent stretch marks. It seems to be working. I honestly don't think I can stretch much further. I saw the gyno yesterday. He said if the baby isn't here in a week he's going to induce the birth. I might take a dose of caster oil tonight to help it along.'

'You poor darling.'

'Don't sympathize with me, Leo, else I'll feel sorry for myself and get the weeps. And don't say anything to make me laugh either because my bladder is touch-and-go.'

'That doesn't leave me with much else to say except I love you. Hold on sweetheart. This time next week at the latest, you'll have our baby snuggling against your breasts . . . the lucky little devil.'

'Behave yourself, Leo. That sort of thinking got me into this state in the first place, and my breasts are now the size of watermelons.'

He chuckled. 'Let's hope it likes its tucker then. It will all be worth it in the end.'

'I know.'

Leo swore when he heard the order to scramble over the tannoy. 'I've got to go, my sweet. I'll ring you again when I get down. Take care. Always remember that I love you.' He hung up.

A little while later he flew out over the cliffs and up through the clouds into a bright blue sky that seemed full of promise. It was a perfect day for flying.

Jerry obviously thought so too. They had sent the entire Luftwaffe out to deal with them.

Fifteen

Esmé had been a little uncomfortable during dinner the previous evening. She'd wondered, as she'd got into bed, if the malaise was caused by the cocktail of castor oil, orange juice and bicarbonate of soda she'd swallowed previously – though once the fizz had died down she was sure she'd retched most of it up.

It was early the next morning – too early, the hall clock having just chimed two a.m. Her bladder was full to bursting. Getting out of bed she stood, and, placing her hands against her back she cautiously stretched, smiling when a weak contraction rippled across her stomach.

'At last,' she whispered, excitement rippling through her as if she were a teenager looking forward to her first date. Patting her baby gently on the bottom she whispered, 'I love you.'

She felt her way to the bathroom, remembering to avoid the buckets of water, gas masks, clothes and torch kept ready on the landing in case there was a fire to extinguish, or just the need to evacuate the house in a hurry.

No need to wake Meggie yet, but she must alert her midwife, she thought.

The operator told her there was no answer. There must be a rush of births on and her allocated midwife was attending someone else, Esmé thought. But she probably wouldn't need her until the morning to do the birth.

'Could you put me through to the hospital?'

'I'm afraid their switchboard doesn't operate this time of morning. Is it urgent?'

'Not at the moment . . . I'll try again later. Thanks.'

There was a rustling noise from the stairs to the basement and she had a moment of fear when she remembered the intruder. She gazed into the dark maw of the stairwell and froze to the spot, her tongue stuck to the roof of her mouth as if glued there.

A torch was switched on and the thin beam bounced up the steps. Meggie whispered, 'Is that you, Aunt Es?'

Esmé's tongue peeled off and her held breath exhaled in a relieved rush. 'You gave me such a scare, Meggie.'

'Sorry . . . it's one of those nights when I keep waking up. There have been no raids on the dockyards and industrial areas yet and it's too quiet. You seem to be having the same problem as me. How long have you been awake?'

'Not long. My labour has started.' That's if one tickle of a contraction could be constituted as labour, she thought, and chuckled. 'It's odd, but despite all those years of training and delivering babies I'm as excited and fearful as any first time mother.'

'Do the contractions hurt?'

'Not yet . . . but it will be painful in the later stages from what I've seen. I imagine that's hours away. Just as well, since I haven't been able to get hold of the midwife to let her know that it's started.'

'Shall we have a cup of tea before we go back to bed. I'm parched.'

'And there's a couple of squares of chocolate left. I was keeping them to celebrate the baby's birth with, but we can do it in advance.'

They navigated their way through to the kitchen, where Esmé lit the candle in its sturdy, Wee Willie Winkie brass holder.

Jack Frost came to rub against her ankles before investigating his saucer. Meggie gave him some tinned milk and he set to it, his tongue lapping noisily. After a quick groom of himself he went to his basket and curled up in it, purring.

The kettle began to boil and Meggie made the tea. 'Shouldn't we telephone the base and let Leo know?'

'No . . . let him sleep while he can. We'll leave a message afterwards, when it's all over so he doesn't have to worry. It's not as if the baby is going to be born in the next four or five hours, and I want to get some more sleep in if I can.'

'I don't think I can sleep. I'm more excited than you are. Just think. In a few hours we'll have a lovely little baby to love.'

A second contraction rippled through her, just as mild as the first. She gazed at the clock, her mind registering twenty minutes, then at Meggie. 'Do you think that bringing a child into the world when we're at war is selfish?'

Meggie grinned at her. 'It's too late now to have second thoughts.'

'Oh . . . I haven't got second thoughts. I just wondered. What if—'

Meggie's finger was placed over her mouth. 'No what ifs – and no, I don't think you're selfish. I think you're lucky. You're married to a man who thinks the world of you, and he will adore the infant you share.'

All thoughts of sleep fled as a quiver of excitement raced through Esmé. 'We'd better get things ready. We don't want to leave everything until the last minute. Why don't you go and get dressed, Meggie. I'll see if I can contact the midwife again.'

Again, there was no answer.

Esmé had just hung up when the air raid sirens began to wail. At the same time her waters broke. She swore as it trickled down her legs, then the trickle became a gush. A strong, prolonged contraction nearly doubled her up and she gave a surprised groan.

Meggie blew the candle out, and was with her aunt in a few seconds as the heavy throb of distant bombers suggested they were flying on full stomachs. The planes were too near to risk going to the Andersen shelter. She was used to planes flying over, but this raid had so many bombers thundering above that she felt uneasy.

Calling out to Judith they swiftly made their way to their hidey-hole under the stairs to the basement with the cat following after them.

'Esmé's in labour,' Meggie told Judith.

'Worse . . . my waters have just broken and I'm soaking. There's pressure and I think this child of mine is going to arrive pretty soon.'

'I'll go up and get you a dry nightdress and dressing gown. I'll bring back some towels and stuff.'

'Meggie, be careful.'

'There's plenty of time yet.' Not quite true, since the noise was now beating against the roof and the whole place was vibrating. She heard a couple of slates ski down the slope of the roof.

Grabbing her torch she ran up the stairs. She snatched a dressing gown from the hook on the back of her aunt's bedroom door and a pile of towels from the linen cupboard, in case her aunt needed to dry herself. There was a nightgown in the drawer, and she dragged the bed cover off the bed on the way out.

She was on the upper landing when there was an explosion that knocked her off her feet. The windows at the front shattered and the curtains billowed as they were sucked out. The bedroom door slammed shut then spookily opened again, revealing a glimpse of bright moonlight outside.

Meggie tried not to panic as a heated draught generated from the blast lifted her off her feet and sent her tumbling down the stairs in the middle of a whirling ball of bedclothes.

At least they'd broken her fall, she thought, as she extricated herself and picked her burden up again. There was a heavy crump at the back of the house and a low rumble that shook it to the foundations. Upstairs, things snapped, cracked and crashed.

Breathing heavily, Meggie shot through the gap in the door Judith had thought to keep open for her and dragged everything in after her. Nerves made her giggle. 'That was close.'

'How close?'

'Across the road and up two houses. Our upstairs front windows are shattered and I got blown down the stairs.'

'Are you hurt?'

The concern in her aunt's voice made Meggie want to cry. She had enough on her plate without worrying about anyone else. 'A few bruises I expect. Otherwise I'm fine. I bounced all the way down. Let's get this space sorted out if we're to turn it into a maternity ward.'

They had a battery lamp in their hidey-hole. Switching it off she opened the door and heaved the two chairs out. 'Judith, you take the other chair and I'll sit on a pillow next to my aunt's feet. Look after Jack Frost, if you would. We'll only use the light when necessary, to save the battery.'

It sounded like an earthquake going on outside with everything in the house jiggling about.

She turned the light back on. 'Actually it's quite cosy in here, like a tent. Aunt Es, you lie on the mattress. It's more comfortable than the stretcher bed. I've brought you a dressing gown, as well. I think it might be Leo's. Can you manage by yourself?'

'I'm not infirm yet.' Her aunt cuddled into the dressing gown and said wistfully, 'I wish Leo was with me.'

'I'm glad he's not; he would take up too much room. Right, now everyone take in a deep, calming breath, then count slowly to ten.'

They'd just finished counting when her aunt gave a prolonged groan.

Judith burst into tears. 'I'm scared.'

So much for deep calming breaths, Meggie thought. 'We've all got the jitters,' Meggie said. 'Try and take a hold of yourself, Jude. Use the stretcher bed. I'll use the upright chair. My aunt needs our help. We can't have her worrying in case we have hysterics.'

'No of course we can't. You're right and I'm sorry. You're so brave, Meggie. I wish I was the same.' She took a deep breath. 'Can I do anything, Mrs Thornton?'

'That's sweet of you Judith. I'll get you to hold one of the torches later if you would – that's if you're not too embarrassed to see my private parts on display. I'll need Meggie to handle the actual birth, since she's been taking instruction from me on childbirth.'

Meggie's heart clunked into her shoes. She could almost smell her aunt smile, as though she'd heard it. 'Is there anything you need from upstairs?'

'We can make do with a first aid kit. I wish I had a mirror though.'

'There's one on the dressing table in a brass frame. I'll fetch it.' She switched on the light again, hoping nobody would see it and think she was sending signals to the enemy.

'No . . . Meggie.'

She took no notice, figuring that the odds against a bomb falling on her at the exact moment she emerged from their lair were pretty slim. In an odd sort of way Meggie enjoyed the danger in the possibility of it.

So she was to be the midwife, was she? It couldn't be worse than digging that bullet out of Nick's arm, she supposed, and hoped she wouldn't faint this time. Secretly, she was quite looking forward to seeing how a baby was delivered. They were so sweet, and she intended to have at least four of her own when she married. Who would they look like though . . . Rennie with his astute fox-eyes and his stuffy manner, or her provocative and delicious Lord Cowan, who she was quite desperate to experience the act of love with. She smiled as she thought, 'Perhaps children from each, like her mother had with her two loves. How romantic it must have been to be in love with two men, both heroes.

With a sudden shock, she realized that that would mean one of them would have to die, like her father had. 'If anyone of importance is listening, perish that thought, I didn't mean it,' she said loudly, and picked up the mirror.

She made her way back, filling a couple of bottles with water on the way.

Above her the planes still throbbed and then laid their deadly eggs as they went by. This must be what hell's like, she thought, pulling the blackout curtain aside and looking at the sky, as red as blood behind the moving black crosses and boiling in an inferno of sparks and black smoke.

She could hear the sound of ambulances and whistles, men too old to fight, but risking their lives to save others.

The raid was targeting civilian areas, and she couldn't help wondering how many children would be robbed of parents tonight, their lives changed for ever. Anger consumed her and she shouted, 'Murderers!'

There would be retaliation, she knew – an eye for an eye. There would be more innocent victims. More orphans, in this culling of human lives.

Judith let her in and switched on the light.

Her aunt was fuming. 'Don't you ever do that again. You were too long. What if a bomb had dropped on you?'

'It would have dropped on you as well, so you wouldn't have needed the mirror anyway. I got angry at the planes flying over when I thought of the casualties this raid will cause.'

'Meggie Elliot, I could slap you for giving me such a fright.' There was no heat in her aunt's words because she understood her – she always had.

Meggie knelt and kissed her cheek, whispering in her ear, 'I love you, Aunt Es. Our baby will be the best baby to have ever been born. Do you know what I'm going to give the baby for a birthday gift, something precious and rare.'

'Tell me, Meggie Moo.'

'All the love you and Uncle Leo gave to me – and that's all the love in the world.'

Her aunt gave a sob, and then she hitched in a breath and placed her palm on her stomach. Eyes closing she grimaced then gave a soft moan. 'These contractions are quite strong. Next time give me your hand and you can feel them.'

Another half hour and the baby was ready to be born. Her aunt had already told them what they must do. She lay on her back, legs apart.

Judith held the mirror and the light, so Esmé could see what was going on.

But the contractions were coming one after another now and she was panting with the pain of the constant pushing.

Fascinated, Meggie watched the head gradually appear. 'You haven't got to be brave. Shout and swear if it helps, I won't mind.'

Her aunt let out a long sigh when the head emerged. 'That's the worst bit over. Lift my head and shoulders up, Meggie. I want to check to see if the cord is around the neck.'

It wasn't.

'The head should turn and then the body will come out. It will be floppy and quite slippery, so take the baby into a towel and support its head, because it won't have the strength to support itself.'

'What if it doesn't come out?'

'Then you'll have to give it a helping hand. I'll tell you what to do.'

Meggie couldn't understand how Esmé could remain so

calm when she was shaking with excitement and nerves. It was a miracle of nature she was watching.

One last contraction and the baby turned and slipped into the waiting towel. It let out an aggrieved howl and then began to bawl.

'It's a boy!' they all said together.

The cat came out from under the blanket, stared at the infant, then hissed at him and went down under again, hackles raised.

The baby was still howling. 'What's wrong with him?' Meggie said in alarm.

'Nothing. He's just getting his lungs working.' Smiling, as if the destruction happening around them didn't even register, Esmé held out her arms for him. 'Now I'll show you how to tie off the cord. You'll need the scissors. There should be two pieces of string in the first aid kit. Tie one part of the cord close to the stomach and the other a bit further down the cord. Yes, there, that's good. Now, cut the cord there. Good . . . that's perfect for now. Bring the light nearer Judith. Let's have a good look at him so I can check him over.'

Esmé handled him firmly, her training giving her the confidence that most first-time mothers would lack. She opened the towel and said, 'You can stop that racket now, young man. You're quite safe.'

The boy stopped crying and stretched. Spikes of dark hair prickled damply from his scalp like the spines on a hedgehog. For a moment his eyes opened. From the glimpse Meggie had they were blue, like Leo's. He stared up at his mother while she made soothing noises. She gently smoothed the waxy remnants of his birth cowl from his face with the corner of the towel and kissed his wrinkled forehead. 'Hello, Johnno, my sweet little angel.'

He grimaced and stretched, arms and legs quivering as they went in all directions, but cautiously now the safety of his barriers were removed. His eyes went out of focus and his head went from side to side as he sought his mother's breast. He found what he was looking for and made his claim, his mouth closing round the nipple with a strong suck. He fell asleep there.

'Look how long his legs and arms are.'

'He's got sweet little toes.'

'Do we have something clean to wrap him in?'

Meggie handed her aunt another towel.

Detached from his mother's breast Johnno was wrapped securely. Esmé couldn't stop smiling as her motherly instinct emerged. 'Isn't he handsome, he looks just like Leo. Thank you both. I don't know what I would have done without you.'

'I'll clean you up as best I can, then we must all try and rest,' Meggie said with tears in her eyes. 'I've only got cold water. I'll go and put the kettle on.'

'No you don't. Not until the all clear has sounded. It's not important. Examine the afterbirth for me. Let me know if you see any small rips in it.'

While Judith looked on from the stretcher, Meggie pulled out the messy towel and bundled it up. Opening the door a chink she shoved it outside, and soaked the end of a clean one by pouring cold water from the bottle on to it.

She washed her aunt, and then dried her with the other end. That one joined the other outside. A fresh towel was placed between her aunt's thighs, and a pillow behind her head. She spread Leo's dressing gown and a blanket over mother and son. She kissed her. 'That's the best I can do for now to make you comfortable. He's so beautiful, I can't wait until Leo sees him. He'll be so proud of you both. Goodnight, Aunt Es.'

'Where are you going to sleep?'

'I'll lie across the end of your mattress with the bedspread over me. My feet will fit under the stretcher bed.' After all, she'd now been downgraded in her aunt's affections . . . and by a gangly scrap of bawling infant.

'You'd make a good nurse now you're over your fear of blood, you know.'

Meggie laughed and switched off the light. 'Go to sleep.'

Despite the racket going on outside they slept as cosily as rabbits in a hat, and when the all clear eventually sounded they didn't hear it. The cat came out from his hole and curled up behind Meggie's knees.

They were woken by a rising tremolo of sound.

'Holy Moses! What's that?' Judith mumbled.

'Johnno Thornton demanding his breakfast. Doesn't he know there's a war on? Did anyone hear the all clear?'

'Vaguely.' Esmé made soothing baby noises that sounded like complete and utter nonsense to anyone except Johnno, who stopped crying to listen intently.

It was something so unlike her aunt that Meggie giggled, and said, 'Who's got an ickle lickle baby boy, then?'

The warble was replaced by a sucking noise. The two younger women and the cat crawled from their lair into daylight, and stretched.

The cat headed for the back door, leaving a trail of footprints in the dust where a chunk of plaster had fallen from the ceiling. When he turned and stared pointedly at them. Judith laughed and opened the door. 'I've got the message, you've certainly trained us well.'

'I'm going upstairs to look around.'

Esmé said from the comfort of her mattress, 'I'll come with you. I need to go to the toilet.'

'No Aunt. You can stay there until I've checked that everything's safe. There's too much glass around. Judith will take you to the outside one. It's closer, and the baby won't mind being left under the stairs for now.'

The house was still intact, except for the sash windows, of which the upper ones were cracked or shattered. Pots, pans and ornaments had been thrown about. A mirror was broken; glass and dust littered everything, curtains hung askew, with big rents in them. She tried to straighten them, to no avail. The upper rail they hung from was bent.

When she gazed out of the window a warden gazed up at her. 'Do you need help?'

'A couple of windows are broken and the telephone is dead.'

'The best we can do is board the windows up, but you won't be able to open them. Gas, electricity and water supplies are still functioning though.'

'Thanks. The rest is just dust and glass. We did have a baby born here last night while it was all going on. Could you take a message to the district nurse? She only lives a couple of streets away.' She gave the man the details then went down to help her aunt.

While Judith made porridge for breakfast, Meggie filled a bucket with warm water and then filled a kettle to make some tea with. 'The window has been broken in your bedroom. I'm going to give it a mop out first, and sweep all the broken glass to the bottom of the stairs. You can rest on the sofa until the window has been fixed. They'll have to board it up, but there will still be light coming through the top. Once the bed is made you can move in.'

'I'll wait until it's been boarded. I don't want strange men clumping about my bedroom when I'm trying to rest. Now, stop being in such a rush and eat your breakfast first.'

Judith went off to work with a message from Meggie to Nick, advising him she wouldn't be in for a few days.

The midwife arrived and helped Esmé wash. She detached the baby from his soiled towel. Both were pronounced healthy, and Johnno now looked clean and deceptively peaceful in his little crib. He slept peacefully, the red pressure patches caused by the trauma of his birth quickly fading.

Taking advantage of the midwife's visit, and remembering the telephone box outside the corner shop, she said, 'I'm going to see if the telephone box is working. If it is I'll ring the base and leave a message for Leo, as well as giving my mother the news.'

It seemed as though every man and his dog had the same idea . . . the queue stretched for miles. Meggie abandoned her quest.

Nick arrived at lunchtime bearing a picnic basket containing egg and bacon tart, smoked salmon and cucumber sandwiches, and a bottle of champagne.

'You have a good cook.'

'I have rather. I'll pass on your thanks.'

Nick admired the infant and said all the right words over him to his proud mother, to which Johnno smugly belched.

Esmé shrugged off his bad manners with, 'I've just fed him.'

'You've gone all gooey over him,' Meggie said. 'I suppose this is all we're going to hear from you . . . baby talk and nonsense.'

Nick looked her up and down, and then smiled. 'Your aunt will be a wonderful mother, I'm sure.'

'I know she will.' Meggie was flustered by that look. She didn't exactly look her best in her paisley patterned apron, and the turban protecting her hair. 'I've been cleaning up the glass and dust from the raid.'

'So I see. You look sweet . . . like a proper suburban housewife. Is there anything I can do to help.'

'Scrub a floor, perhaps.'

His gaze said the idea was totally insane. 'Don't be ridiculous.'

Esmé asked him. 'Could you find a way to contact Leo at the air base? Our phone is out of order.'

'The office phones are still working. I'm going back later. I'll do it then. If I can't get hold of him I'll leave a message. Write down what you want to say.'

'Would you ring my mother as well, just to let her know that both Esmé and the baby are well.'

'Of course I will. He placed a piece of paper on the table. 'By the way, as of now you're on a fortnight's leave. Here's your pass.'

Sixteen

24 August

A son called Johnno. What a beauty! When they got back to Australia he'd teach the boy how to fly a plane, and they'd go to visit his cousins at Fairfield Station and take him out horse riding. He might even teach him to shear a sheep, if he could remember how himself. Leo felt like thumping on his chest. As soon as he got back from this sortie he intended to try and wrangle a couple of hours off so he could go and see Es and his son.

His mind wandering, Leo had chased a Messerschmitt halfway across the channel. He came down to earth when a line of tracer bullets from a Dornier nearly cut his wing in half. They missed the fuel tanks by a couple of inches, thank God, but silenced the radio in mid squawk.

His aircraft shuddered, and then slipped sideways.

He managed to get out of his straps and pulled the canopy back, and then pushed himself out when the plane began to roll. As he was trying to make sure he was clear of the aircraft he collected a passing blow. Something gave a crack as he pulled the ripcord and the lines tangled and knotted. He swore when the chute only partially opened. The person who'd packed it had been careless. He counted his few blessings. Better than not having a chute at all, he supposed, as he descended a little too rapidly towards the grey, rippling expanse of water, and better than landing on hard ground – though water wasn't that soft when put to the test, either.

He was having a quick thought or two on Isaac Newton's law of gravity when the plane hit the water. It gave a muted whump. A spark ignited the fumes in the almost empty petrol tank, causing it to explode in a large bubble of air.

Leo landed safely, yelping at the pain in his leg as he hit the resistance the water presented. His parachute billowed. Collapsing on top of him it was caught on the tail of his Spit. Dragged under, he collected a clout on the head, so hard that for a moment dizziness nearly got the better of him.

Be damned if he was going to die here!

The insufficient air he had in his lungs was slowly depleted as he was dragged down, struggling with the parachute straps and cords, which were now tangled in knots. The fire hissed out as the sea swallowed the aircraft, taking him with it. Bubbles of escaping air rose to the top.

Then he was free of the plane. His life jacket carried him to the top. He sucked in a huge breath of cold air tainted with petrol fumes. He tried to swim away from the fuel floating in the water but his leg wouldn't work properly and he cried out and swore with the pain. The left one was broken. At least it wasn't the femur.

Praying nothing would ignite the fumes he discarded his boots with some reluctance as they filled with seawater, swiftly unbuckling the front tag and swearing when he eased the one from his broken leg. It would have made a fine splint without the boot attached. With a small penknife he kept in his pocket he was able to make a hole in the parachute silk and tear off a long piece of the silk. He wrapped it firmly around both legs, using the good one as a splint.

'Some bloody merman I'd make,' he muttered, splashing around like a stranded fish as he tried to find a direction.

Blood clouded his vision. He washed it away and used another strip of the silk as a bandage for the gash in his head. He pulled his helmet over it. It would provide some pressure, which would help stop the bleeding. He wasn't too worried about the cut though. The head always bled like crazy, on account of its many blood vessels.

It was only twenty miles across the channel. He might be able to swim back to England. He *had* to get back for Esmé and the baby.

A son. *His boy, Johnno!* He couldn't wait to get home and see him.

Judging from the position of the sun it was late afternoon. He could see land but couldn't quite make it out. His ears began to buzz. Elevated blood pressure, probably caused by concussion, he thought. That would cause problems if he wasn't careful.

Hampered by his broken leg and the awkward splint, which meant that he couldn't use his legs, only drag them behind him, he headed for the land. It was hard going. Now and again he turned on his back and floated, resting. He heard planes fly across the sky, hundreds of them. Something big seemed to be happening.

The second time he woke it was dark, and he was cold and shivering. Hypothermia and shock, he thought . . . a combination that could easily prove to be fatal. He must stop himself from falling asleep.

There was the smell of tobacco smoke and he heard whispered French nearby. There was a hollow sense of disappointment in him. He thought he'd been heading for England, but the land he'd seen must have been France. His head ached too.

He could make out the scruffy, peeling hull of a fishing boat and took hold of an anchor rope, knowing he was at the end of his tether, literally as well as metaphorically. When they pulled the anchor up he'd go with it, however bleak the pain. There were faint signs of dawn on the horizon.

'Help,' he whispered.

After a moment of silence he heard a cautious, *'Qui êtes-vous?'*

Leo filtered it through his school French system. 'I am *Anglais* pilot – no *parler* French good *comprenez-vous? Fracturé* . . . leg. Concussion. *Aide s'il vous plaît.'*

Someone whispered in accented English, 'Can you see us?'

'I'm at your stern holding on to a rope, and need urgent medical attention. I can't walk and I'm concussed. Where am I? I was trying to swim to England.'

'France.'

'Would you take me to England?'

A man gazed down at him, eyes concealed under the peak of his hat. He spread his hands and there was a gleam of a smile. *'Impossible!* You haven't even seen us . . . *comprendre?* We'll get you to shore.'

Leo did understand. Fifteen minutes later he had a tot of brandy tucked under his belt and was in a dingy. Carried ashore in an aroma of fish and sweat, and in a lot of pain, he was gently deposited on the beach at the high tide mark, with the tide going out. Someone stuck a peppermint in his mouth. To disguise the smell of the brandy, he supposed.

His shoulder was patted and there was a whispered, *'Bonne chance mon ami.'*

He heard them scuffing the sand as they left, so it would look as though he'd crawled from the sea. He began to shiver as the mist closed around him and the pain made him seek some respite in sleep.

He woke to a thick fog and a muted murmur of voices that his knowledge of French soon exhausted.

Someone put a finger over his lips when he groaned. He was bitterly cold, in pain, and ravenously hungry, in that order. His body was racked with shivers and his head and body bumped on a wooden floor.

The engine noise said he was in the back of a truck.

He tried not to yelp when the movement stopped and he

was lifted on to a stretcher. He supposed he'd be forced to spend the rest of the war in a prison camp somewhere.

A man bent over him. He was pale, as though he spent most of his life indoors.

'I need a doctor, my leg is broken,' Leo said.

'I know.' The man opened a box and took out a syringe. 'Morphine . . . I fix.'

'Are you a doctor?'

'No.' Leo felt a prick in his arm. His tongue dried and he fell asleep. When he woke again his leg was in a plaster cast. It throbbed like hell.

'My brother and I had to pull it back into place. You won't be doing much for the next six weeks.'

He felt like vomiting, and his face must have told its own tale because someone thrust a bucket within his reach. He dry retched into it.

He became aware of a smell in the room and looked around. It was an ordinary room with an operating slab, a sink and several dishes. A suspicion formed in his mind. 'If you're not a doctor, what are you?'

'A medical orderly.'

'And where am I?'

'In the morgue. You were pronounced dead by drowning. The death certificate says you are Louis Gaston.'

'By whom?'

'A cousin. He's a doctor in the hospital here. You need not know his name.'

Leo realized he was naked. 'Where are my clothes?'

The man smiled. We had to take them off and hide them. They'll be returned to you later. In the meantime you will be loaned something less noticeable to wear. Try not to worry, *mon ami*, you are in the hands of the Resistance. We will have you out of here in a day or two.'

Leo relaxed.

The telegram boy had handed over the yellow envelope later that afternoon.

Esmé hadn't opened it, of course. Leo had promised to telephone her – and he would. Her husband always kept his word.

She had been seated on the chair next to the telephone for two hours, the baby tucked up next to her in his pram, a shining navy blue conveyance with chromed fittings and frilly furnishings. Leo had brought it home, balanced upside down on top of the car and tied in place with ropes.

'What do you think?' he'd said, looking slightly anxious. 'The salesman said that this is the very best money can buy. It has a weatherproof hood and cover, coach springs and a foot pedal brake.'

Esmé had smiled and said, 'What's the engine like, Leo?'

'Very funny.'

'It's a splendid carriage, Leo. Our baby will look like royalty in it.'

She wasn't smiling now. Everything inside her was a tangle of knots, that only one bright thread could unravel, if only she could find it.

She was thirsty and generally uncomfortable. Her back ached. But by leaving the chair she knew she'd be tempting fate.

She and Leo had achieved nearly everything they'd set out to do, and together. They married, worked and saved, and produced a beautiful son. It wasn't fair that he should be raised without Leo as his father.

It was a shame that the war had intervened in their plans, but that was an interlude. When it was over they intended to go to Australia and she'd give him another child, and they'd live happily ever after in the sunshine.

If the phone rang and she missed Leo's call she might never hear from him again. So she sat there and waited for the telephone to ring. She didn't know what else to do.

Meggie discovered her aunt there when she came back with the shopping. 'The queues are getting longer and longer, but I managed to get some pork—' She scooped in a breath. 'Something awful has happened, hasn't it?'

Her aunt didn't answer. She gripped the seat on either side of the chair; her face pale and set.

'Aunt Es,' Meggie said gently, her voice thickening with tears when she saw the yellow envelope in her lap. 'I think we need to get you to bed.'

Esmé's fingers tightened, anchoring her to the chair. 'I'm waiting for Leo to call. He promised to ring me yesterday.'

Plucking the envelope from her aunt's lap she said, 'You haven't opened this.'

'I can't. What if he's . . . what if he's not coming back. He said he'd telephone me. I'm waiting for his call.'

It was likely that he might not be coming back if she'd received a telegram. 'The telephone is still out of order.'

'No, it's not. It rang earlier, someone asked for you.'

Tearing the envelope open Meggie read the message out loud. *'Regret to inform you that Squadron Leader Leo Thornton did not return from an air operation, and at this time is reported as missing.'*

When Esmé made a little moaning noise, Meggie told her, 'They go on to say that this doesn't mean he's been wounded or killed, and if they get any further information they'll let you know, to alleviate any anxiety the news may have caused you.'

The sudden clamour of the telephone made them both jump.

A smile appearing on her face, her aunt snatched it up. 'Leo?'

Her face suddenly crumpled. She dropped the telephone and buried her face in her hands. 'It's not him . . . it's someone called Constance Stone. She rang before.'

Picking up the receiver Meggie said, 'Mrs Stone. It's Margaret Elliot. If it's not urgent, may I call you back?' Bad news couldn't strike twice in one day, surely. 'Is it . . . Rennie?'

'No, my dear. It's Foxglove estate business so it can wait. Is everything all right?'

'We've had some rather disturbing news. I'll get back to you as soon as possible, probably tomorrow, and if necessary will make an appointment to see you. Thank you for calling.'

As soon as she'd replaced the receiver Meggie put an arm round her aunt and encouraged her to rise. 'Come with me, Aunt Es. You're going back to bed while I cook dinner. I'll call you if there's any news.'

'I don't feel like eating dinner.'

'You must, for the sake of Johnno. We eat little enough as it is on rations. I'll sleep up here too . . . keep you company, so you won't feel you're alone. I have two weeks off so I can look after you. I'll make you a nice cup of tea. And don't worry about the telephone, I'm here to answer it.'

'Tea . . . the panacea for all evils.' Esmé got to her feet and gazed into the baby carriage at her son. 'It would be a shame if he never knew his father.'

'He will know him. Stop thinking the worst. Go on, off you go and get into bed. I'll bring Johnno up when he wakes for a feed.'

Meggie gazed at the child. How brand new and dear to them he was, sleeping soundly in all innocence of the devilry going on around them. He didn't know there was a war on, and he didn't know yet that he'd picked out a wonderful mother for himself. And he'd know his father was a man to be proud of, whatever happened, as Meggie had known her father, because he was part of a family who loved and cared for each other.

As for Leo, she was sure he'd come home . . . if not today, then another day. And the war would end and they'd all start rebuilding their lives.

Dashing away her tears she rang her mother, nearly crying again at the sound of her calm voice.

'Meggie, my dear. Is everything all right?'

She lowered her voice to a whisper. 'Leo is missing in action.'

'Oh . . . how dreadful.' In the poignant silence Meggie imagined her mother staggering back on to the chair kept by the instrument, her palm pressed against her chest. 'How's Esmé taking it?'

'All right I think. It hasn't really sunk in yet. I found her with the telegram unopened in her lap, waiting by the telephone for Leo to call. I've just got her up to bed. I don't know how to handle the situation. It's so very dangerous in London now. The house up the road was bombed and there are raids day and night. Leo wanted Aunt Es to go and stay with you, but she refused. Now she has the baby to look after, and it would be horrible if anything happened to them − especially since Leo might turn up.'

'She must come to me as soon as she's over the birth. Denton has some time off coming. He can take the train up to London and persuade her. Better still, I'll send Chad up. Their twinship has always made them close, so she'll listen to him.'

'Leo's car is garaged. Chad could drive that back. There's probably enough fuel in it, and if not I know someone who can get us some.'

'Black market?'

'It's a way of life here, Mummy. People aren't as honest as those in the country . . . probably because there are more of them.'

'Country people help each other out.'

'So do Londoners. They're so wonderfully brave and resilient in the face of the danger.' Nick came into her mind and her mouth drew into a smile. 'Sometimes they can be foolhardy too.'

'Tell Esmé she and her son can live in Nutting Cottage. Chad and Sylvia have bought their own place now . . . one more convenient for Chad's rounds. He does a duty drop-in every day at the convalescent home though. There's no chance that you could come down with Es, I suppose? I haven't seen you for ages, and I do miss you.'

A warm feeling lodged in her heart. 'I miss you too, but I can't at the moment. I'll try and get a weekend pass in a month or two.'

'What is it you do that's so important?'

'Secretarial work.'

'Can't you get a posting? I'm sure we could find room for you here. I could put the refugee children in the sitting room. Their mother came down to visit, and there was a scene when she had to return to London. Poor little girls were so unsettled after she left.'

'Yes, I suppose they would have been. You don't understand, Mummy. I like what I'm doing. It's challenging.'

'What's challenging about typing up other people's letters? It all sounds rather dreary to me. I suppose it's that boyfriend of yours . . . the one with the odd name.'

'Rennie? What a coincidence that you should mention him. His mother rang me earlier . . . something to do with Foxglove House. By the way, Rennie is fighting overseas and his mother is now acting as trustee.'

'Ah, yes . . . of course, he would be. It's hard to think of war down here, though it's only a hundred and twenty miles away. It's something to do with the entail, I expect. Who can understand all this legal mumbo-jumbo that goes on? Denton got a letter just the other day. Apparently an estate that's no longer viable to maintain can be disposed of.'

'Oh . . . good.'

'I'm sure the solicitor can explain it to you much better than I, but that's the gist of it. In another year you'll be of age. If you decided to dispense with it, act sensibly. There will be hidden costs.'

Johnno gave a huge yawn then a few fretful whimpers of discontent.

'Your latest nephew is beginning to wake up.'

'I'll leave you to it then. Ask Esmé to ring me when she's able. I'll try and talk some sense into her.'

Johnno managed a long, warbling high note and waved a fist around before cramming the whole hand in his mouth and taking great smacking sucks on it.

'That bad, huh?' she whispered, and lifted him from his pram. His little flannel nightie, the yoke smocked in blue knots, was damp. She took him upstairs and laid him on the bed to change his nightie and tackle his napkin.

Folding the corners into a kite shape like she'd seen her aunt do, she brought the ends across and the last one up through his legs. She pinned it in place. 'There,' she said, and kissed him. 'You mustn't munch on your fist, you're not old enough for solids.'

When she lifted him the nappy slid down his legs on to the bed. 'You did that on purpose, you rogue. Stop showing your manly bits off.'

There was a chuckle from behind her, and she turned.

'I'll show you how to do it properly. Who were you talking to on the telephone?'

She could have lied, but she didn't.

'It was my mother. I was asking her advice.'

'And she planned it all out for you . . . my life and that of my son.'

'You frightened me, Aunt Es. She only wants what's best for you and Johnno.'

'I know, and I'm sorry. I scared myself. Shock affects

people in different ways. For me, it was as if the world had come to a halt. I'm well aware that Leo is missing . . . but he's not dead. He's alive . . . I know it. What was Livia's plan?'

'She's sending Chad to persuade you to return to Eavesham. You and the baby can live in Nutting Cottage, which is now vacant. That's the first place Leo will think of if he can't find you here. My mother wants you to give her a ring.'

'I will . . . in a day or two, when I decide what I want to do.'

'It would be better for the baby.' But her aunt already knew that.

A week later there was a rattle of a motorbike outside and a young man presented himself at the door. 'I'm Eddie Richards . . . I was the Doc's wingman.'

It took a moment for Meggie to think of who the Doc was, and the man's face was vaguely familiar.

'We met once before. You were taking a flying lesson and I was rude to you, I think. For that I apologize, Mrs Thornton.'

'I'm not Mrs Thornton. I'm Margaret Elliot . . . Doc Thornton's niece. And it was me who was rude to you, I think.'

He gave a faint smile, as though he remembered their meeting. 'Sorry, of course you are, I recognize you now. It seems a long time ago that we met, and now we're much older. It's nice to see you again, Miss Elliot.'

Esmé came down the stairs, the expression in her eyes wary. 'Thank you for coming, follow me into the sitting room if you would. I'll get us some tea.'

'I'll make it,' Meggie said.

As she walked away, she heard, 'I was with the Doc when he was shot down. His chute didn't open properly and he ditched into the channel. His cords caught on the tail of his Spit and it pulled him under when it sank . . .'

So Leo had drowned. How could Eddie Richards be so matter-of-fact about it, and so insensitive in telling his wife what had happened.

Eddie Richards's report knocked the stuffing out of her aunt, and robbed her of hope. The colour ebbed from her face and she buckled at the knees.

When Meggie heard her sobbing her heart out that night she got into bed with her and held her tight. She couldn't bear knowing her aunt's heart had been broken.

'I could kill that man with my bare hands for telling you that.'

'It's all right, Meggie. He needed to tell me and I needed to know.'

'Leo has given you Johnno to love,' was all she could think of to say, but despite that, she was in tears herself.

When Chad arrived a few days later Esmé was packed ready to go.

Dear, sweet Chad . . . so responsible and kind to his twin sister, as he had been since their time together in the orphanage as children.

'Oh, my poor, dear Es,' he'd said and had held Esmé tight while she cried and cried.

Leaving them together, Meggie walked to the garage and fetched the car. It was difficult to start, but finally came alive with the help of a man polishing a motorbike in the adjoining garage, who fiddled with this and that under the bonnet, and then said with great satisfaction when the engine fired, 'There she goes. The engine's been lying idle and needs a bit of coaxing. Drive her around the block a bit.'

She remembered Leo calling the car a cantankerous old cow, his accent flattening the vowels a little. She smiled and whispered. 'If you're still alive you'd better find your way home, Leo. Es needs you.'

They piled her luggage into the back of the car, and tied the pram Leo had been so proud of on the top.

'There's an extra can of petrol in the boot,' she told him.

Meggie hugged her aunt and whispered, 'Don't you give up on him.'

She had a strong feeling that Esmé still held a little hope inside her, for she found Leo's clothing neatly folded in the drawers, and his best uniform hanging in the wardrobe along with a change of clothing, as if it had been placed there, waiting for its owner to come back. There was an envelope addressed to him on the dressing table.

Not that Meggie didn't believe Eddie Richards's account of

what he'd seen, but he'd been in a fast moving aircraft dodging the enemy planes and was probably as exhausted as he'd looked.

Was her aunt being stupid, choosing to believe that Leo was still alive? Was she? Meggie didn't care. All she knew was that she'd rather hope he was alive than know that he wasn't.

Seventeen

As Meggie's mother had told her, the Foxglove estate, which was no longer affordable as a country house and was entailed to the Sinclair bloodline, could be sold if permission was gained from the courts.

Constance Stone said, 'I've spoken to your stepfather, Doctor Elliot. He suggests that I prepare a case to put before the court, with your permission. By the time it's gone through the system you will be of age I expect. The law acts slowly in such matters, especially when dealing with the estates of minors.'

Meggie felt a small quiver of remorse, but mostly relief. It was no longer the grand country home her father had grown up in, but a sad, decaying house she couldn't afford. She'd never really felt pride of ownership in it . . . but then she'd never known her father . . . only her grandfather, who'd suffered from delusions. Meggie thought he'd been disillusioned, and must have certainly been depressed to have tried to take his own life after his actress wife had left him.

She frowned for a moment, chasing away the last image she'd had of Major Sangster, dead in his chair in Nutting Cottage. He'd just told her that he'd fathered her and she'd gone to make him some tea to calm him down. When she'd come back with it he was dead. It had been years of nightmares before she could think about that without being scared.

Her mother, who'd detested the old man, had made a bonfire out of the chair he'd died in, and his bed.

Her mind came back to Constance Stone and the problem of Foxglove House. 'I don't want to sell it while it's still providing a useful service for our war casualties and bringing in a regular rent.'

'Once the entail's lifted it can be disposed of at any time, though the government department responsible for caring for the wounded has a lease arrangement that will carry it over the period of the war. You will, of course have to manage the business side of it yourself once you turn twenty-one. There are options. You might decide to still leave it with us to manage, or you can place it in the hands of a rental agency, that will charge a percentage fee for the service.'

She nodded. 'We'll see what the circumstances are at the time. Have you heard from Rennie lately?'

'Yes . . . he's well.' Constance dug the point of her pen into the pad of blotting paper in front of her. She looked slightly embarrassed. 'There's something I must tell you, dear. Rennie is due for some leave soon. When he does, he intends to get married to Pamela.'

Relief rolled over her, yet she couldn't help but be peeved with him for leading her on. 'Couldn't he have told me himself?'

'Actually, it was my idea, and he agreed it might be a kind thing to do. He's very fond of you. We all thought that your affection towards him was a sort of hero worship though.'

She wasn't going to let him get off scot-free. 'I wouldn't go that far. Perhaps Rennie thought I was one of those loose types of women, and lost interest when he discovered I wasn't.'

Constance Stone looked horrified. 'Oh, I don't think that's the case. Rennie is not that sort of man. He's a gentleman like his father.'

Who had once pinched her on the buttock and laughed when she'd passed him in the corridor with her arms filled with files. It had been so unexpected that she'd nearly dropped them. She had it on good authority from Nick that all men were that sort of man, but refrained from saying so.

'Rennie thought you were a sweet girl, if a little naive. He'd just had an argument with his fiancée and she'd broken off the engagement. It was flattering for him to know a young girl like you admired him. Now they've sorted their differences out he and Pamela have realized they still love each other. Anyway, for what it's worth I'd like to tender an apology on behalf of my son.'

'It's not worth much if the delivery method of the message is anything to go by? For goodness sake, I had a bit of a crush on him, that's all. Rennie encouraged me in the beginning. He soon changed his mind and put me straight, and we agreed to remain friends.'

'That's what he told me. Nevertheless it caused quite a bit of reactive consternation in the family, especially when he asked us to employ you. After all, you are a client. We thought then that he might be serious about your relationship.'

'Why should that have caused consternation? I come from a perfectly respectable family.'

'I'm not suggesting you don't. It's just that you were rather young at the time, my dear, and having a relationship with a client makes for bad business practices.'

She snorted.

'There, now I've made you angry, and that was not my intention.'

'I'll be honest with you, Mrs Stone. Yes, I am a little angry. I feel insulted by the way you brought me here on a pretence of business, which was rather underhand, and a waste of my time and yours.'

Meggie thought it might be better to be gracious now her first attempt at love had failed. It was galling to be given marching orders by a man's mother. 'You needn't have worried. Rennie was only being kind to me. He knew I wanted to become a lawyer, and thought I might gain some useful experience in a legal office, that's all.'

'And you did very well.'

'I enjoyed it, but I doubt if I'll take it up as a career because I rather like office work now I'm doing it. Perhaps I'll become a legal secretary, which would satisfy my mother.' Or perhaps she'd start her own business specializing in the training and supply of secretarial services. She'd only just that minute thought of it, and it had possibilities.

'We'll be quite happy to furnish you with a reference if need be. Rennie didn't want to hurt your feelings, and intended to write you a letter. I thought it would be better if I prepared you first.'

'Rennie didn't ask you to talk to me about our relationship, then. You just assumed it was all right for you to do so.'

'He's my son, Miss Elliot.'

How crushing this was. Meggie had already counted to ten twice, and now started on the third time. This woman was as insensitive as a steamroller.

'If you'd like me to pass on a message when I write to him, I'll be happy to.'

The two-word message she instantly came up with was too vulgar to say out loud. A man of Rennie's age who hid behind his mother was weak in her book, and be damned if she was going to use his mother as a go-between.

But no – it wasn't something the Rennie she knew would do. Anyone would think she was a troublesome fly to be brushed off in such a way.

'I don't think so, Mrs Stone. I'm capable of passing on my own message the next time I see him.'

She rose to her feet and smiled, said out loud, '*twenty-nine, thirty*,' and let her have it, convinced that Leo's method of anger control was outmoded. 'Lord but you're an interfering woman. You should cut Rennie free from your apron strings. I'm quite sure he can manage his life without you.'

'You're very rude, Miss Elliot.'

'I could be ruder. I do hope you're not going to charge me for this consultation after you brought me here on false pretences, since it's been a waste of my time . . . and of yours.'

Constance Stone was still spluttering when Meggie closed the door and walked off.

The empty house weighed heavily on Meggie's shoulders. When she thought she heard creaks or footsteps overhead she kept creeping up the stairs to find it was either in her imagination or the cat prowling around.

Having someone living upstairs had been comforting, now the place seemed to be full of ghosts and she was lonely without her aunt and uncle living above her.

Meggie had a talk to Judith and suggested that they move

upstairs. 'If my aunt decides to come back I'd like to keep the place lived in. Leo might come back, yet. He's a strong swimmer and may have made it to shore.'

'But surely he would have turned up by now. Didn't they exchange the names of prisoners of war?'

'Perhaps he's lost his memory,' Meggie came up with.

They both knew the odds against that had happening were close to nil.

'Eddie Richards said he was nearer France than England when he went down. He might be injured and be in a hospital or in a prison camp on the Continent. We might be able to find out.'

With hope in her eyes Meggie gazed at Judith. 'How?'

Judith chuckled. 'Despite your high IQ you can be so dim sometimes, Meggie. We work in intelligence. Find out if you can make it work for you. Ask the charming Lord Cowan. I'm sure there's more to him than meets the eye, and he's fond of you. He can't keep his eyes off you when you're outside the office, and you lap it up.'

Meggie blushed. 'I do not.'

'I know we're not supposed to discuss these things, but do you ever wonder what he's up to when he's not in the office? I'm sure you and Gordon Frapp are a front for whatever he really does.'

Meggie remembered Nick going off for several days when she'd first started working for him, sailing to Dunkirk with the small fleet to help rescue the stranded troops, she'd thought, but he'd never said. His face had been grey with fatigue when the operation had finally finished. Another time she'd fished a bullet from his arm. Where had he collected that? She grinned, recalling his explanation. Was he some sort of secret agent? It would certainly suit his personality.

'Yes . . . perhaps you're right, Jude.'

Oh Lordy! Nick wouldn't help her if he'd found the Blessing file among the other files. She had to get it back!

She went into work ten minutes early. There was a red carnation in a vase on her desk, another in his buttonhole. His office door was open a chink.

It creaked when she cautiously pushed it open, only to find

him relaxed in his chair, eyes closed, long legs stretched out, crossed at the ankles and propped up on the desk.

Meggie could see the gleam of his eyes through his lashes. 'Have you been here all night, or are you pretending to be asleep?'

He opened them and the smile he offered her was pleasant. 'You're just in time to make your boss a cup of tea.'

There was a gas ring plugged into a connection near the fireplace. She lit it and put the chipped enamel kettle on it. 'I'd like to speak to you in private while that's heating up.'

'We'll be entirely private today. Frapp's caught a cold and I've told him to stay home for a few days and keep his germs to himself. So you can make us both some tea, and there's some gingerbread my cook made for me.'

She took the seat opposite him.

'I was just about to start on my files,' he said.

Her glance skimmed down the four files and she reached out for them. 'I can check some of those.'

As quick as a flash he was upright, his palm flattening against the files. 'You know, Meggie. You disappoint me sometimes.'

Her heart thumped in her throat. 'You know, don't you?'

He made a low humming noise in his throat that could have meant anything. 'What did you want to talk to me about?'

'Leo Thornton.'

'Ah . . . your aunt's late husband. What of him?'

She shrugged. 'I thought you might be able to locate him . . . that's if he was taken prisoner.'

'That's a big ask. What makes you think I can do something like that?'

'I thought you might know someone who knows someone who knows something.'

His glance went to the map on the wall. 'Leo Thornton went down over the Channel.'

'To know that you've already anticipated that I'd ask.'

'It would be the logical thing for you to do.' He turned back to her and tapped a finger on the files. 'I might be able to work out time, currents and possibilities – if his body floated ashore. It might still be pinned under the plane.'

Mouth dry, she whispered, 'What if he's still alive?'

'Do you think he is, or hope he is?'

She shrugged. 'However illogical it seems, intuition tells me he is alive one minute, then it tells me he can't be. Then I start to hope all over again. I do hope he is . . . for the sake of Es and the baby.'

'I see. I do know a couple of people who might be able to find out.'

Relief rushed through her. 'Thank you, Nick, I'll be forever in your debt.'

'Not forever, my sweet. Let's discuss the payment of that debt in advance, shall we?'

'I don't know what you mean.'

'Allow me to lay it on the line for you. Nothing buys you exactly nothing. This sort of fishing expedition is expensive.'

'I haven't got much money to spare.'

'I'll expect something in return, Meggie mine. How about this . . . If I get a positive result I'll expect you to spend a weekend with me . . . and I'll come prepared. After that, if I'm in a position to bring Leo home, I will, though it will take time, and will place me in extreme danger, and there's no guarantee.'

An uneasy feeling shivered through her at the thought of going through with his demand, and a bigger one at the thought that she'd be placing him in danger. 'Can I think about it?'

'Of course you can. You did say you'd wait for the four-poster bed and satin sheets, something I can now provide. So what is there to think about?'

'Nothing, I suppose. You intend to use my body in payment for your services.'

'You've got it in one. In addition, as this operation will be unauthorized I will tell you nothing about what I'm doing or when I'm doing it, unless I need to know something. Don't ask me for progress reports. And if one word of it gets out to anyone, inside the office or out, the whole operation will be abandoned. Do you understand?'

To her relief he pushed the files towards her. 'Go and make the tea now. You might like to ponder on what's at stake while you're at it.'

'I needn't ponder. I accept.'

While she was waiting for the tea to brew she flipped open the Blessing file and stared at it. The contents were all there. Placed on the top was a cryptic crossword with two clues left to fill in down and across. The down was easy. *Jungle Rex*. 'Lion,' she muttered, and gazed at the longer word going across. *Ear potion under the knife*. It was an anagram. Operation Lion. He'd outguessed her.

Feeling stupid she poured the tea, placed some gingerbread on the plate and carried it through to him. 'I suppose you think that was funny.'

'Nothing I do is funny, and it all had a purpose. What is it, Meggie? Don't you like being outsmarted? I found that file ages ago. What the hell did you think you were up to placing it in the cabinet? Who was it intended for?'

'Considering it was in your drawer, who did you think it was for? I wanted you to know that I'm on to you.'

'You also tampered with the lock on the filing cabinet, didn't you? That makes you as bad as me.'

She shrugged. 'So why did you give me the file back? Have I missed something out?'

'Several things, the most obvious being that nobody would believe it.'

'I had no intention of showing it to anyone. I came in early to see if I could retrieve it. You don't check the cabinet often.'

'I see.'

Her anger rose to the surface. 'No . . . you really don't see, Nick. I don't know why you did what you did, and I don't really care, but my aunt reacted badly to it. Till the day she left for Dorset she was scared to go into the house in the dark – both of us were. She used to put a chair under the door handle when she went to bed at night. Neither of us liked being there alone after you invaded our privacy. She's too nice a person to be treated like that, especially when she likes you so much. I knew you were duping her, which made it worse. The more I kept quiet about you, the more I felt like a conspirator.'

'I know, and I feel ashamed. I tried to make it up to her, and to you. I don't know why I did what I did, just boredom I guess. You haven't told your aunt it was me, have you?'

'No, the only reason being that I don't want to disillusion her. She still thinks you're a fine, upstanding young man, not the mercenary petty thief who rifled through her personal things just for the kick it gave him. And now you're trying to blackmail me into going to bed with you, and using her missing husband as an excuse. Leo Thorton has more guts in his little toe than you have in your entire bloodline.'

'You make me feel ashamed. I love you, you must know that,' he said.

'It's not something worth having. You can keep your four-poster bed, your satin sheets and your damned charm, and whatever you imagine loving someone is.' Well, for the time being anyway, she thought. 'And you can keep your damned games. To hell with you.'

He sighed. 'I'm not ready for hell yet, and now I'm suitably flagellated and contrite, will you please forgive me, since you know you're going to? I'll still make enquiries, and I'll cancel the debt and give you my piece of gingerbread as a bribe.'

She was so relieved she could have hugged him to pieces. 'Do you mean that?'

'You have my word.'

'Which is devious by any standard.'

He chuckled. 'Be careful, Margaret, Eloise, Sinclair, Sangster Elliot . . . Meggie for short. I might have you charged with insubordination.'

He had a remarkable memory to remember all of her names in order, especially after all this time. The only time he'd heard them was the day they first met. He grinned when she scowled at him.

'By the way, that was a good fight you put up in defence of your virginity, Meggie. Well done . . . though I still intend to claim it, one of these days, probably when you least expect it.'

Picking up the gingerbread she took a big bite out of it, then smiled at him. 'Bargain,' she said.

Eighteen

Meggie, on hands and knees, was polishing the linoleum on the hall floor when the postman arrived.

There was a scruffy-looking letter for Leo and Esmé that had been sent several months earlier from Fairfield Sheep Station in Australia, which Leo's family owned. No wonder the envelope was scruffy. Australia was 13,000 miles away. Meggie couldn't quite visualize that sort of distance.

The second letter was for her, dispatched from the legal firm that handled her legacy.

Slipping Esmé's letter into her pocket she sat back on her heels and opened it.

> *Dear Margaret,*
>
> *I feel I must apologize for the way you've been treated. I had intended to inform you personally of my impending marriage, but I understand from my mother that she spoke to you recently about the friendship we share. She suggested she might have upset you, in which case I think I need to clarify the position that exists between us, so you are under no illusion.*
>
> *In view of my impending marriage to Pamela, and my current commitment in the defence our country, it would be better if we knew exactly where we stand with each other. This is something that had been adequately dealt with previously, in my opinion.*
>
> *I'm given to understand that Doctor Thornton has been posted as missing. I'd appreciate it if you'd pass on my best wishes to your aunt. I only knew him for a short time but he struck me as being a decent man with high ideals, and I do hope any news of him proves to be positive.*
>
> *If you happen to be passing St Martin's Church – as you know it's a short distance from the office – and if you have*

*the time, do attend the wedding service to wish Pamela and
myself well.*

With best wishes for your future.

Yours sincerely,

Rennie Stone.

'Keep your sincerity, you stuffy bag of legal pomp and circumstance!'

Having insulted the composer Edward Elgar, as well as Rennie, she screwed the letter up and threw it at the wall.

Receiving this type of letter from someone she'd looked up to was humiliating. Meggie had no intention of going to the wedding – mainly because Rennie hadn't advised her of the date, so she knew he didn't really want her there. Secondly, she didn't wish them well at all. She said loudly, 'I hope it rains heavily on the day, and Pamela turns out to be a miserable nag of a wife. And I hope any babies you have are really, really, ugly.' She conjured up a couple of grimacing creatures with big noses, elf-like ears and sharp, crooked teeth. Then she relented. It wouldn't be their fault, and besides, she couldn't do that to babies, which were so lovely and cuddly and sweet. Besides, Rennie would be a proud caring father to any children he had, even if they did look like garden gnomes.

Going into the kitchen she turned up the radio, then clumsily tap-danced back to the hall, where she sang out with Flanagan and Allen. '*Run rabbit, run rabbit, run, run, run. Here comes the farmer with his gun, gun, gun . . .*'

One good thing about getting in a temper, it gave you energy and added elbow grease to your arm, or so her mother's cleaning lady had told her.

The drummer was all over the place and she frowned. She started to sing as she got down to polishing again. When she stopped to refold the polishing cloth a voice said softly, 'Meggie.'

She looked around her and saw nothing but Jack Frost sitting on the stair watching her. 'Brilliant . . . I can hear voices coming from a cat now.'

'Here at the letterbox, you idiot.'

A pair of grey eyes gazed at her so she laughed and moved closer and gazed back at him. 'Woof! Woof!'

'I'm terrified. Didn't you hear me knock at the door?'

'Actually I thought it was Gene Krupa doing a drum solo.' She needed a distraction after that letter. 'What are you doing here, Nick?'

'Teasing the guard dog I think. I'm beginning to feel like a peeping Tom.'

'You have lovely eyes when you're peeping.'

'This letterbox is too low for comfort and I'm growing meaner by the minute. I've got something for you . . .'

'I'm only bribable to a certain extent . . . what is it?'

'Diamonds and emeralds.'

'Not good enough. I'd settle for chocolate.'

'Chocolate . . .? Perhaps.'

'That's better.' When he slid through the door Xavier Cugat was playing 'Amor'.

He held out his arms. 'May I have this dance, miss?'

Laughing, she slid into them, her pelvis already doing some Latin moves to the beat of the music. He lifted her palm to her mouth and kissed it. 'You smell like lavender polish.'

'It's the latest perfume for ladies who clean.'

He was a good dancer, and she was able to anticipate his moves easily. Xavier Cugat segued into a Glenn Miller dance tune and she was pulled closer to him. He said, 'All right?'

Her eyes lifted to his. It was more than all right. His mouth was luscious. She was on fire for him. 'Where's my chocolate?'

'I said chocolate *perhaps*. It turns out to be, perhaps not. Will you accept a kiss instead?'

Nick didn't bother to wait for an answer, but just helped himself. His body was warm against hers and she could feel the result of his positioning nudging against her stomach as they danced.

'Yum,' he said when the kiss was over. 'That was better than any chocolate I could name. Tell me, what were you rattled about when I arrived?'

'I received a letter from my solicitor friend saying he was getting married.'

'I'm sorry.' He shrugged. 'Cancel that. I'm really not sorry. I'm just sorry if he hurt your feelings.'

'Oh, it's nothing like that. It's my pride that's injured. I told you we'd decided to be friends, but it seems that his family thought it a bad idea. A pity really, because I like them, and I liked him.'

'And now you don't?'

'Well, it does feel a bit like a stab in the back. It's just that Rennie brought our friendship to an end by putting it in writing, as though I was an employee being sacked. So I got in a temper and called him a few names, none of which he deserves by the way. But while I was letting off steam like an engine driver's stoker, I was also working my temper off in a flurry of productive activity, so the outcome was a lovely shining floor . . . until you interrupted.'

He pulled the turban from her head and threw it aside before ruffling her hair. 'I do love your way of thinking, Meggie. It's as curly as your hair.'

She became conscious of her apron and the old dress she usually did the housework in. She tried to straighten the creases.

'Stop fussing with yourself.'

The music changed again, becoming dreamy. Meggie was pulled a little closer. They seemed to be swaying on the spot and she imagined herself dancing, alone with him in a ball-room, expect for the orchestra. Her gown was a white misty drift of chiffon, sparkling with pearls. No! No! That was too bridal, and Nick was not the marrying kind, she thought. She changed the colour to midnight blue, with one strap covered in silver sequins. Crystals were scattered over a skirt that sparked moon gleams as they moved.

His mouth was a mere inch away from her. The skin of his face was smooth, giving off a slight fragrance of sandalwood. Moving slightly she tentatively kissed one corner of the quirky little smile he wore.

I love you, she thought in surprise, when he turned to gaze at her, but it was different to the way she'd loved Rennie . . . more savage and needful. Nick was a loner, but he put up a good front. He engaged her eyes until the music stopped, and then kissed her again, making her mouth pliable under his as he gently nibbled at her bottom lip.

The hall clock struck ten thirty, making her jump. This couldn't be happening to her in the middle of the morning.

Nerves attacked her. She *did* love him, and that thought was just as unnerving as the first time she'd thought it, for he challenged her at every turn. 'Rennie's letter is somewhere on the floor if you want to read it. It's awfully stuffy. He sounds almost middle-aged.'

'Forget Rennie. He's in the past. I'm glad he's gone because it gives me a better chance with you. Can I take you to bed?'

She gave a nervous sort of laugh. 'Just like that?'

'It's as good a time as any. Yes or no?'

She blushed. 'Yes . . . I suppose you might think so.' She drew in a deep breath. 'But what makes you assume I want . . .'

A grin spread across his face. 'You're a healthy young woman. Of course you want to. You looked as though you were going to eat me when we were dancing. But such a chaste little kiss.'

'You're being conceited . . . but perhaps I did want to.'

'Then why didn't you encourage me?'

'I didn't know how. I only know I wanted to kiss that little bit of you at the side of your mouth.'

'Now you get to kiss a bit more of me. Come on then. Let's get it over with.' He swept her up in her arms and headed for the stairs.

'I look a mess.'

'It doesn't matter since I'm about to remove all your clothing and ravish you, after which you'll be more of a mess.'

That one sentence left her already feeling naked. Her courage wobbled as she delved into a barrel of prissy excuses designed to keep him at bay. 'My bed squeaks,' she warned, almost breathless, something which was quickly followed by, 'I forgot to patch the rip in the bedspread.'

He laughed. 'You should have insisted on the four-poster and the satin sheets. It's too late now.'

She didn't bother to ask him how he knew which was her room. She already knew. Setting her on her feet he gazed down at her, and then removed her apron. When he'd finished he said, 'Undo the buttons on my shirt.'

The wound on his arm had healed leaving a scar that resembled a smallpox vaccination. She gently touched it. The small scar would wrap them in secrecy and bind her to his thoughts until he was too old to think straight any more.

Opening her blouse Nick cupped her breasts. He smoothed his fingertips over the satin cups supporting them and teased her nipples. 'That's lovely,' she said, and when he took one into his mouth and ran a hot, moist tongue over it her knees almost buckled and she gave a tiny cry.

There was a swift intake of breath from him. 'You're exquisite, Meggie.'

Easing the clothes from her he pushed her on the bed in a seated position and swiftly stepped out of his clothes. She closed her eyes. 'You know, I feel awfully hot and bothered . . . and a bit shy.'

'Damn it, Meggie,' and his voice was full of laughter. 'You're allowed to feel shy and you're allowed to look. My penis won't bite you. As for feeling hot and bothered, you should be. Try being in my skin at the moment.'

When she opened her eyes she wasn't so sure that she wanted to be. There it was, springing from a little nest of dark hair that arrowed up to his neat, aristocratic belly button. He was bigger than she'd expected.

Drum roll please. Where was Gene Krupa when she needed him?

Taking her hands he snugged his length inside them. 'Caress me a little, but gently.'

His skin felt like silk stretched over the hard muscle. She explored him, feeling the change as his testicles hardened to her touch. She'd learned about this from her aunt's lectures, and relaxed. She'd even practised rolling a condom on a stiff rubber penis that the midwives called Dangerous Dan. She'd become quite proficient at it. But this one was nothing like Dangerous Dan. It was wonderfully warm and alive. As she gained in confidence he grew even larger. She wondered how big he would get—

'Enough now.' He pushed her on to her back, joined her on the bed and looked down at her.

'I've got the jitters, and I keep thinking things I shouldn't so I want to laugh.'

'Laugh if you want. Sex should be fun, and you'll be serious when the time's right. You have lovely, firm, jutting breasts.'

The admiration made them jut even more and her nipples pushed against the skin. Inclining his head, he licked each tip into a frenzy. She shuddered and he smiled and kissed her, his tongue probing the depths of her mouth, so when he walked his fingers down her body she didn't really take much notice until he slipped his finger inside her already sensitized cleft.

She tensed for a moment, and then decided she liked what was going on there. Nick seemed to know how to go about pleasuring her. 'Oh!' His soft caress made her melt and she opened to him, hot and pulsing. She closed her eyes surrendering to him without restraint. Her hands wandered his body, over his firm and powerful buttocks, and her pelvis lifted to the touch of his hands and his tongue. Little moaning sounds were coming from her own mouth and his breath was harsh against her ear as she lifted against him, entreating him.

He'd been right, and her concentration had slipped to what was happening right now.

He stopped for a moment, finding a moment to slip on the rubber, and then he rolled over her and gazed into her eyes. His were as dark as storm clouds as they looked into hers.

Centred between her thighs, the touch of his hand was seductive in its caress, inciting her body into something eager and demented as it responded to him. She gave a shuddering little groan . . . another . . . several, until she could barely control what she felt. Only then did he invade into her warm wetness, lifting her thigh with an arm under her knee and pushing into her. She gave a small yelp when something gave. He paused for a moment. 'All right?'

'Yes . . . don't stop.'

But it was just the beginning. She abandoned herself to Nick's touch as he stroked into her, again and again. Aware of the power of him, and that was being restrained, she could barely breathe. When she did take a breath she inhaled a warm, feral musk that acted like an aphrodisiac, so her skin prickled and the sensitive surface of her breasts, and her vagina, previously untouched-by-mankind, were in a hot fermenting turmoil that nearly had her jumping off the bed to be satisfied – as if she could leap up from her supine position and impale herself on her lover upside down.

He prolonged the pleasure for a short time before he lost his control, then he came faster and faster. She clung to him, her pelvis lifting to his assault, her legs around his waist, keeping him anchored to her. She shuddered over the edge a moment before he did, the squeak of the bed making rusty protestations in the background. Wrapped as they were in each other's arms, Meggie barely heard it and enjoyed every moment of their togetherness.

After Nick got his breath back and they'd disentangled themselves he shifted his weight to one side, and then moved a strand of her hair from her eyes. 'Well?'

She grinned, out of breath and wondering why he needed reassurance on such a splendid exercise. 'A wonderfully immoral rampage, my good man.'

He ran a finger along the curve of her mouth. 'That was the basic model of debauchery. There are variations to explore and we have all day and all night to do it in. Let's take a bath before lunch.'

'What a wonderful idea.' She'd fill the bath to the brim, and there were some scented bath salts that made the water soft and a small amount of bubble bath in a bottle that her aunt had left behind.

A problem raised itself. Lunch! He'd be staying for dinner and breakfast as well. Her mind journeyed into the larder with its almost bare shelves. Apart from bottled rhubarb and apples from home, 'I have two sausages –' she grinned, not missing the symbolic nature of the sacrifice – 'so I can manage a toad-in-the-hole and some tinned peas.'

He shuddered. 'I've got no intention of eating your rations. My man, William, will deliver a hamper at noon that should take us through the weekend. There might even be some chocolate in it. Tell me something.'

'What?'

'Anything . . . the first thing that comes into your head on the count of three. One, two, thre—'

She flung out at him, 'I . . . I love you, and it's nothing to do with what's just happened.'

'Ah, Meggie, I hoped you'd say that, because I adore you.' When his smile slowly came she knew she'd die if she never saw him again.

The warm glow she was feeling vanished when it hit her. He was going off on one of his operations, and now she knew his job was dangerous she'd worry all the time he was away in case he never came back. Sliding her arms around him she held him tight and bit her tongue, so the words couldn't escape.

In the back of her mind she wondered if Nick had found something out about Leo. She was dying to ask him. After all, she'd just paid the penalty Nick had demanded of her, even though it had been a pleasure rather than a payment. But no, it was too soon.

She daren't press him. He'd already said he'd cancel whatever he had in mind, if she did mention it, because his own life would be placed in jeopardy. She believed him.

'I need to go to the bathroom,' he said a few minutes, later, and was gone.

A few seconds later came the sound of the bath water running.

Pulling on her dressing gown Meggie gazed at herself in the mirror. Apart from pink cheeks and messy hair and a feeling of smug gratification supplied by the former exercise, she looked exactly the same as she had before.

He came up behind her, and sliding his arms around her, nibbled the junction of her neck. She shivered.

Lunch came in a hamper, driven to the house by a man of nearly middle years on a motorbike and sidecar. Apart from that there were a couple of boxes carried in, containing enough to see them through the weekend, and more beside.

For lunch there was a flask of home-made cream-of-celery soup, salad, and cold chicken breast. The rolls were crispy, the middles still slightly warm and doughy from the oven, so the butter melted into its surroundings.

'I haven't tasted real butter for ages.'

'The dairy staff make it and my father sends me up a pot every so often. He believes in me eating well.'

'What's your father like?'

'To look at the earl is handsome, and he's well-mannered and quiet. As a person . . . he's proud of his lineage, manages his estate competently and is a little bit self-satisfied. As a father, he was — and still is — a bit remote. He was a better father to me than I was a son to him. I think. There was a period where I ran a bit wild, and he got me out of a couple of scrapes. Sometimes I wish I'd been a better son to him.'

'Do you love him?'

Nick appeared to ponder the question, and then he smiled. 'D'you know, Meggie, I've never really thought about it. He isn't a demonstrative man, but yes I imagine I do. Father and sons don't usually put on a public display of affection, or a private one either, come to that. He's always treated me like an equal rather than his son.'

'And your mother?'

'She ran off with another man, then my father came to the school one day and told me she'd died. I was in the middle of exams.'

'Did you miss her?'

He shrugged. 'All I can really remember of her is that she wore red lipstick and told me she loved me. I was upset, and I turned my back on her.'

'That must have hurt her.'

'Yes it would have, but no more than it hurt me. When you're a child you don't think of such things. She left me a villa that overlooks the sea in France and my boat, *Petite Cochinelle*. My father kept the yacht in a boatyard where she was maintained; then he taught me how to sail her when I was old enough. We used to go out in her during the school holidays. A German general is living in the villa now.'

She was curious. 'How do you know about him?'

The smile he gave was wry. 'I'd forgotten how quick-minded you are. It doesn't matter how.'

'I never met my father. Richard Sinclair Sangster died before I was born.'

'I know everything there is to know about you Meggie.'

'Including all my names.'

'I have a good memory. I didn't think you'd notice my slip over your nickname and hunt me down though. It's best to let sleeping dogs lie.'

'There's something you probably don't know. I suspect that my grandfather was my real father. That's what he told me. My mother said he assaulted her, and Major Sangster told me the same thing just before he died.'

'I know that too. Does it worry you?'

'To be honest, I'd rather have not known. It used to bother me, but not any longer. Richard Sinclair Sangster is on my birth certificate as my father. Denton Elliot adopted me and brought me up though. He was the best of fathers. He and Richard had been friends since childhood, and he gave him an identity for me. I just wanted you to know about the major. You're good at keeping secrets.'

He smiled a little at that, seeing right through her. 'Let's not talk shop. Have you had enough to eat?'

'I'm bulging at the seams.'

'So am I. Another glass of wine?'

'I've had two already, and it's made me feel sleepy.'

'Then we'll go and have a rest so you can relax.'

'How very transparent of you.' He grinned when she laughed.

She got very little sleep in the next twelve hours. The siren went off during that time. The planes thundered overhead, the bombs came down like rain and they ignored the noise and the danger.

Meggie woke in the pale promise of dawn, the all clear sounding in her head. Nick was nowhere to be seen, though she'd felt his kiss warm against her mouth a little earlier. She called out to him, but with no result, and went looking. The remains of their dinner littered the kitchen table . . . the crystal wine glasses and linen napkins with his family crest.

'Oh, Nick,' she whispered. 'You forgot to say goodbye.' But she remembered the kiss and knew he'd forgotten on purpose. She could still smell the spicy odour of his body on her and could almost taste his delicious flesh on her tongue. Her skin was still in a glorious tingle from his kisses, and although she ached in odd places, had a small bruise on her breast and was a little bit sore, she wasn't even a tiny bit sorry.

She quickly washed and dressed and headed out towards the river, to where *Petite Cochinelle* was usually moored.

A patchy fog was reinforced by stinking smoke; gathered from burning buildings that had once sheltered the families who lived, loved and worked there. The moist particles roughened her throat and made her cough, so she was forced to press a handkerchief against her nose.

Poor London, she thought, skirting the night's smoking cinders of dwellings as much as she could. Her heart went out to the newly homeless.

There was a defiant stoicism about people now, a sense of endurance that brought them together. They stood in small groups, holding treasures they'd dug from the ruins of their castles to take with them – a child with a doll, a woman with a picture of her wedding day and a man with his best suit. In case he needed to be buried, perhaps. A canary in a cage whistled in the dawn from on top of a pile of rubble.

Those without someone to own them waited like lost dogs to be told where to go, some making jokes about their predicament, because not to do so would make them feel like cowards.

The wardens busily herded them like a flock of sheep, joking, 'Off you go to the church, you lot . . . you can get a cup of tea there and it will only cost you a prayer,' and to Meggie as she tried to slip past. 'Oiy . . . you can't go down that road, miss. There's a UXB. We're waiting for bomb disposal to come along and disarm it.'

She reached the river only to find the nothing she'd expected. Even so the sight of the empty berth was disappointing. A thin mist writhed from the surface of the Thames and barges butted busily through the chilly grey water, appearing out of the mist to scuttle across her available landscape and disappear back into the mist again. There was a scrap of white paper impaled on a grey splinter. It was attached to a weathered post supporting a faded red and white life preserver.

I'll always love you. Remember that, it said.

Fear stabbed at her. 'Sail in safety *Little Ladybug,*' she whispered, folding the precious little scrap into her purse.

When she arrived back home she cleared away the dishes and unpacked the two boxes. It was a veritable feast, and she felt guilty as she packed it neatly in the larder. There was a bar of chocolate, and a small velvet box tied together with a green velvet ribbon.'

'*Diamonds and emeralds,*' he'd said.

Her answer to that? 'No, not good enough, Nick. Chocolate . . . perhaps?'

He'd given her both. There was a piece of paper inside the box, folded up small. *Would you consent to becoming The Right Dishonourable, The Viscountess Cowan?*

'The dishonourable Lady Cowan,' she said, and laughed, because it sounded like the title of a rather lurid novel. She rarely remembered that Nick was a Lord now, even in the office. Her brothers would tease her unmercifully when they found out.

It was a beautiful ring; a clear white diamond flanked by two emeralds, and in a setting set of white gold.

She thought of the career she'd wanted so desperately to pursue. Her values had shifted. It took years to become a lawyer. It didn't seem so important to her since her thoughts had turned to having her own business, which was much more appealing. At least she wouldn't have to take orders from anyone else. If she married Nick her career path would be as his wife – if they both survived the war.

She'd probably be called on to open village fêtes and judge baby shows or measure the circumference of pumpkins on the biggest vegetable stall.

Lord . . . she'd probably have to wear a hat. Placing a table napkin on her head she smiled graciously at her reflection in the mirror and then closed her eyes and whispered, 'Good morning, Lady Cowan.'

The ring was pure and honest, a promise from Nick to her. The rest didn't matter. All her plans were swept aside in the face of this overwhelming declaration of love from the most complicated of men.

But she could do both.

She ran a fingertip over the cool, hard surface of the gems – gems that glittered like pebbles in a sun-dappled brook. He was right. She'd never get to the bottom of him, so why try? She would never settle for an ordinary man and Nick had an air of danger about him that she loved.

'If you slip past the knuckle it means we are meant to be,' she said. Holding her breath she dropped the ring over the tip of her finger and gently pushed . . .

Nineteen

Meggie did attend the ceremony of Rennie's wedding, despite her first pathetic intention that she wouldn't. Her absence wouldn't punish anyone or give her any satisfaction, since it wouldn't even be noticed. Her attendance might dispel the rumour that she was Rennie's popsie. It didn't rain, as she'd once requested from anyone who'd been listening. It was a perfect autumn day, alive with colour like a Monet painting.

She'd been petty. Rennie wasn't the type of man to cut her out deliberately. He'd probably just forgotten to put the date in his letter. The notice in the paper provided her with it. She took a seat near the back in case she needed to escape.

The church was full of the dust of war. It floated in the beams of sunlight, like the crushed hopes of many endeavours through the decades. It coated the upper reaches of the church and its statuary, where nobody could reach to wash it away without erecting a scaffold.

Perhaps an unpublished Shakespearean sonnet lingered there, fourteen lines of perfection composed when the bard was supposed to be praying. Had it drifted up in several million thought particles and waited to be put together again and discovered? The churchyard was filled with the ancient bones of plague victims, and she hoped a bomb wouldn't disturb their resting place.

She wore her WRNS uniform because it made her feel responsible and adult, and she was proud to be wearing it. She was miles away from the young girl who'd once imagined she was in love with Rennie. She was somebody doing her best to help Britain win the war, though what that best actually consisted of in the job she'd been allocated, she found hard to define.

Rennie arrived with his father, who gave her an embarrassed look, and with Cousin Ambrose, who pinched her on the cheek and whispered, 'I knew you'd put a brave face on and come, my dear, that's the ticket,' before moving on down the aisle.

Constance Stone offered her a barely-there smile and lingered next to Rennie. In case Meggie picked Rennie up and ran off with him tucked under her arm perhaps? In any case, Rennie wasn't about to have their conversation overheard and sent her on her way, with, 'Excuse me please, Mother.'

Collectively, the lawyers had beaten her, but by the use of deceit. She'd never have believed they'd be so devious or two-faced. It was a hollow victory though. Rennie never had any intention of making things permanent and had made that clear.

He stopped, his foxy eyes wary and his smile coming and going. 'You made it then, my Mags. I rather hoped you would.'

They both knew he was lying. 'Would I miss my best friend's wedding?'

'I'll certainly miss the irony in your words. You're the only person who could make me laugh. You look good in uniform.'

'Like some sort of clown? Service life is nothing like I expected.'

'Life rarely turns out as planned. You were always ready to embrace it with enthusiasm. You brought something fresh and lovely into my life.'

He looked tired, but then, most men of serving age looked tired. He was wearing his uniform too. He deserved more than she was giving him. 'I don't believe in going out with a whimper, Rennie and neither did I want us to end on a sour note. Sincerely, I do hope you and Pamela will be happy together. I'm sure you will be. Goodbye, Rennie dear.'

'Thank you, Mags.' He took her hand in his and kissed it. His gaze went to the ring on her finger and he raised an eyebrow.

She grinned, liking this little show of defiance in the face of the curious gazes of the congregation and lowering brows of his family. 'I did say I'd dazzle you, but somebody else ended up dazzling me.'

'Anyone I know?'

'I doubt it.' She didn't enlighten him since it wouldn't be official until she'd accepted Nick in person.

Ambrose appeared at his elbow, bristling with annoyance. 'Time to take your place, Rennie.'

She issued instructions to God as Rennie walked away from her to join Cousin Ambrose. 'Look after him.'

The organ played part of Mendelssohn's wedding march and Pamela appeared, looking lovely in a pale-blue knee-length suit worn with a silk-flowered pillbox hat. A short net veil covered her eyes. She was on the arm of a small man in grey pinstripes, one who looked rather insignificant and colourless in the company of the silks. She recalled that he owned several factories that manufactured weapons of war.

Pamela's smile washed over Meggie, faltered, and then came back again, frozen brilliantly in place like a butterfly on a pin.

Meggie smiled reassuringly at her. She had never been a serious contender for Pamela's man, and now she had a perfectly good one of her own . . . somewhere . . .!

Nick had hidden *Petite Coccinelle* in a small indentation in the rock below his villa. It was hardly visible, even when the tide was out because there was no beach below the villa, only a series of steps hewn from the rock and a small wooden jetty that could be swung aside to allow the yacht access. The wall curved inwards through the rock that formed the Cotentin Peninsula that surrounded Cherbourg, providing an effective, but small buttress to hide behind.

Its mast was barely allowed a yard of headway when the tide was in. It was not a place one could escape from easily if cornered, but he had to hide somewhere and he knew the coast pretty well. Even so, every minute placed him in extreme danger.

He waited, dozing on and off, and coming alert in an instant when something bumped gently against his hull. When the shadow of a man's head emerged over the side Nick placed the barrel of his revolver against the man's temple.

The man froze, whispering his code name in rapid French, 'It's Henri. Did you bring the weapons and ammunition?'

Nick relaxed and answered in kind. 'You'd better come aboard. Where are you going to hide them?'

'We'll take them up to the villa and hide them in the cellar.'

'What about the General?'

Henri spat into the water. 'He won't be home tonight. We'll smuggle the weapons out next week.'

'I'll pass them down to you. What news of my pilot?'

'Your pilot has been with the Resistance for the past seven weeks and has been kept on the move and passed from hand to hand. There are rumours and I think he'll be betrayed. He's noticeable because of his unusual blue eyes. I've brought him with me. His leg was broken, but is more or less healed. Don't expect him to run on it yet.'

'I won't.'

'I also have a package for you to deliver, my friend. Make sure it falls into the right hands.'

'You have my word.'

'It would be better for you not to linger tonight. You'll have to take the flyer with you now. I understand he's not a British national. If he's caught he'll be classified as a terrorist and a spy, and will probably be sent to Buchenwald concentration camp and eventually shot. I've heard the conditions for prisoners there are horrendous.'

Nick nodded. 'I'll take him off your hands, Henri. What's the wind like?'

'The water's choppy and the sky is overcast, but it's early and you have a good following wind. You should be able to slip away unnoticed and make good speed.'

'Can the man climb aboard without help?'

'If he's careful.'

Nick switched to English. 'Come aboard flyer, but be careful you don't slip. I'll help you from this side.'

'That depends where you're taking me?'

'This is no time for heroics, my friend, but you do have a

choice. Either get on board or my French friends will drown you. They've risked their lives to hide you and keep you alive. You know too much so they're not about to hand you over to the authorities alive.'

'Put like that, I think I'll take my chances aboard with you, mate.' There was a grunt as Esmé's man bumped into him. Nick put out an arm to steady him, and guided him down to the cabin. 'Duck your head. Good. I'm going to leave you here while I unload some cargo.'

'Can I help?'

'Just stay out of the way. There's a bunk behind you, Doctor Thornton.'

'May I know who I'm speaking to?'

Nick grinned and turned the key in the lock. He took the top from a fire extinguisher that was securely fixed next to the cabin door, and dropped the package inside before returning the top and securing the catches.

Leo slept for a short time. He woke, feeling disorientated. They were at sea. The boat was lively, skewing around and skipping from one wave to another. He began to feel queasy and felt his way about the cabin until he found the door.

When he opened it a blast of wind snatched the air from his lungs and nearly blew him backwards. It cured his queasiness though, until the yacht suddenly canted over on its side and he only managed to stay on deck by clinging to the door.

His rescuer seemed to have eyes like a cat because he called out of the darkness, 'She's all over the place and the tide's running fast. It would be sensible for you to stay inside the cabin, and with the door shut until we reach England, especially if your leg is likely to be unstable. You don't want to break it all over again, or worse . . . fall over the side.'

'I wouldn't mind a little fresh air.'

'If we sail in these conditions with the cabin doors open the wind will cause enough drag to slow us down and I'll be fighting it every inch of the way.'

The boat took a dive and Leo was forced to put some muscle into his bad leg. He grimaced. His rescuer was making sense.

'It will be getting light in about fours hours or so, and the conditions will be calmer when we leave the Cherbourg current behind. Perhaps you can come out then. There's a life jacket in the locker under the seat for you to wear, and a bowl under the bunk if you're going to toss up.'

'Who are you?'

'That doesn't matter. What matters is that we make the crossing, and as quickly and quietly as possible. I hope we have luck on our side, because it's going to be an eight-hour run, at least. I don't usually sail during daylight hours, but the Germans are on to you.'

'We'll be sitting ducks if the Luftwaffe see us.'

'Let me worry about that. They'll be attacking the convoys come dawn so they won't be looking for us. Besides, only a fool would sail a small boat in these conditions – they know that,' Nick said.

'And our boys will be there picking them off,' Leo said with a great deal of self-satisfaction.

'If we're sunk we'll have to swim for it.'

A huff of laughter came from Leo. 'I've already tried that.'

'The cloud is almost down to sea level at the moment, which will help, as long as we don't run into a warship or two. There's a torch, and I don't have to tell you to be careful in its use. See if you can find the picnic hamper. There's a flask containing coffee, and some food. Try and rest after.'

'What about you?'

'I've eaten. I have my own coffee, and I need to keep my wits about me.'

Leo soon found the picnic basket. It contained hard-boiled eggs, a chunk of crusty bread and an apple. He ate it quickly, washing it down with the coffee.

Hearing the sound of a Spitfire patrol droning above in the clouds he experienced a feeling of security, and pulled the blanket up to his chin. His baby son was nearly two months old and he'd never seen the little tyke yet. As he lay on the bunk to rest he felt a rapid downward spiral into sleep . . . as if he'd been given a strong sleeping pill. He applied his will against falling asleep . . .

What seemed to be an instant later Leo saw light and

realized the boat was no longer moving. He yawned and stretched. It was the best sleep he'd had in weeks, but it had left him fuddle-brained.

Judging from the position of the sun it was late afternoon. He gazed around him, his eyes sharpening. He was in a park! 'What the hell!'

A warden was crouched by his side. 'Are you all right, sir?'

'I think so. Where the hell am I?'

'London – Hyde Park to be exact. A woman walking her dog saw a man bring you here. The man used the public telephone, and then walked off. You're wearing uniform and are in a wheelchair, so I thought you might either be drunk, or injured.'

Leo gazed around, bewildered. 'But I was sure I was on a boat.'

'Yes, I'm sure you did think that, sir,' he said, obviously humouring him. 'Perhaps you dreamed it, or perhaps your friends were playing a trick on you. Here come the authorities. They'll soon sort it out for you.'

The two men walked towards him. They wore RAF security badges. 'Can you tell me your name and number, sir?'

He was suspicious. 'Can you tell me yours?'

The second man smiled. 'Squadron Leader Thornton, isn't it? Doc for short. Don't worry, sir. You're in good hands. We'll soon sort this out. You've been missing for nearly eight weeks.'

It was unlikely anyone outside the squadron except family would know his nickname, obvious as it was. He needed someone to sort it out. Even so Leo's mind had begun to work overtime. He was sure now that he'd been drugged. Someone had brought him here to avoid being identified. But why keep his identity a secret?

Because he worked under cover! Leo wished he'd been given the opportunity to thank the man.

'Who alerted you?'

'A phone call sir. The man refused to give a name. He told us who you were.'

The rescue must have been unauthorized.

'He said he came on a boat,' the warden chipped in.

'What was the name of the boat, sir?'

It hadn't had one. The name had been blacked out, and the

skipper was just a shadowy figure. He'd taken care not to be seen, and Leo wasn't about to say anything that might identify him or incriminate him. 'I don't know.'

'Would you come with us please, sir. We have instructions to take you to hospital for a check up.'

Leo was itching to see Esmé. She'd be worried sick about him. 'Do I have any choice. I'd like to ring my wife.'

'No, sir,' and although the speaker sounded apologetic, there was steel in his voice. 'You're going to hospital first.'

First had been the interrogation. Leo found it hard to lie, but he had very little to say, apart from repeating French gossip. Something that was hard for him to do because, apart from a few common words, he didn't speak the language and most of the conversation had gone over his head.

He did his best to report everything he'd seen in Cherbourg, the number of troops, etc. He pointed out, 'I had a broken leg and mostly saw the inside of barns, attics and cellars, when I wasn't blindfolded. They were very careful. He had nothing but praise for his rescuers. The Resistance cell who'd rescued him had been a well-run operation and he wasn't about to jeopardize the lives of the people who'd looked after him by revealing so much as a name.

'Did you see the person who brought you back home?'

Leo felt the need to protect the man. 'No . . . it was totally dark and I slept for most of the way. I woke up where I was found.'

'Perhaps he was a black marketeer. Some of them smuggle goods back and forth. Did he have any cargo on board?'

Leo remembered the guns and ammunition being unloaded at the other end, and hoped they'd been put to good use. 'Unfortunately, it was too dark to see anything.'

After the interrogation the remains of the decaying cast was removed from his leg. He enjoyed a soak in the bath before being poked and prodded.

'Hmmm. The person who set this fracture was an expert. I'm going to give you some extra calcium to take. Go easy on it for a while. I dare say you'll know when it's ready.'

He was issued with a pair of crutches, a clean uniform and a chitty for a month's leave before he needed to return to duty.

Discharged the next morning he made his way home to Queen Street and banged at the door. There was no answer.

Some of the windows had been broken, and there was damage to the panel in the front door that had been covered with cardboard. He pushed it in, then pushed his arm through the aperture and opened the front door.

'Esmé,' he called, and the cat came trotting out of somewhere to weave around his ankles. He tickled him under the chin.

Limping up the stairs he pushed open the bedroom door. It was clean and tidy, the bed bare of covers. There were a couple of letters on the dressing table.

One was from Esmé, the other from his sister-in-law in Australia, Minnie. He slid it into his pocket and opened the one from Esmé. She'd gone to Dorset to be near her sister.

> *I can't believe you won't come back, Leo darling. Johnno is thriving, and we'll be living at Nutting Cottage for as long as it takes.*
>
> *Call me, my love. Please, please call me. I'll never give up hope.*
>
> *Yours always, Esmé.*

Leo hated hearing his wife cry, but on this occasion he thought he might enjoy it.

A few seconds later, the telephone in Nutting Cottage began to ring. He imagined Esmé coming down the stairs, wearing her favourite brown slacks and her long pink cardigan with pearl buttons over a cream blouse. Or was it a blue cardigan? It didn't matter. She would be holding their precious baby in her arms.

There was a choking lump in his throat just thinking about it.

She picked up the receiver right on cue and said, 'Esmé Thornton speaking.'

'This is Leo. Have I told you recently that I love you, my sweet bonny Esmé?'

There was silence for a few moments, then cautiously, 'Leo Thornton?'

'How many Leos do you know?'

'Leo, you beastly creature, where have you been for all this time?' she scolded. The big sniff she gave was followed by a bigger sob, as if all her tension was being released like a cork from a bottle as she wailed, 'I've missed you.'

Baby Johnno gave a bit of a bellow and she soothed him with. 'Why are you complaining, my little man? It's your father. He's come home? I told you he would.'

Now it was Leo's time to cry, and he choked out, 'I'll be there as soon as I can . . . on the next train if I can get there on time.'

Twenty

Meggie usually walked to work unless she was late. She always took a detour to the river, just in case. It was odd how the landscape kept changing. Streets once lined with buildings were demolished, or partly demolished. Rows of houses had gaps in them and windows were blown out or boarded up, as though the houses were sightless. Street trees lost leaves and limbs.

Some houses had lost their fronts like doll's houses. Beds and dressing tables teetered from ledges, held by a leg or two. Drawers were open and sheets and blankets hung down like bunting. People hunted among the rubble piles, looking for precious keepsakes. Some furnishings had their innards exposed, chunks of lathe and plaster, held by whiskers of horsehair that had helped strengthen the mix. Springs sprung from chairs.

There had been retaliation since the blitz. The RAF had abandoned their policy of industrial bombing. No longer were just the German factory and dock areas targeted, but they flattened civilian areas as well. The game of war had become ruthless. The gloves had come off.

The day was overcast and the wind had a bite to it, a reminder of the coming winter. It would be her birthday in October. Her mother had planned a party for her.

'It won't be as grand as we would have liked, Meggie dear, but we thought you'd prefer something more subdued, so it will be the family.'

Meggie missed her aunt, though they talked on the telephone now and again. She had a yearning to see her mother again. Sometimes she felt as if she was playing at being grown-up. What she wanted was a big hug from someone who loved her.

She wondered if Nick would come home. She had never known him to be away for such a long time. Even James Bethuen had called her into his office and quizzed her on Nick's whereabouts two days before.

She told him the truth. 'I have no idea, sir. He doesn't take me into his confidence.'

Bethuen gave her an odd look, then smiled his tight smile and said, 'Quite.'

Judith told her that night, 'Bethuen works under someone else, and they must be getting worried about his long absence. I think he knows about Nick socializing with us. You should be careful, Meggie.'

'About what?'

'That nobody finds out about you two. His father knows a lot of people, and I doubt if he'd approve if you had any ideas of grandeur. I mean, look what happened when you set your sights on that lawyer. Nick is much further up the scale.'

Judith was unaware of how social Meggie had been with Nick, and Meggie wasn't about to tell her. Her housemate wasn't exactly discreet.

Meggie was also worried. When she reached the river her heart leaped. There was a yacht at the berth. It was Nick's boat but it was different in that it was battered, scratched and scruffy. The name had also gone.

She went on board, her footsteps echoing on the planked decking, and softly called his name, 'Nick.'

There was no answer, and the cabin doors were locked.

When she got to the office Bethuen called her in again. 'I'm given to understand that you and Lord Cowan are . . . *close.*'

She kept cool. 'From whom?'

He didn't answer but avoided her eyes. 'You do know, my

dear, that any relationship that might develop between staff members is frowned upon. I could make an exception in certain circumstances. Has Lord Cowan told you what he does and where he goes during his absences?'

Wild Spanish bulls stampeding around Bethuen's office wouldn't make her betray Nick – not that there were many of them in Whitehall, she imagined.

She counted to ten, adding an imaginary *Olé!* at the end, knowing she could answer him truthfully, and more. 'I'm not privy to Lord Cowan's work schedule or activities, and I object to the inference that there's collaboration of some sort between us. If you have any complaints about my work or feel that I've violated the Official Secrets Act in any way, or even brought disrespect down on the service I represent, please contact the appropriate department of the service.'

Judith winked at her when she left the office.

Expecting Nick to turn up at work she was on tenterhooks all day. Gordon Frapp gave her a heap of aerial photographs to pore over. Barely able to concentrate, she did her best to discover anything looking remotely sinister.

'What did Bethuen want?' Frapp asked her, and too casually to be taken as such.

'He asked me if I knew where Lord Cowan was.'

Frapp gave a knowing grin. 'Do you?'

'Of course I do.'

His eyes took on the avid eagerness of a dog waiting for a titbit. 'Where?'

Rising, she closed the door then looked under the desk. 'We're not bugged are we?'

'I'd know if we were.'

'Good, because I'd hate this to get out, Mr Frapp . . . I keep Lord Cowan in the pickle jar in my larder.'

Frapp's grin failed. 'Very funny . . . I can see where your loyalty lies.'

'It is a pity yours doesn't coincide with mine.'

She didn't tell him the boat was back at its berth. He could find out that for himself if he bothered to look. It occurred to her that Nick seemed to thrive on intrigue, perhaps boredom had driven him to it before the war, but it was something entirely different and dangerous now if the bullet in his arm had been anything to go by.

She didn't even know where he lived, which, considering his declaration of love and the engagement ring, was rather odd. Perhaps that had been play-acting too. Her heart sank. Life was suddenly getting complicated.

It was getting complicated for Nick, too. Eight weeks of sailing the French coast and the Mediterranean while trying to catch up with his contacts and gather information had been wearying. If he'd been caught running guns he'd have been shot out of hand.

Thankfully, Leo had recovered enough from his injuries to be handed over – to the visible relief of the Resistance. He was sorry he'd had to give him knock-out-drops. The man was too sharp. Thornton had already seen Nick's face once, when he'd taken the jewellery back. What on earth had possessed him to play such stupid games?

A quick phone call from a nearby telephone box and Nick's man had arrived with a wheelchair. He'd cut it fine, and Leo was already beginning to recover by the time they'd got him away from the river. They'd watched from the shadows of the trees as the appropriate authorities had come for his passenger.

William had taken Nick home, and he'd been staggering from fatigue by the time they got there.

'Your father, the earl has rung several times, My Lord. He's heard rumours.'

In his absence Nick had thought a lot about his father. Rumours had a habit of reaching his ears quickly. He took a shot in the dark. 'Call him and put his mind at rest, William,' he croaked. 'But I imagine you don't need me to tell you that.'

'As you say, sir!'

'Tell him I'll talk to him tomorrow. I need a few hours of undisturbed sleep.'

'And your young lady. Isn't it about time he met her?'

'Since you enjoy running my life so much, arrange something then.' Nick smiled, thinking of Meggie. She was never far from his mind, and he couldn't wait to see her again. I'll visit her this evening and surprise her. Though he didn't think it would be much of a surprise, since she had it all worked out, he was sure.

William eyed him critically. 'That beard will certainly surprise her. It's most unkempt.'

'This beard will be removed once I've slept, William, so start stropping the razors. And pack a hamper and add a bottle of champagne if you would, the best we've got.'

'A special occasion, sir?'

'Every time I see her is a special occasion. You're being inquisitive William.'

'Yes, sir, I'm aware of that, but one couldn't help but notice that you have more than a fondness for the young lady.'

'One should mind his own business.'

Unperturbed, William said, 'I dare say, but the welfare of one's master *is* one's business. Wouldn't it be more convenient for the young lady to visit you here, since the area where she lives has been subjected to heavy bombing lately, and there's a lot of rubble to navigate.'

'I'm more than fond of her. I adore her, and I'm going to marry her if she'll have me. And yes, you're right. I shall visit her personally and escort her to dinner. By the way . . . the boat needs urgent maintenance. In particular the fire extinguisher needs to be replaced.'

'Yes, sir. I'll let the maintenance people know right away.'

Meggie did her usual detour to the river on the way home. She stood there in the evening mist staring at the empty space where the boat had been. She couldn't believe it . . . it had gone from its mooring!

Had everything he'd said to her been lies? She knew he was back in England, she could almost smell him.

She headed for home, changed out of her uniform and into her best dress, just in case.

As usual, Judith was seeing her latest boyfriend. They were off to the cinema to see a film. 'I'll get myself some beans on toast for dinner,' she'd said.

'There's a slice of corned beef to go with it. And I made a jelly.'

Meggie would sit in the empty house, except for the company of Jack Frost. There was a tin of caviar in the larder, left over from Nick's last hamper. She opened it for the cat to eat.

A pity it wasn't tinned herrings in tomato sauce. Her mouth began to water at the thought. There were no fresh eggs now. Somebody had stolen the hens from the back garden when they were at work.

After Judith had gone she went to the kitchen and made herself a cup of tea.

There was a note propped against the salt and pepper pots. She stared at it, and then her heart seemed to explode. It was from Leo! He was alive! She snatched it up.

Meggie, I'm home again. I'm taking a month's leave and have gone to Dorset to see Es and the baby.

Racing into the hall she rang the number of Nutting Cottage, her smile a mile wide.

Her aunt answered and said in a breathless rush. 'Somebody rescued Leo. He'd been injured and the Resistance found him and looked after him. He came home in a yacht and security picked him up. They wouldn't let him ring me until after he'd been interrogated.'

Nick's yacht, she thought with some pride. He'd done it for her. Nick had risked his own life to rescue Leo. 'Did Leo say who his rescuer was?'

'He didn't see anyone, though he formed the impression that his rescuer had a beard. He said it was all so very mysterious. He fell asleep. He thought he'd been given some knockout drops, because he woke up in Hyde Park.'

That was definitely a Nick touch. Imagine him giving Leo knockout drops? Goodness, she hoped Leo never found out. Stifling a giggle she quickly changed the subject. 'What did Leo think of Johnno? I would have loved to have seen his face when he saw him for the first time.'

'Leo thinks he's the cat's whiskers, and vice versa. I could swear that Johnno knew he was his father as soon as they set eyes on each other, and without me telling him. They can't stop smiling at each other. I'll tell you about it when you come down for your birthday. You'll be here for it, won't you, Meggie Moo? Livia is dying to see you.'

'I'll try and get some time off. Aunt Es . . . would you mind not calling me Meggie Moo any more. Just Meggie will do.'

'Oh, dear, you have grown up, haven't you? I'll try to remember not to. You must ask that lovely boss of yours to the party. Bring him with you, he's such a gentleman that he'll impress your mother no end.'

'I will if he wants to come.'

The doorbell rang and she finished her phone call hurriedly with, 'I'll call you again tomorrow, Aunt Es. Lots of love to Leo and Johnno.'

The nights were drawing in rapidly and there was a nip in the air. When she opened the door it was dark in both the porch and the hall.

She knew who stood there, a shadow against a darker shadow in the sandlewood-scented twilight. She breathed him in and his presence filled her.

In an instant she was in his arms, hugging him tight and feeling his body against hers, warm and reassuring. 'Nick . . . oh, Nick. I'm so glad you're safe.'

He kissed her, the sensation so tender, loving and possessive that she wanted to cry.

'So am I. Fetch your coat and scarf. You're coming home with me for dinner tonight. It was all William's idea. He wants me to impress you, with champagne in crystal and candlelight, so you'll accept my proposal when I offer it properly and officially.'

She pulled him inside and took him through to the kitchen where a candle glowed. 'Offer it now.'

He took her hands in his, and his grey eyes engaged hers. They were soft in the candlelight. 'My dearest lady, words can't express how much I love you. Will you forgive me for all my faults and become my wife. I promise I'll be good from now on.'

She threw an unbelieving laugh at him. 'Not too good, I hope.'

He chuckled.

'Does that mean you won't keep disappearing.'

'I can't promise that, my love . . . not while there's a war on.'

'But you will promise to be careful?'

'I've got everything to stay alive for.'

She took the ring from the chain around her neck and handed it to him. It slid easily on to her finger, as she knew it would. 'Will your father mind? He might think I'm not good enough for you.'

He ran a finger down her cheek. 'He'll adore you. He wants to meet you at the weekend.'

'By the way,' she said. 'Bethuen carpeted me this morning. He demanded to know where you were and warned me of the danger a relationship with you would represent.'

'The devil he did!'

'I told Bethuen I didn't know where you were, and to contact the appropriate authority if he had any complaints about my work. Then Gordon Frapp asked me the same thing.'

'They're both transparent. Gordon wants to be in charge, and Bethuen wants to go back to not doing anything much. What did you tell Gordon?'

'That of course I knew where you were . . . I kept you in a pickle jar in the larder. He was not amused.'

Nick burst into laughter. 'You've got more tricks than the two of them put together.'

She could have kicked him. 'You're not going to tell me anything I want to know, are you?'

'I shouldn't think so. You can keep on keeping me in your pickle jar for the time being.'

'I can add two and two together, you know. I know much more than you know I know.'

'Obviously you're pickled too . . . which is why my wedding gift to you will be Girton College for a couple of years, if that's what you really want to do. Once we're married you can leave the Wrens if you want.'

When she opened her mouth he placed his finger over it. 'You needn't say anything.'

She pulled his finger away long enough to say, 'But I want

to say something. Unfortunately, Nick, I'm totally and utterly speechless . . . well almost. I thought I might go into a partnership with Judith, and open a secretarial school when the war ends. What will you do?'

'Learn to run the family estate. It will be in my charge one day, and it's what my father wants and expects of me.'

Epilogue

Spring 1946

Arms around each other, Nick and Meggie strolled around Foxglove House, recently vacated.

'You know, Meggie, it looks as though it might be rather beautiful under this institutional paint. If you want to keep it, you can. It has lovely ceilings, but it's a pity they painted over the oak panelling. I suppose it could be restored. We could put an estate manager in to manage the farming side.'

'I made my mind up long ago that I didn't want to keep it. I've got a good offer for it, from someone who wants to convert it into four flats. The money will go to charity, probably to children in need. You won't mind, will you?'

'Not at all.'

She ran her hand over the piano; the once glossy top was covered in scars left by cigarettes and rings from drink bottles. The underside had names scratched into it.

'We could get that repolished.'

'I like it as it is. This piano has been played by heroes, including my father, and that's a good way to remember it. Goodness knows how many of them died in our defence. Could we store it somewhere, in case there is a war museum set up? I'd rather like to preserve it.'

She fell silent. Although Rennie Stone's name wasn't on the piano lid, he'd been killed in France by a sniper's bullet some eighteen months earlier. He was buried in France somewhere. Poor, dear Rennie.

Sliding on to the piano stool she began to play, and sang, wincing at the flat notes issuing from the ill-used instrument. *'I'll get by.'*

'As long as I have you,' Nick whispered, sliding next to her and planting a kiss on her cheek. 'Does it still hurt?'

Here was a man who knew her better than she knew herself.

'Sometimes. Rennie was a good man. He knew I had a crush on him. Luckily he wasn't the type to take advantage of my feelings, and he let me down as sensitively as he could.'

'Not like me then.'

'It always felt as though we were right together, even when we argued. Allow me to tell you something you don't know. In about six months' time there will be three of us.' She laughed when his mouth fell open, placed her fingertip under his chin to close it, then kissed him. 'See, I can have secrets too.'

There were tears in his eyes now. 'I love you, Lady Cowan.'

'Come on you big softie, let's go and inform my mother she's going to be a granny.'

They walked through a misty, pale amaranth evening, the earth bursting with spring growth and the breeze stirring fresh and rousing with promise.

There was a faint smell of smoke in the air for it wasn't yet warm enough in the evening to go without some sort of comfort.

'Do you know what I miss the most now the war is ended, Nick? The sound of the planes flying over,' she said. 'It's so quiet now.'

Nick missed the excitement of the danger that came with them. But he'd always known he'd have to grow up sometime, and Meggie was compensation for that.

They fell quiet.

Leo had worked under Denton for the past few months, refreshing his surgeon's skills. He'd been offered a job with the Royal Flying Doctor Service in Australia, and they were leaving the next day from Southampton.

Meggie's mother, Livia, was shedding a few tears over it. Meggie crossed to where she stood, gave her a hug and whispered something in her ear.

Nick tried not to grin as Livia's eyes widened. So did her smile.

He watched the news pass round, and the hugging began. Meggie had warned him that they hugged a lot. He liked this family he'd married into. Mostly, he liked being part of a family.

They had mastered the art of precedence. Meggie was

hugged, first by Livia, then Esmé and then Chad's wife, Sylvia . . . all delighted by the news. Livia had gained a certain cache in the neighbourhood by having a viscount for a son-in-law, but she wasn't a person who would show off for the sake of it, just enjoy her pleasure in it quietly.

As for his own father, the earl, he'd accepted Meggie with more than a little relief, alerting Nick to the fact that he'd always been aware of his son's foibles.

His little unit had been dissolved, but Nick's services hadn't been dispensed with. He'd worked under cover for the rest of the war, by which time the adventure had become a chore, and he'd experienced a need to settle down.

Denton slapped him on the back. 'Congratulations, my boy.'

Nick nearly said 'my pleasure' before he remembered he'd taken his pleasure with the man's stepdaughter – on many occasions, and it just got better and better.

Denton was followed by Leo with, 'Ever since I first met you I've been puzzling about where I know your face from. Now I remember.'

'Enlighten me,' he said.

'Have you ever been a postman?'

Chad laughed. 'It sounds like you've had one too many, Leo. There wouldn't be too many lords of the realm out there delivering the post.'

'Could be. All the same, I'm sure we've met before. I'll remember it eventually.'

Not until he was safely back in Australia, Nick hoped.

Meggie joined him and took his arm. 'I'm sure you'd make an excellent postman, darling? I can just see you on your little bike delivering parcels. Have you been offered a job then?'

Leo laughed. 'I've been trying to remember where I've seen Nick before.'

'There was a picture of his father in the paper last week. They look rather alike.'

'That was probably it.'

Nick exchanged a grin with her and planted a kiss on her mouth. 'I could smack your bottom,' he whispered.

'Not here, you couldn't. I must go and get the champagne glasses. Daddy wants to make a toast.'

She gave her two brothers a gentle shove when she passed them. They were tall and looked like Denton.

Nick listened as Denton made his farewell speech to Esmé and Leo. The surgeon was grey-haired, conventional, calm, and satisfied with his lot in life. Livia Elliot was a good-looking woman, like her sister Esmé Thornton, though not quite as elegant. She was a motherly type.

Denton lifted his glass a second time, and he looked at Meggie and Nick and smiled. 'And to our darling Meggie, who has finally decided what she's going to do with her life . . . with a little help from her husband.'

Meggie blushed.

After the laughter died down Denton made another toast. 'To peace.'

To which they all raised their glasses.